AMBUSH

Amanda should have been delighted that her stepsister Emily had joyfully accepted the Duke of Norwood's marriage proposal.

Certainly this irritatingly proud nobleman and the impeccably proper Emily deserved each other.

Just as surely Amanda's father would be pleased by so exalted a family alliance.

As for Amanda, she had to be relieved to have the matter settled so firmly. And no longer would she have to be concerned about the unwanted attentions of the Duke—and even more troubling, about her own unsettling response.

No longer would Amanda's head have to battle with her heart. No longer would she have to fight with all her good sense against surrender to folly.

Amanda should have known that in love, as in war, there was always danger of a surprise attack. . . .

The Prodigal Daughter

Allison Lane

A SIGNET BOOK

SIGNET
Published by the Penguin Group
Penguin Books USA Inc., 375 Hudson Street, New York, New York 10014, U.S.A.
Penguin Books Ltd, 27 Wrights Lane, London W8 5TZ, England
Penguin Books Australia Ltd, Ringwood, Victoria, Australia
Penguin Books Canada Ltd, 10 Alcorn Avenue, Toronto, Ontario, Canada M4V 3B2
Penguin Books (N.Z.) Ltd, 182–190 Wairau Road, Auckland 10, New Zealand

Penguin Books Ltd, Registered Offices:
Harmondsworth, Middlesex, England

First published by Signet, an imprint of Dutton Signet,
a division of Penguin Books USA Inc.

First Printing, November, 1996
10 9 8 7 6 5 4 3 2 1

 REGISTERED TRADEMARK—MARCA REGISTRADA

Printed in the United States of America

BOOKS ARE AVAILABLE AT QUANTITY DISCOUNTS WHEN USED TO PROMOTE PRODUCTS OR
SERVICES. FOR INFORMATION PLEASE WRITE TO PREMIUM MARKETING DIVISION, PENGUIN
BOOKS USA INC., 375 HUDSON STREET, NEW YORK, NY 10014.

No man is an Iland, intire of itself; every man is a peece of the Continent, a part of the maine; if a Clod bee washed away by the Sea, Europe is the lesse, as well as if a Promontorie were, as well as if a Mannor of thy friends or of thine owne were; any man's death diminishes me, because I am involved in Mankinde; And therefore never send to know for whom the bell tolls; it tolls for thee.

—John Donne (1573–1631)
Devotions XVII

Chapter One

Voices murmured in staccato German behind a heavy door, the sound nearly inaudible through the waltz tune reverberating from the nearby ballroom. "Cannot permit . . . treachery . . . look like an accident . . . what about the Russian . . . French . . . tell . . ."

A frustrated listener pressed an ear against the keyhole, straining to hear that rapid conversation. Vienna was crawling with spies. Who did these two work for? Had they engineered the disappearance of that officer last week? Footsteps suddenly echoed from around the corner, raising panic. To be caught at all meant failure. To be caught here could mean death. Fingers grasped a hidden knife, their tension belying the listener's assumed nonchalance. But it was only Jack.

Suddenly the hall dissolved into twilight, the listener now a searcher, frantically crisscrossing the battlefield after Waterloo. Images rose in stark horror—shattered bodies, burning gun carriages, mud—all permeated by the eternal smell of smoke and gunpowder. He had to be here somewhere. Trembling hands turned over an officer wearing a familiar green uniform. Dear God, it was Andy. And over there was Robin; poor Robin who had always been so cheerful, even during that hellish march across the Pyrenees when altitude sickness nearly drove them mad . . . The grim search continued. Another body, and another. Repeated shock deadened all sensation. A shattered leg, a severed head, pools of blood, carnage, death . . .

A man pinned under a horse . . .

Amanda awoke screaming. She was shaking so hard it was a wonder the bed did not shatter. Both hands covered her mouth, trying to force back the sobs. That had been a bad one. Burt had warned her against searching for the body herself. She should have listened to him. A year later she still dreamed of that day. Jack. Her husband. Dead.

She said the word deliberately, repeating it aloud. The finality of the sound woke her fully, dragging her from the half-slumber in which she had still been trapped.

"No!"

Her senses pricked to attention even as her body froze. No wonder the nightmare had returned after an absence of a month. Smoke teased at her nostrils—not the faint scent of cooking fires that permeated this run-down wing of the inn, but wood smoke. And it was thickening even as she identified it.

Throwing on her gown, she grabbed the valise she had not bothered to open when she had fallen, exhausted, into bed immediately after dinner. A peek around the door verified that the hallway was still clear of flames.

"Fire!" she shouted, running to the end of the corridor, banging on doors as she went. Turning to retrace her steps to the stairs, she repeated the call. "Fire! Fire!"

Surely she was not the first to awaken. She could hear the crackling flames now, loud above the wails of those that she had disturbed. The noise increased as she approached the central block of the inn. Merchants and farmers were crowding behind her, pushing and shoving in their frenzy to escape. But the more important guests were housed in the second wing, the one that now burned.

"Has anyone roused the others?" she shouted as the innkeeper stumbled into view and began organizing his servants to fight the blaze.

"Too dangerous," he replied shortly.

And on the first floor that was probably true, she conceded. The fire had apparently started on the ground floor and had already roared into the rooms above. There was movement there. But the arrogance that was nearly universal among the aristocracy would prevent them from alerting their servants. Racing up to the second floor, she repeated her call, banging on doors to awaken whoever might be ensconced there. Having done all she could inside, she escaped into the yard.

People were huddled near the stables, some in shock,

others cursing the innkeeper—as though he were at fault for disturbing their sleep—and the rest milling uselessly about. She had witnessed similar scenes after sudden, violent action too many times to bear remembering.

"Are any of you local?" she demanded, unconsciously employing the same brisk tone with which Jack had always kept his troops in line.

A boy nodded.

"Is there a doctor nearby?"

He nodded again.

"Good. Fetch him." The lad turned and ran into the darkness.

"You, sir," Amanda next addressed the most intelligent-looking of the nervous men.

He glanced at her in surprise.

"Yes, you. You seem capable. Form the uninjured into groups and try to prevent the fire from spreading."

He glanced where she was pointing. There was a gap between the burning wing and the stables. The grooms were already throwing water on the thatching under the direction of the ostler, but there were not enough of them to stop the blaze. His back straightened. "Right."

She had judged well, she reflected as she turned to the others. He was already forming bucket brigades and moving off to the task. She had not dared suggest that the landlord needed help to save the second wing. Guests would hardly be agreeable to entering the inn again, but the relative safety of the stableyard would keep them occupied.

The wounded were already in evidence, though those with serious injuries had not yet escaped. Would she never be free of death?

Sparing a moment to reflect on how familiar it all was, she set to work. Within minutes she had settled the injured as far from the fire as possible and had established a treatment center. Ripping up the petticoat that was in the valise she still carried, she ordered one of the inn's maids to get what supplies she could from the portion of the old wing that was still intact. It would not be much, of course. Pray God the doctor would arrive soon.

A loud bang woke the Duke of Norwood from a peaceful sleep. He had already growled a blasphemous complaint before he smelled smoke and heard a distant shout of "Fire!"

Pulling on his pantaloons as he ran, he jerked open the door, only to discover that the hall was engulfed in flames. Damnation! He slammed it shut again, trying to consider the situation calmly. Escape through the hall was impossible, promising certain death if he tried. A glance at the window made him grimace. Flames already licked up the outside of the building. Under his horrified gaze, the wall erupted in fire. Was he doomed to die here?

His mother had been pressing him for years to secure the succession, but he had not agreed until three months before. Had he left it too late? Would the dukedom wind up in the hands of his incompetent cousin after all?

Imbecile! he cursed himself, dragging on his boots. *Bloody fool!* This was hardly the time to evaluate his life. Striding to the other door, he tried the handle. Locked, of course. He had not hired both rooms of this potential suite. Cursing again, he repeatedly threw himself at the door, nearly frantic before he succeeded in breaking the latch.

It opened into a corner room that had two windows, only one of which was yet affected by the fire. But the smoke was much worse than in his own room. The door to the hall stood open, the occupant having fled. Dropping below the thickening cloud, he slammed it shut, then turned his attention to the second window, wasting precious seconds trying to force it open. He finally picked up a chair and smashed at the panes of glass. The chair was reduced to kindling and his nerves to near hysteria before he finally broke through the network of leads.

"Damnation!" he growled, choking as he flung a coverlet over the shards still in the frame. He had no time to pick them loose, and the opening was barely large enough to accommodate him. New clouds of smoke were billowing around his head. The ground was a good deal lower than under his room, the inn ending on the edge of a ravine. Flames already licked up from the window directly beneath his. But he had no time to reconsider his plan. The door to the hall was ablaze and his own room was a raging inferno. Forcing down panic and an image of his smashed and broken body sprawled across sharp stones, he jumped.

•   •   •

The stable yard teemed with people, Amanda noted absently as she applied lard to yet another burn, loosely binding the arm with strips of sheeting to protect it from the night air. At least a dozen townsmen had arrived to fight the blaze. She prayed a doctor would turn up soon. There were injuries she could not treat alone.

Her corner was becoming organized. She had enlisted the help of two young men who sorted the injured according to the severity of their wounds. While the innkeeper's wife tied up minor scrapes, she did what she could for the moderate and severe cases, though it was not nearly enough. Was the doctor away delivering a child?

"Mrs. Morrison!" exclaimed a familiar, jovial voice as she straightened to move on to the next victim.

"Dr. Matthews!" A smile of pleasure and relief stretched her face. "So this is where you retired to."

"Yes. What do we have here?"

"Aside from minor burns, eleven people need your attention so far," she reported. "There's a broken leg on the end." She pointed to a young curate who had jumped from his window. "Next to him is a head injury, then two guests whose gashes need stitching, and seven severe burns. I am looking after the lesser wounded."

"What are you using?"

"Lard and wrapping. There is nothing else. Have you basilicum powder?" She nodded to his bag. "We used all the innkeeper had."

He handed her a packet and set to work, commandeering one of her assistants.

A loud crash elicited screams from most of the women. A harsher scream sounded from inside the inn. Amanda shivered and glanced over her shoulder. The roof had collapsed, sending flames roaring into the sky, but the fire fighters seemed to be gaining the upper hand. The second wing remained free of fire, its slate roof protecting it from the storm of sparks that rained upon the area. Two men were atop the stable beating out a small blaze. She returned her attention to the injured.

Three critical cases joined the queue, a dozen more being shunted into her holding area.

"Dr. Matthews needs your help," murmured his helper.

"Right." She hurried to Dr. Matthews's side to find him frowning over the latest victim.

"Was it he who screamed?" she asked, sickened by the sight. Both legs were burned, with one smashed too badly to ever recover.

He nodded. "A roof beam caught him."

His voice was drowned out by an arrogant newcomer. "Stand aside, lad! I will see the doctor now!"

"But you've nought but minor burns, sir," protested Amanda's assistant.

"I've a broken arm, not that it matters. He will attend me now."

Obviously a nobleman, decided Amanda. No one else could be so odiously haughty.

"We'll have to amputate," murmured Dr. Matthews. "The right might recover, but the left is hopeless."

"The boys can move him into the stable," she suggested. "We've enough people in shock as it is. I will take care of his lordship."

She turned to examine the gentleman who was trying to shove past her helper. He was half a head taller than herself, with an almost perfect physique, but his dark eyes and hawkish face blazed with enough anger to send most people running for cover. Disapproval marred his forehead and pulled his mouth into a permanent frown. His black hair hung longer than was currently fashionable and was plastered with mud. He wore only torn pantaloons and a filthy nightshirt with a scorched left sleeve. Amanda snorted.

"You will have to wait your turn," she addressed him coldly.

"Obviously, you do not know who I am," he said through gritted teeth, eyes contemptuously raking her from head to toe.

"You are an arrogant lord with no manners, no sense, and a grossly inflated opinion of your place in the universe. There are half a dozen people in worse condition than you. I refuse to deal with you until later," she stated, hands on her hips.

"*You* refuse!" He glared.

"Absolutely. The man who was just brought out will die

without immediate attention." She turned to follow Dr. Matthews, but a hand shot out and pulled her back.

"I am the Duke of Norwood. Where is the nearest doctor?"

"I don't care if you are the Prince Regent, Wellington, and God Himself rolled into one," she shot back, drawing herself up and donning an expression every bit as haughty as his own. "You will sit down and shut your mouth, your bloody grace. The only available doctor is trying to save lives." It was time to take this toplofty beast down a peg, she decided as his face turned an interesting shade of purple. She sweetened her voice. "Or if you wish to be attended sooner, we could use some help. Your arm will heal just as well if it is set later, and your strength will make treating that gentleman easier."

Tearing herself free, she hurried into the stable.

Norwood stared after the retreating figure, unable to move. Was she descended from Medusa that she could freeze him so easily? No one had ever spoken to him like that. Her flashing brown eyes had impaled him like a butterfly on a pin. Yet there was nothing notable about the woman. Her sisters were everywhere—nondescript, brown-haired females clad in widow's weeds. But her words reverberated through his mind. Was he really so important that he would condemn a man to death just to get his arm set a few minutes earlier? Phrased that way, his request sounded ludicrous.

Pain stabbed his arm, his leg, his neck. Damn, but he hurt! The jump had gone about as badly as possible. Broken glass had sliced through his clothes. He had landed on a slope, his foot twisting to drop him in the exact spot where a burning timber crashed moments later, snapping one of the bones of his left forearm.

The wench's words again teased his mind. They sounded almost like a dare. A scream of agony erupted from the stable. Unwillingly, almost without thought, his feet moved in that direction.

"There you are," she snapped as he appeared in the doorway. "You're late. Grab that leg and hold it still."

Hardly realizing what was happening, he did as he was

told, wedging the foot between his thighs and holding the knee immobile with his good hand. Only then did he note the others' actions.

The woman was leaning heavily on the victim's shoulders, pinning them to a rough table. A doctor had applied a tourniquet to the other leg, tied the foot down, and was positioned above it with a knife and a saw. The patient screamed again.

Norwood blanched. The man he was holding was his own valet. His grip loosened.

"Damnation! Hold him still!" snapped the doctor, slicing deep into the burned flesh.

Fitch bucked, kicking upward with his free foot. New pain exploded through Norwood's body but he grimly held on. A few quick strokes followed by the rasp of a saw, and the injured leg twisted free of its former body, spilling blood onto the floor. Fitch lapsed into a coma.

Norwood convulsed in horror. Staggering two steps away, he cast up his accounts against the wall, unable to absorb the brutal reality of the past half hour. Neither the doctor nor his assistant took any notice of his prolonged retching. They worked quickly, discussing the fire victims and other patients they had known. Their voices finally broke through the fog that had descended on the duke's brain.

"Will he recover?" she asked softly.

"Maybe, Mrs. Morrison. The other leg may heal, or it may have to go as well. We should know in a couple of days. The burns are the worst of it. His reflexes are certainly working properly." They shared an amused smile.

"Poor man. I hope he has family that will take care of him. It is brutal on the streets."

"Is that where you have spent the last months?" inquired the doctor as he finished sewing up his handiwork.

"Not quite. I have been teaching music in London since I returned, though it is not enough. But things will improve."

"You deserve far better, my dear," he said briskly.

"I doubt it. Set his grace's arm while I see what new casualties have arrived." She called the boys to move Fitch.

Norwood grimaced as the doctor prodded his arm.

"Did Mrs. Morrison refer to you properly?" Matthews asked as he maneuvered the bones back into position.

"I am the Duke of Norwood," his grace managed through gritted teeth.

"And I am Dr. Matthews. Thank you for your assistance."

"Will Fitch really recover?" Norwood asked.

"You know the gentleman?"

"Yes. Will he recover?"

"Possibly. His chances are better if he is well cared for."

"He will be."

Amanda returned. "There is another bad one, Doctor. I doubt he'll live, but perhaps there is something you can do."

He nodded. "See to Norwood's wounds, then come help me."

Norwood gasped as she spread lard on his arm. "How do you come to be so capable?" he said, trying to distract his mind from the pain.

"Too much practice. Thank God Matthews lives here. If anyone can save that fellow, it will be him. Too many country sawbones are inept."

"You know him well?"

"We worked together for several months after Waterloo," she replied in a voice that terminated the topic. "Thank you for your help."

"I did little but disgrace myself," he muttered.

"Nonsense, though you'll remember that there are better ways to hold down a leg." She grinned as he flinched in discomfort.

"Wretch. You could have warned me."

"Experience teaches best." She finished wrapping his arm and tied off the bandage. "There. Most of the burns are not deep. You will have a scar on the back of the hand and another near the elbow, but the rest will heal without a trace."

He had not even thought about possible scars. His face drained of color, dizziness again assaulting him.

"Put your head down," she ordered, pushing it toward his knees. "I should not have mentioned it. You've had enough shocks for one night."

"You must be a witch. How did you drag me into this?"

"You dragged yourself in, your grace. It is good for even the highest to reduce themselves to being human once in a while. And don't feel guilty over your reaction. It is nearly universal the first time."

The traumatic events of the evening had left him floating in a dream—the mad sort where people said and did mad things, and events raced illogically from crisis to crisis. Or was it a dream? The witch had said something about being human.

"Is that why you coerced me into helping with this?" he asked as she smeared salve on his cuts. "Were you trying to bring the aristocrat to his knees?"

"Not really," she lied. "We needed the help, you needed something to occupy your time until Dr. Matthews could set your arm, and my other patients needed to be spared a temper tantrum."

"You make me sound like an infant," he growled.

"Think about it, your grace," she suggested. "I've got work to do."

"Poor Fitch," he murmured again as she disappeared, leaving him sitting in a blood-stained stall with only a mangled leg for company.

Amanda thought about the Duke of Norwood as she assisted Matthews. It was the only way she could keep the memories from crowding too close. If her nightmare had cracked the door leading to the past, the surgery and Matthews's presence threatened to burst it wide open.

There was something about the duke that piqued her curiosity. Despite the hauteur that must be expected from so lofty a lord, she sensed a softness underneath, a vulnerability that she had not expected to find there. Had she misjudged him? Perhaps his initial tirade had been a reaction to the fire rather than his usual demeanor. She really should not have pushed him to help. The sight was bad enough for anyone unprepared, but he had already suffered other shocks while escaping the blaze. The fact that he had coped as well as he had indicated a strong character. She owed him an apology.

In retrospect, her own behavior had been unconscionable, reverting to the deliberate perversity she thought she had shed along with her childhood. Now she knew that nothing had changed. The trigger had merely been missing—that icy arrogance she so heartily despised. The realization did not bode well for her errand.

Dawn finally broke across the eastern sky. The worst injuries had been treated. Those still fighting the waning blaze bore only minor burns.

A yard of tin sounded as another London-bound mail coach approached this busiest of coaching inns. Several stages and private carriages were already being harnessed for departure. Horses whinnied. Shouts arose as people scrambled for possessions.

Taking leave of the doctor, Amanda picked up her valise and boarded her stage.

Chapter Two

Amanda jumped down from the wagon and thanked Mr. Wilson for the ride. Nervous terror almost paralyzed her. Somehow, her imagination had left off at this moment, never considering the actual confrontation with her father. And she had to admit to cowardice. Jack would have been disappointed, but there it was.

Sighing, she turned down the oak-shaded lane that led to the dower house. If anyone would welcome her back, it would be her grandmother.

Tears stung her eyes at the familiar sights and sounds. The double-arched stone bridge that carried the main drive across the stream was beautifully framed by a pair of trees, the ancient willow still shading its far end. Old Gordy whistled his dog into action, the sound immediately followed by the bleating of several sheep as a brown blur chased dots of white over a distant hillside. The creak of the wheel wove through the musical trickle of water as she neared the ancient mill, precariously perched on the banks of the stream. Even the heights that marked the moor brought a lump to her throat. Oh, how often she had dreamed of escaping that sight, wishing for adventure, for excitement, for the least glimpse of something beyond this valley. And she had found it. Her life had not been dull since she left. Nor had she suffered any regrets. Not once had she wished to return. So why was she suddenly overwhelmed by this feeling of coming home? Thornridge Court had never been home.

Angrily, she repressed her thoughts, afraid of becoming maudlin. The last thing she needed was to face her grandmother while thinking of the past. Both marriage and age now left her free. The family could control her life only if she allowed it. Pigs would fly first. This was no sentimental journey, but a business trip. She would say her piece, listen to her father's response, and then leave. But she must remain calm. Anger would defeat her purpose.

The lane topped a rise and she could see the dower house. It was in perfect condition, of course. Every landowner had a duty to maintain his possessions, and if there was one thing all Sternes understood, it was duty. Only Amanda had failed to learn that lesson.

She shook away the memories. Details of the house became clear as she moved closer. The freshly pointed stone was bare of ivy, though new vines already poked up near the foundation. Blinking at this first sign of change, she looked around for others. Instead of the familiar flower beds with their rigidly geometric blocks of color, the herbaceous border now enclosed a riotous collection of miscellaneous blooms. The topiary animals that had gazed across the stream for a century were gone, as was the ancient yew that had always marked the gate. The house suddenly appeared alien, the home of a stranger. Nine years was a long time.

Forcing her feet to continue, Amanda drew in a deep breath, letting it out in a controlled sigh as she tried to relax. There was no reason to be afraid. The worst that could happen was being turned away, and that would leave her situation unchanged. She would survive. If she could not face this least fearsome of her relatives, she might as well retreat back to town. *I need some of your courage, Jack,* she mouthed silently. And it was there.

Buck up, my dear. You know that courage mounteth with the occasion, his voice whispered in her ear. *Remember Badajoz . . .*

Her back stiffened.

The butler was new. For a moment she panicked, terrified that the house was now occupied by strangers, or worse. But that was impossible, she reminded herself as she clutched at her fraying composure. She would have heard of her father's demise. And Englewood had spent the Season in town.

"Is Lady Thorne at home?" she asked.

"I will see." The butler's eyes flicked disparagingly over her nondescript black gown.

"Tell her that Lady Amanda would like a few words with her," she ordered in a voice she had never before employed, even when living at the Court.

He motioned her to a chair in the foyer and left. She bit her lip, pushing the snub aside. It was no more than she deserved. At the very least her father would have disowned her. Seeking her grandmother's home first was a deliberate ploy to circumvent whatever standing orders he would have issued regarding her. Why had she come? Surely her situation was not so bad that she must grovel at the one place she had sworn never to visit again.

Questions chased themselves around her head, but the answers were as elusive as ever. If only Jack had not died. If only she had been able to support herself. If only Jessie had not decided to remarry. If only, if only, if only . . . Had she been wrong to try to establish herself in London? Perhaps some other town would have been better. Bath? York? Birmingham? Any one of them would have required less money to live decently. She would not have had to work as hard to scrape out her share of the expenses. But would she have found as many students in those places? Could she have charged the same fees? The questions never ceased. The answers were unavailable. She had made her choices. It was too late to repine.

The butler returned, his face as impassive as before, but his eyes seemed slightly warmer. It gave her hope.

"Follow me, my lady," he intoned.

The drawing room was exactly as she remembered it. French furniture dating to the middle of the last century was arranged on a beautifully worked Axminster carpet. Rich red silk adorned the walls. Gold and scarlet draperies had already been closed as the sun dipped below the horizon.

The lady sitting regally on the settee had not changed either. Her height was hard to judge, but Amanda knew she was tall, taller even than herself. Not a flicker of emotion showed on Lady Thorne's face or warmed her pale blue eyes. Snowy hair peeped from under a lacy cap, but the effect was icy. Her spare frame was as straight as ever. As usual, she held a piece of exquisite needlework in her lap. As a child, Amanda had often wondered how someone so cold could produce such beauty. It still seemed incongruous.

"Amanda." She spoke the single word without inflection.

"Grandmama." Amanda returned the greeting the same way.

"Why are you here?"

"I must speak with Father and wondered what reception to expect."

"A needless question, as you must know."

"I presume he disowned me." Amanda still stood just inside the door of the drawing room. There had been no invitation to sit. But her demeanor in no way hinted that she was poised for flight. She returned her grandmother's stare unflinchingly.

"Of course. And repudiated all connection. Few people even remember your existence."

Amanda suppressed a shudder. She had expected no better. "But he remains a slave to duty," she commented as if mentioning that the sun rose in the east.

Lady Thorne nodded.

"Then I will see him." She turned to leave.

"Sit down, Amanda," commanded her ladyship.

Amanda raised her brows in question.

"I believe the shock has receded enough that I can actually take in the fact that you are here. I have prayed for you every day since you left, my dear. Thank God you are safe." Her voice broke.

Tears were suddenly streaming down Amanda's face. She stumbled forward to join her grandmother on the settee. For the first time in her life, Lady Thorne pulled her into her arms and wept.

"You are in mourning?" her ladyship asked at last, noting the nondescript black gown, the thin figure, and the signs of hardship around Amanda's eyes.

"Jack died at Waterloo." Her voice cracked on the name. The unexpected outburst of emotion had penetrated some of the armor that normally protected her heart from pain.

"You loved him, then?"

"Yes."

"You look poorly, and that dress is hardly worthy of a servant."

"True, it is not one of my better gowns." But it had

served its purpose. Traveling on the stage, she had not wished to draw attention, though if she were honest, none of her blacks were much better.

"Are you ailing? You seem thin."

"Do not upset yourself, Grandmama. I suffered a rather nasty chill last winter, but I am completely recovered."

"What is that on your skirt?"

Amanda looked down. She had forgotten, not that she could have done anything about it. "Blood."

"What?"

"The inn I stayed at last night burned down. I was helping the injured. One of them needed to have his leg removed." She shrugged.

Lady Thorne blanched. "Why was a well-bred young lady dabbling with such things?"

Amanda almost laughed. "Grandmama, I am no longer young. I was married for eight years and followed the drum the entire time. There is little I have not seen. I often worked with the surgeons, especially after Waterloo."

"Lady Amanda should be above such things." Hauteur filled her voice.

"I have not used that title from the time I left home until speaking to your butler just now. It has no place in the life I have chosen. I am Mrs. Morrison, widow of a soldier."

"Nonsense."

"Do not think that I have come back to stay, Grandmama," warned Amanda. "I need to speak with my father. Then I will return to London. It is useless to push me into a mold I cannot fit. Besides, unless he has changed beyond all recognition, the Marquess of Thorne will never allow Lady Amanda to enter society."

Lady Thorne pursed her lips in thought. "I never approved of the Sterne character," she finally admitted. "But I was powerless to change it. Very well. But at least promise me that you will keep in touch. I wish you had done so earlier."

"I dared not," admitted Amanda. "Father could have caused trouble for Jack with his superiors. I hoped that he would either bid me good riddance or be unable to trace us. That is why I was so vague."

"I do not know how hard he pursued you," said her

grandmother. "But there were so many young men who left to join the military at that time that he let it go in the end."

Amanda smiled. "Good. Jack was not one of them, though I implied such in my note."

Lady Thorne widened her eyes in surprise, but Amanda was not disposed to discuss her marriage further.

"May I change into something better than this old gown before I go to see my father?"

"It would be inadvisable to call tonight," warned Lady Thorne. "He is hosting a house party and is doubtless at dinner. The gentlemen are riding early tomorrow. Perhaps you can see him when he returns."

Amanda sighed. "Very well. Is Hudgens still there?" The butler was one of the few servants who had supported her, though never openly.

"He retired two years ago, shortly before Lady Thorne died."

Her head shot up at that news. "So he is alone again?"

"And will remain so. Everyone is home just now except Englewood, who went to Brighton for the summer."

A frown creased Amanda's brow. Turning the topic, she asked, "What is the house party?"

"Emily made her bows this spring, attracting a great deal of attention, as was inevitable. Her breeding and dowry were unmatched, and her looks are beyond passable. Her most eligible suitor is due to arrive today. Thorne expects an offer for her hand."

"I see. So the house is full of young men and women. He will not keep me waiting for an answer then. It would never do to expose his guests to my undutiful influence."

"Just so."

Amanda accepted her grandmother's offer of a room for the night but would not commit herself beyond the morrow. They dined in style, something Amanda had not done since Brussels. But she did not mention it. In fact, she spoke little of her marriage or her life since leaving home, and not at all of her errand.

The Thornridge Court butler glanced at the note she carried and frowned. It was from Lady Thorne.

"Follow me, ma'am," he ordered, a hint of reluctance in his wooden voice.

Amanda tried to ignore her surroundings as they traced their way to the library. Little had changed in nine years. The Court had always been an austere showcase rather than a home. Suits of armor lined the marble hall; the main drawing room was expensively ornate, but cold; the formal dining room remained as dark and forbidding as always. Even the morning room they had just passed felt cheerless. Thorne's unyielding character had imprinted so firmly on the house that she doubted anyone would ever be happy there.

But the library . . . She almost quavered when the butler showed her in and closed the door. The room was empty of all living creatures save herself, but ghosts pressed around her, leaving the air hot with anger and hatred and rebellion. All hers, of course. Thorne considered any show of emotion to be beneath his dignity. Time rolled back to the last time she had seen this room . . .

She had obeyed his summons. One did not defy the Marquess of Thorne no matter how much one wanted to. At least not to his face. What had she done now? she wondered as she approached the library. It was his favorite room and the one in which he always meted out discipline. That nearly all punishment landed on her was too old a truth to even register. Was it her latest visit to Granny Gossich? The woman was the area healer. She had also been Amanda's only friend for many years, and her teacher. Much of her knowledge of herbs had been learned from Granny. And it was through Granny that she had met Jack.

The older Amanda shook her head, trying to dislodge the memories. Her position would be weakened if she succumbed to the anger of their last confrontation. But the library was too oppressive, her nine-year-old fury too intense. She could not stop the images from parading before her eyes or the voices from echoing mockingly in her ears.

"It is time you wed," Thorne had announced once the door closed.

The seventeen-year-old Amanda tingled with anticipation. Was she really to go to London at last? She had never traveled farther than Middleford, the market town only a few miles from the Court, but she longed to see more of the world, to meet ladies and gentlemen of her own station. But of course Thorne did not have that in mind. She should have known better than to hope. His next words shattered the dream.

"I cannot chance you mocking your breeding by misbehaving in town," he announced coldly. That had been a continuing complaint since her birth. Her conduct was inconsistent with her exalted position in society—lacking dignity, lacking propriety, and above all, lacking the condescending devotion to duty that formed the mainstay of Thorne's life. "You will wed Mr. Anthony Fontbury next week. The settlements are already signed."

"No!" Her scream of anguish reverberated from the walls. She knew better than to counter him, of course, but this was too much. "You cannot do this to me! Even you cannot be that cruel. He is hateful! I won't do it. I won't!"

"Stop this!" A hard hand smashed across her face, bringing her back to the reality of the library. "I have had enough of your intransigence. You are a disgrace to the family. God knows I have tried hard enough to teach you proper conduct, but you refuse to learn. You are a child of the devil, right enough. Fontbury has the sense to keep you from embarrassing us all in public."

It was the death-knell. She had met the man only once, but she knew enough about him to understand what the future held. He was a penniless younger son who would have jumped at the fortune Thorne must have offered, even if it meant taking Amanda with it. Fontbury would keep her locked on his estate until he had beaten her into submission, and probably afterward as well. It had taken all of Granny's skill and a month of bedrest before Billy had recovered from Fontbury's single visit, and even then he could not return to his position as stable boy.

The six-and-twenty-year-old Amanda discovered that her hands were pressed tightly to her ears, as though they could stifle the echo of her father's voice. He had continued his tirade for a good ten minutes, listing every fault that had come to his attention since his last lecture. But her real crime was inheriting her mother's disposition.

The first Lady Thorne had been a sad disappointment to her husband. Despite being a duke's daughter, she had fraternized with people of the lower classes, actually allowing warmth into her contacts with them. She had laughed a good deal, even at herself, and rarely found fault with anyone. She had also committed the unpardonable sin of addressing her maid by the girl's given name. Amanda suspected that the worst transgression was laughing and calling Thorne a stuffy prig when he chastised her for that last. She had heard the tale from one of the servants. He would never have publicized so mortifying an occasion.

The second Lady Thorne was very much more to his liking, as were their four very proper children. If Amanda had copied their demeanor, they would have accepted her, but she had not. Despite her sunny nature, when it came to Thorne, she perversely dug in her heels and refused to obey his edicts.

Which was exactly what had happened that last day. Upon leaving the study, under orders to remain in her room until Fontbury arrived the next morning, she had fled to Granny Gossich's cottage, tears streaming down her face at every thought of the wretched future her uncaring parent had arranged. But Granny was not at home.

Hoping that she was tending Jack, Amanda had gone there. She had first met him three months earlier when she accompanied Granny on her healing rounds. He was temporarily back from the wars, recovering from wounds. They had become friends, nothing more. But she drank in his tales of the faraway places he had seen and the exciting things he had done. It was so different from her own life. He shared her zest for living and was in the enviable position of controlling his own destiny.

Granny was not there, but Jack took one look at her face and urged her to talk. Between sobs she managed to choke out a confused tale of Thorne's perfidy, Jack's handkerchief pressed to her eyes. It was when she expressed the hope that Granny might know of somewhere to which she could escape that he made his own suggestion.

And so they were wed.

The rattle of the door handle pulled her attention back to the present. Her heart began to race but she kept her face impassive. It would never do to let him guess that she needed him.

The Marquess of Thorne paused just inside the door, shock clear in his gray eyes. It was the most emotion she had ever seen on his face. His fading brown hair had turned to dirty gray in the intervening years, but his regal carriage and imposing height remained the same. The lines of stern disapproval were deeper than ever. Several unidentifiable expressions twisted his countenance before it settled into hauteur.

"Well, Amanda, why are you calling yourself Mrs. Morrison?"

"It is my name."

"So the blackguard married you, even without a dowry," he scoffed, disbelief evident. "Or was it some other fellow who decided exclusive favors were preferable to sharing his slut with others?"

Anger thrust fear and nervousness aside. She had often wondered if she could have reasoned with him had she not lost her temper that day. Now she knew. And nothing had changed. It had been lunacy to come here. She nearly rose to leave, but Jack's voice sounded in her ears. *Never retire from the battlefield until you have accomplished your goal or exhausted all options. Only then should you retreat with dignity.*

"I'll not argue with you except to state that my behavior has never been less than ladylike. And as I have no intention of staying here, you needn't fear for your guests."

He stared silently as he stalked over to slam a letter onto his desk. The action was so familiar, Amanda nearly cringed, but this time whatever bad news lay in that missive could not concern her—except that she had apparently arrived at an inopportune time. Something else had already put him in a fury. Cold eyes raked her from head to toe, taking in the changes in her appearance.

"Then why are you here?"

"I know what store you set by your name," she stated baldly. "I have come to a crossroads and felt you deserved a voice in which path I choose, since it may reflect on you. My husband died at Waterloo, leaving me little but his back pay. I have been supporting myself in London by teaching, sharing a house with another widow who was likewise occupied. But Jessie will remarry at the end of the month. Without her contributions, I cannot keep my home. There is no other lady with whom I could live in amity, and so I have two choices. I can advertise my breeding to justify increasing my fees and to recruit a better class of students than the daughters of merchants. Or I can ask you for a small allowance. A hundred pounds a year would maintain my present status."

Fury was growing in his eyes. Either the double shock of her appearance and that letter had loosened his control, or the years had undermined his rigid composure. His face was more expressive than she had ever seen it.

"You are working?" he snapped, imparting so much scorn into the words that he might as well have accused her of whoring on the streets of Middleford.

"There is nothing wrong with work," she countered. "I teach music and French. There are less genteel ways to support oneself."

"The daughter of a marquess does not work for a living," he stated coldly.

"I repudiated that designation nine years ago, as did you. I have never regretted it, nor do I now. It makes no difference to me which course I take, but I felt you deserved the option of keeping my origins quiet if they matter to you."

His face was glaring with rage, its features twisted into a caricature of one of the gargoyles she had seen on Notre Dame. "Your place is running a proper home for a proper husband and providing his heirs—if you can. I will not condone your continued intransigence."

"My lord, this discussion is pointless," she interrupted him, steel underlying her voice. "I have no intention of marrying again. I could never find another man like Jack. Nor will I give up my teaching. All other considerations aside, I enjoy it. The only question is the one I already stated. Will you provide me a small allowance or shall I trade on my aristocratic connections to attract more business?"

"You have already cost me a small fortune," he snapped. "I had to pay off Fontbury to keep your stupidity quiet."

"Don't you dare blame that on me," she snarled. "You signed a contract without consulting me. It was your affair and your responsibility. I will allow no one to force me into an untenable life. Nor do I care a fig if people know I eloped, so any face-saving you indulged in was strictly for your own benefit. Now, enough of the past. Have you a preference about how I conduct my business in the future? If not, I will do what I must."

His hands balled into fists, but she no longer quailed under his stare. She had seen too much in recent years to be cowed by one arrogant nobleman. That fact alone gladdened her heart as some of the weight of her childhood slid from her shoulders. Jack had told her many times that she would never fear Thorne again. She had always replied that she knew he would protect her. But Jack had not allowed that to be the last word, pointing out that because Thorne was powerless to coerce her, she would find the courage to face him down the next time they met. And she had. She could feel her muscles relaxing as she watched her father pace restlessly around the library under the disapproving frown of the previous marquess, whose portrait hung above the chimneypiece.

Several minutes passed in silence.

"You will have your allowance," he conceded finally. "But there are conditions."

Amanda kept her face impassive with an effort.

"I will provide one thousand pounds a year," he continued. "But you must move back home. You will behave like the proper widow you should be and may choose between overseeing this house or looking for a new husband."

She burst into laughter. "You surpass yourself in arrogant blustering," she said, once she had regained her voice. His face resembled a thundercloud, but she was no longer intimidated. The freedom that fact brought swelled her heart. "I will never again live in this house. You have no legal authority over me, and I thank God every day for that." She rose to leave, but a gesture stayed her.

"Perhaps I have been too hasty."

She could hear the effort it cost his pride to admit even that small error. Her heart began to race.

He continued slowly. "I repudiated all connection with you when you cast aside your breeding to elope with a common soldier. If you refuse to come home, I will continue to disown you. But it is improper for a woman to live in London alone. The offer of an allowance stands, but only if you move to a cottage in the country where no one knows you, and comport yourself as befits your station."

"You are being deliberately obtuse, my lord," she stated

coldly. "My station is what I choose it to be. And what I chose was to sever all connection to a family that has done nothing but denigrate me since the day I was born. Unfortunately, fate seems to have other ideas and I am left with making a damnable decision between openly declaring a connection or secretly accepting an allowance. But I will not give up my freedom. I am not ashamed of my life and will never act as though I were. Nor will I give up teaching."

Thorne again paced the room. In his newly opened countenance she could read his conflict. He despised the idea of reneging on his word, yet duty demanded he assist his daughter. Playing shuttlecock between those extremes were his ingrained beliefs on the proper role of ladies.

He finally halted next to his desk, absently fingering the letter opener as he spoke. "Aside from propriety, it is not safe for a woman to live alone in London. I cannot offer you even a shilling in support of so foolhardy a notion. Nor will I allow you to trade on the family name to make a living there. If you persist, I will make your name a byword in town until no family of any class will employ you."

Amanda remained motionless. That possibility had occurred to her before, but she had not believed that he would drag his own name through the mud to such an extent. She still did not.

He continued. "If moving elsewhere smacks of cowering in shame, then live in Middleford. Show the neighborhood how low you have sunk. But don't expect to trade on the family connections. We will have nothing to do with you and you will not be welcomed here again."

She considered his words, trying to discern his real thoughts. Manipulating people was second nature to him. The demand that she hide away anonymously in the country was irrelevant. He must have known that she would never consider it, just as she knew he would never openly blacken her name in town. So the choice lay between surviving alone in London without help, or moving to Middleford and accepting an allowance.

He probably wished her to remain where he could watch her, but having come into the open, he could do that anyway. Middleford was a charming market town of several hundred inhabitants. She knew many of them, though he might not be aware of that. And if she were honest, London was not the most congenial place for a woman alone. She had to walk to most of her lessons, and the streets were never safe—even in the respectable neighborhood where she and Jessie lived.

"The allowance?" she asked, for he had not actually connected it to Middleford.

"A thousand pounds a year, but nothing if you remain in London."

It was more than twice what she had had to live on in even the most affluent times of her marriage and would allow her to survive in comfort for the rest of her life.

"I will not claim any connection with you," she agreed. "But I must visit my grandmother on occasion. She will wish to see me if I live so close, and you can hardly dictate her behavior."

He frowned, but finally nodded.

"I will continue teaching music and French if there are students who wish to study those subjects," she continued. "And you must understand my past. Many people in this area, including several in Middleford, know me. I have not changed that much since my marriage. You are mistaken to believe they will think poorly of me. Quite the reverse. I will not trade on your name, but I cannot control the tongues of others. Very soon, everyone in the district will be aware both of the connection and of the antagonism that exists between us. If you cannot accept that, then you must allow me to return to London." Even as she spoke the words, she knew they would not matter. Thorne regarded the lower classes as little better than animals. Their opinions would affect him as much as those of a sheep. But she had to point out the obvious, lest some higher-ranking individual criticize his decree. She would no longer allow him to blame her for anything.

Thorne paced the library, face contorted in thought. Finally, he turned back to Amanda. "As usual, you live in a dream world. But even if you prove correct, I care nought for the opinions of a bunch of motley peasants. Make yourself a laughingstock if you must. Every family has its black sheep, so worthy gentlemen will not blame me. But you will not interfere in my family's life."

"Agreed."

Chapter Three

Amanda paused to admire an arrangement of roses on the hall table before joining her grandmother for tea. She had not seen the lady in nearly a fortnight, her own affairs keeping her too busy.

After leaving the Thornridge library, she had walked back to the dower house deep in thought, trying to decide whether she had handled the confrontation well or had botched it. Though she was not unhappy at the thought of leaving London, perhaps it would have been better to live someplace that was not under Thorne's nose. Had he outmaneuvered her? She had little experience in manipulation. Yet there was another side to his terms.

She laughed aloud as the truth suddenly became clear. Instead of the choice she had offered, she had won both options. The allowance was many times what she had requested, and enough people knew her identity that she would have little trouble securing students. An unexpected benefit was that Thorne was proving to all and sundry that he really was the unfeeling monster she had always known him to be. She doubted that he even realized she had won everything. Despite her efforts, he had not believed her. He was the one living in a dream world, a place where lords not only received obedience and respect from their inferiors, but could control their minds and thoughts as well. He truly believed that his peers would follow his lead and condemn her, and that the lower orders would ridicule her every move. This was but another skirmish in their lifelong war, his latest attempt to shame her into adhering to his standards.

Lady Thorne did not see it in that light, of course. When

Amanda admitted she was leaving London, the dowager was delighted.

"I always thought he regretted the rift between you. This is the first step in making amends."

"Fustian!" Amanda exploded. "He has never rued an action in his life. He is again trying to make my life miserable."

"It is true that he has never openly admitted a mistake," agreed Lady Thorne. "Even as a child he was adamant. But that never prevented him from correcting his behavior."

"Enough, Grandmama," protested Amanda. "I have agreed to his conditions, but that is the end of it."

"It is right that you return to your home," she stated firmly.

"Not home, Grandmama," she countered. "I would starve first. I will live in Middleford, where I will continue teaching."

Lady Thorne frowned, but did not offer new arguments. "There is a cottage on the edge of town that was recently vacated. It is not large, but you seem not to care about that."

Her grandmother had been right, Amanda decided as she toured the house that afternoon. Too large to deserve the designation of cottage, it nonetheless suited her. The parlor was roomy enough to house a pianoforte, something Lady Thorne had already insisted on providing. A small stable would permit her to keep a horse and gig, allowing her to accept students from farms as well as town. The garden included a selection of common herbs that she could use for making healing draughts. The adjacent forest and water meadow contained others. Yet the house was small enough that it could be run by only a couple of servants.

She had returned to London the next day to close up the house there and ship her belongings north, arriving back in Middleford only two days before. Now that she was settled into her new home, she had accepted her grandmother's invitation for tea.

"You pour," requested Lady Thorne once they had exchanged greetings. "Are you established at last?"

"Reasonably. I could have been back a week ago, but I wanted to stay in town until after Jessie's wedding."

"She shared rooms with you?" asked Lady Thorne.

"Yes. Her husband also died at Waterloo."

Her voice precluded further conversation on the subject. She did not wish to discuss her marriage. She missed Jack. She missed so many old friends. Talking about any aspect of the last nine years would reduce her to tears, something she could not do again in her grandmother's presence.

"Is the house party still in progress at the Court?" she asked instead.

"No." Unexpectedly, the dowager chuckled. "It was a dismal failure."

"There was no betrothal?"

"The suitor excused himself from attending. Thorne was livid." Her voice held an odd inflection.

"What happened?"

"The gentlemen sent word that he was suffering from an unspecified injury and must return home. Personally, I suspect that he was not ready to commit himself. He has a reputation for avoiding society. That is one of the reasons Thorne chose him—proper disdain for frivolity."

Amanda shuddered. It sounded like Emily was having as little voice in choosing her husband as she had had. "And he must also have the requisite title and wealth. Who is this paragon?"

"The Duke of Norwood."

Surprise flooded Amanda's face as she recalled Thorne's fury in the library and the letter he had slammed onto his desk. He must have received it along with the note from his mother. No wonder he had been unable to control his face. Two such massive shocks in succession were too much.

"Do you know him?" Lady Thorne asked, raising a quizzical brow.

"I met him once," Amanda admitted. "You needn't fear that he is vacillating. His injuries are real and more than slight. He was a fellow guest at the Blue Boar the night of the fire. His valet was the man who required the surgery."

Lady Thorne shook her head at this coincidence, though it was really not that surprising. The Blue Boar was the natural stopping place for those traveling to Thornridge Court from London. "I have never met him, though his grandmother was a close friend. She claims all virtues for the lad, but her mind has been wandering so much these last few years that it is difficult to know what to believe. Will he make a suitable husband for Emily?"

"Speculation is useless," Amanda reminded her. "I have not seen Emily since she was eight years old. Is she like her parents?"

"She has been raised to be a dutiful daughter."

"Then they will probably suit. He is as toplofty and arrogant a man as I have ever encountered, save for my father, though there does seem to be a softer streak buried beneath. I presume his visit will be rescheduled." Knowing the duke's injuries to be real, she did not for a moment believe that he would cry off.

"Emily is already talking of a shooting party when the partridge season opens in September," admitted Lady Thorne. "They have not yet heard back from the duke."

Amanda merely nodded, not particularly interested. Her siblings had never been close, especially the girls. Emily was the oldest female, being nine years younger than Amanda. Marianne had been only five when Amanda left. The boys had arrived between her and her sisters, but they had spent the years before her own departure at school. She had not minded. All of them followed their father's lead and despised her, tormenting her ceaselessly until she deliberately avoided their company. Likewise, her stepmother had disdained her, noticing her only when she wished to encourage her own children by comparing them favorably to the hoydenish Amanda.

She turned the conversation to her own affairs and spent a pleasant hour describing her plans for the cottage and her hopes that she could establish herself as a teacher of music and French. Or other languages, if there was a demand for such. She was fluent in several.

"There was quite a scandal here last week," commented Lady Thorne when tea was over and they went outside to admire the rose garden.

"And what was that?"

"Do you remember Lord Quinn?"

"Yes, a curmudgeonly old gentleman in rather ill health."

"That was the former viscount. He died several years ago and was succeeded by his grandson."

"Toby?" asked Amanda in surprise.

"Yes. Toby is now married to Elkington's eldest daughter and has two small children—both girls, to his disgust."

"What scandal could he be involved in? I cannot imagine him changing so much. He was always one for propriety. In fact, he and Edgar shared so many ideas, they might as well have been brothers." Edgar was Thorne's heir, Lord Englewood.

"His cousin is visiting for the summer," reported Lady Thorne. "Mr. Hawkins has already earned a reputation for rascally tricks, according to Lady Beatrice."

"I've heard of Lady Beatrice," admitted Amanda. "She is said to be a most knowing gossip."

"She always was," agreed her grandmother. "Inquisitive as a cat, even as a girl. And just as cruel. Anyway, Mr. Hawkins is acquainted with Mr. Raintree and Lord Peter Barnhard, who were guests at Thorne's house party. They were schoolmates, I gather, before Hawkins was sent down for misconduct—some prank involving a performing bear, I believe, though it happened some years ago. Apparently the three stole away last Friday to play ghost in Sir Timothy's stables. In the resulting chaos, one of the stable lads broke a leg."

Amanda, who had been trying to stifle giggles, suddenly sobered. "Poor boy. Is he all right?"

"It was a clean break. But Thorne was not impressed with the scoundrels' behavior, ordering Raintree and Barnhard to leave. Their departure caused more stir than the prank did."

"That is understandable. Most people do not condemn such harmless pastimes, even though damage was done in this instance. What did the other guests think?"

"I only know what Emily reported when she told me of it the following day. She was upset over the giddy laughter with which her female guests greeted the news. Miss Simpson even derided Thorne as a pretentious old goat. I doubt we will see her in the future. Emily's own reaction was all that was proper. She vows to never speak to the perpetrators again as her way of showing disapproval and will cut them if their paths cross in town."

"Why? Because they injured an innocent party?"

"Of course not. He was only a stable boy. But they should not have abandoned their dignity to engage in such tricks. And they certainly should not associate with servants. They must have done so or they could not have learned of Tom's belief in spirits."

Amanda paused a moment, but decided that she must be herself. If her grandmother did not approve, there was nothing she could do to alter the situation. "I see nothing wrong with normal high spirits," she declared, brushing the petals of a velvety red rose, her face half turned away. "It was unfortunate that they did not consider the potential consequences, but there is no reason to condemn them as scoundrels because of one boyish prank. They will grow up in time."

"You sound as though you endorse such behavior," said Lady Thorne chillingly.

"No, I do not. But I understand them. This accident will remain in their minds as an object lesson. I have seen it happen too often to doubt that they were appalled at the lad's injury. We often saw young men who bought colors on a lark or from some romantic notion of vanquishing the evil Napoleon. Only after their first battle did they realize how serious war is, and how dangerous. Such a shock can produce a more sobering effect than any number of lectures."

Lady Thorne snorted.

"Was Thorne satisfied to throw the lads out?" Amanda asked, not believing that the man could have changed that much.

"No, he read Quinn a loud and very public lecture on his own moral laxity after church this past Sunday, decrying the viscount's lack of supervision, his failure to set an example of proper behavior, and his inability to control his wife—the girl laughed over the incident before services. Thorne finished by calling Quinn's propriety into question for allowing Mr. Hawkins to continue his visit and swore to get him dismissed as a justice of the peace. It has raised quite a furor."

"I can imagine."

"Quinn actually cut Thorne in the village yesterday."

"Thereby prolonging and intensifying the disagreement."

Amanda sighed. "But one can hardly blame him after such a mortifying attack."

"Yes," agreed Lady Thorne. "Whatever the merits of his complaint, Thorne's choice of fields on which to wage battle was unfortunate."

"I heard that Granny Gossich passed away recently," Amanda commented, hoping to change the subject. Her father's self-righteousness was too familiar to be interesting.

"The old witch who lived in the woods outside Middleford?" Lady Thorne asked, surprised. "She died last month. Why?"

"She was a close friend for many years," admitted Amanda. "But she was no witch. Only a healer. Her skill with herbs was greater than all but the most enlightened doctors, and she knew much about treating injuries. I have often been grateful for what she taught me."

"How was it that Thorne allowed such an acquaintance?"

"Do you seriously believe I let him dictate my friends? I was an undutiful child—as he lost no opportunity to remind me—and often went off on my own. Sometimes it was to ride the moor or visit the tenants, but most often I went to Granny's cottage. She accepted me for what I was rather than dictating behavior because of who I was. I didn't think of it like that, of course. I only knew that her home was comfortable and she cared for me."

Lady Thorne had blanched. "We all cared for you, Amanda."

"Speak for yourself. My father was cold and disapproving. He declared his hatred more than once. The others followed his lead. You showed warmth on occasion, but think back. There was little to choose among the lot of you for stern haughtiness. Or should I term it *the Sterne Hauteur,* that arbiter that not only condemns all joy, but coerces others into its mold, thus perpetuating itself for all eternity. Has Father ever smiled? Or laughed? Has he ever approved of anything that brought pleasure to life?"

"You are harsh, Amanda. He has many responsibilities."

"I would never argue his devotion to duty. But duty and enjoyment need not be incompatible. Now, enough of this. I've no desire to waste a perfectly lovely day discussing the

Marquess of Thorne. Do you know where Granny was laid to rest? I must pay my respects."

"Not in the churchyard. The vicar despised her practice of witchcraft."

"Then he was ignorant, for she was no witch. But I am not surprised. He owes his living to Thorne. Where is she?"

"I know not. Tales claim her body was spirited away by the devil."

Amanda sighed. Granny's friends probably feared desecration at the hands of a bigoted vicar, possibly with the approval of Lord Thorne. Perhaps John Timmonds would know. He was a tenant who had blessed Granny many times for curing his wife of a raving fever.

Their conversation was interrupted when a young lady arrived.

"Good afternoon, Emily," said Lady Thorne. Taking the bull by the horns, she turned to Amanda. "Mrs. Morrison, this is my granddaughter, Lady Emily. Emily, my granddaughter and your sister, Amanda."

Amanda hardly took in the fact that Lady Thorne had introduced her as a granddaughter, despite Thorne's edict that she claim no connection to the family. Emily was a petite miss with pretty blonde ringlets. Her jonquil muslin walking dress trimmed in lime ribbons was obviously a product of a London modiste, and a charming chip-straw bonnet framed her heart-shaped face. With a smile, she would be lovely, and her position as Thorne's daughter with a generous dowry would make her a very desirable candidate on the marriage mart. But just now she appeared dauntingly unapproachable, her brown eyes staring icily.

"What is she doing here?" demanded Emily, delivering a direct cut as she turned to her grandmother.

"I invited her. This is my home, you might recall," Lady Thorne gently chided in return.

"You know Father repudiated her," Emily protested.

"Your father's edicts do not concern me." The dowager's voice was stern. "I will entertain all my relations whenever I choose."

"You needn't fear I will bother you," commented Amanda dryly. "I have no intention of trespassing where I

am not welcome. Nor will I waste my time with people
who do not interest me."

"What a taradiddle!" exclaimed Emily. "No one can ignore the Marquess of Thorne."

"You make him sound like God. Sorry to disappoint you,
Lady Emily, but I care nothing for the family. Fate has led
me to make my home in Middleford, but I doubt we shall
see each other to speak." She turned to her grandmother.
"Thank you for the tea."

"You needn't leave yet, surely," protested Lady Thorne.

"There will be better times to chat. Good day." Nodding
silently to Emily, she departed.

Amanda pulled herself from another nightmare and sat
up. It promised to be a long night, the fourth in a row. Donning her dressing gown, she wandered over to the window.

The dreams were getting worse as well as more frequent.
She should have expected it. By returning, she had
breached a barricade that had been in place for nine years.
Ghosts were bound to emerge.

This one recalled one of the more painful memories of
her childhood. Thorne had castigated her many times for
associating with the tenants, but she had refused to give in.
Aside from sheer stubbornness, the tenant children were
her only friends. But the year she turned twelve, Thorne
had shifted tactics, inflicting his will by turning her own
character against her.

"You were with Willy when he broke his ankle this afternoon," he charged. As usual, she was standing before his
desk.

"Yes." She hadn't understood where his words were
leading. The accident had been unavoidable, her presence
in no way affecting it. She had only stopped a moment to
exchange greetings on her way to Granny's cottage. Fif-
teen-year-old Willy had been perched high in an apple tree,
thinning the buds to improve the size of the fruit. She was
already moving on when the branch broke.

"You demean yourself and insult the entire family by
such behavior," he continued, his voice even icier than
usual. "The distraction of being singled out by one so high
can only contribute to inattention in the lower orders. Your

presence caused him to fall. And now the Randalls are short a worker. I cannot allow their fields to suffer. They must leave."

"You can't throw them out because of Willy," she cried, aghast.

"I can, and I have. Think about it, Amanda. Your refusal to learn proper behavior has cost the Randalls their home. Remember that next time you are tempted to overstep your position."

Amanda had hated him that day more than at any other time in her life. She had immediately rushed to their cottage, but they were already gone. It was five years before she discovered that Thorne had not thrown them out. They had been a hard-working family that deserved more than the poor farm they rented at the Court. When a larger one opened up on one of Thorne's other properties, he offered it to them. The arrangements were completed before Willy's accident, though Mr. Randall had not yet informed the children.

Amanda shook her head. Thorne had lied, using the coincidence to impose his will. It was one of the few times she had capitulated to his edicts. Never again had she played with the tenant children, which had left Granny as her only friend.

She turned from the window and crawled back into bed. Granny was gone now. Already people were turning to her for healing and advice, rumor crediting her with all Granny's knowledge. Some even whispered that the fates had brought her home as the reincarnation of Granny Gossich. What would Thorne do when he discovered that?

Chapter Four

Nicholas Blaire, tenth Duke of Norwood, stretched his left arm toward the ceiling, so pleased that it was finally out of the splint that he almost smiled. Unfortunately, it had been so long since that expression had broken out on his face that the muscles had forgotten how, but it felt good to move freely.

After weeks of convalescence with little to do but contemplate, it was obvious that he had been drifting for years. His life had no purpose beyond daily routine. He rarely socialized. Everyone knew him for what he was—cool, remote, and happier in his own company. Even lords with eligible daughters no longer schemed for his duchess's rooms.

That had changed six months earlier, of course. His mother had long bewailed his neglect of duty. He needed an heir. The second cousin who would inherit if he died without a son had not been trained to the responsibilities of the dukedom, with its eight estates, dozen other properties, and thousands of dependents. He owed it to his position to marry again. It was time. He had ceased mourning Annabelle several years earlier, though he had not yet forgiven himself for his mistreatment. Older and wiser, he would not make that mistake again.

And so he had forced himself to London for the Season, back to the scene of his shame. Hiding his discomfort behind an acceptable mask of controlled *ennui,* he had danced, driven in the park, pretended interest in wailing singers and hesitant pianists at boring musicales, and allowed himself to be ogled at the theater. He had visited clubs he had not seen in ten years and looked in on Parliament, finally assuming the seat he had inherited eight years before. And through it all, he had conducted a cynical analysis of every chit he met.

He had found the perfect wife, he decided, dispassionately reviewing her credentials. Lady Emily Sterne. Even her name was suitable. The daughter of a marquess, she had the breeding he required for his duchess. Barely seventeen years old, she promised to be a conformable bride. She had been well trained in the responsibilities inherent in her new position, and possessed a devotion to duty that mirrored his own. Thorne was a proper fellow who was wealthy and frugal, with no vices that might affect his daughter's marriage.

His mother approved his choice, having known Lady Emily's mother since the latter staged her come-out. The duchess often recounted Lady Thorne's cool propriety and adherence to strict decorum. Her eldest daughter would make a perfect duchess. Surprisingly, Norwood's grandmother also approved, citing her own long friendship with the dowager Marchioness of Thorne. The lady's eldest granddaughter was the best possible choice for dear Nicholas's wife. It was the first time Norwood could recall his mother and grandmother agreeing.

So why did he entertain doubts about offering for the chit? She was not in love with him, and that was good. He wanted no complications in his life. She would provide an heir and oversee his household, but not demand constant attention. His son would be properly raised by the usual sequence of nurse, tutor, and public school, needing personal attention only when he reached the age at which Norwood must sponsor him into the clubs. Everything would work for him exactly as it had for his own father. A perfect marriage of convenience.

He wandered over to his bedroom window. The park laid out by Capability Brown stretched into the distance, every tree and shrub placed and tended for maximum effect. It was time to take charge of his life. He had drifted long enough. Taking his seat in Parliament was the first step. He had survived the Season intact, putting the past irrevocably behind him so that living in town no longer bothered him. Marriage was another step. The arrangement was strictly business, but having a wife would place demands on his time. He was prepared for that, though he had no intention of being thrust into a giddy social whirl. That was something he must make clear before making his offer.

The duke added it to the list of topics he must discuss with Lady Emily. Not that he expected any problems, but this time he was making no assumptions. Unpleasant surprises had no place in his well-ordered life. He had already accepted an invitation to attend a shooting party at Thornridge Court. It was all very much like his departure from London two months earlier, except for the nagging questions about embarking on a new marriage. Why? The girl conformed perfectly to the characteristics he demanded in his wife. There was no reason for the lurking suspicion that the fire had saved him from making a ghastly mistake. It had merely postponed his journey.

The fire. Now there had been an unpleasant surprise, leaving vivid images imprinted on his mind. If only he could put the experience behind him! But it refused to fade, causing nightmares that still awakened him several times a week. The pictures were always the same—utter helplessness at facing a flame-filled hall; abject terror as he jumped from the window; shock and humiliation surrounding Fitch's surgery. Every detail was magnified in his dreams—fiercer flames, a higher window, louder screams, denser smoke, more blood . . . Even his emotions intensified until they rose up to choke him. Then he would awaken, screaming and gasping for air. But he could not believe that the fire itself was responsible. It was his own dishonorable behavior.

He shuddered every time he recalled his arrogant demand for immediate attention. Never had he expected to react that way; the surprise of it shocked him as much as the events of that night. A duke should conduct himself in a more seemly fashion. That widow who had been treating the injured had certainly not been impressed.

And why would he wish to impress so lowly a creature? he asked himself disparagingly as a pair of swans glided effortlessly across the distant lake. He did not demand adoration from everyone he met. *Obviously, you do not know who I am . . . I am the Duke of Norwood.* In retrospect, his words sounded like a command to toadeat him. He shivered. Granted, his position required deference, but he could have achieved it in a more gracious manner. The widow had not hesitated an instant before knocking him down a peg.

He turned back to his bedroom with its blue velvet hangings and heavy gilding. That must be why her image haunted his dreams. He knew next to nothing about her, but he could not seem to forget her. Perhaps it was because she had refused to bow to his authority. Never before had anyone treated him like a servant. Of course, it might be nought but the novelty of the situation or the calm efficiency with which she faced a crisis, but he could not make himself believe it. He had wanted to thank her for her care and commend her on her efforts, even apologize for his behavior. But the opportunity never arose. Before the last few wounded were treated, she had boarded a stage and was gone.

He had decided to ask Matthews for information. The doctor had known her before and might know where the duke could send his thanks. But Matthews was inside the inn. Someone was trapped under another section of collapsed roof. The only way to extricate the fellow was to amputate the crushed leg on the spot.

Norwood's stomach twisted with the memory. He had slipped into the stable when the doctor appeared to find assistants. His splinted arm was too cumbersome to be of any use. At least, that was the excuse he murmured to himself. In truth, he was a coward, unwilling to make an ass of himself by vomiting in front of yet more people. His ducal dignity would suffer too much. And so he had been safely hiding when a wall came down, killing the victim, the doctor, and his two helpers.

It was that dishonor that he could not forget. It contrasted badly with the image he held of himself. Nor could he impute his behavior to shock. Succumbing to shock was also unacceptable. And so he had been left to ponder his character. What lack led him to disgrace himself? First to Annabelle. Then when he faced a genuine crisis. Unless he could answer the question, there was no guarantee that the future would differ.

There had been nothing to do but search out another doctor and arrange to transfer Fitch to a nearby inn. Given the plethora of wounded and the paucity of nurses, he found himself caring for Fitch himself, a situation the valet loudly decried in his few moments of lucidity between lengthy bouts of delirium. He had even tried to tend Norwood's own injuries.

A surgeon arrived from the next town the afternoon of the fire. Dr. Martin was a florid man who reeked of wine. He prescribed leeching to remove noxious humors and opined that the other leg must come off. Norwood balked. The experienced Matthews had stated that it would be impossible to tell for a couple of days. The duke dismissed Martin and sent for a learned physician from London, but in the end it made no difference. The burns festered and Fitch died of fever.

Norwood had returned to his estate. The Season was over. With his arm broken, there was little he could do in town anyway. Dr. Harris found no reason to fear for his own recovery, but blue devils dogged him every mile of that journey. He might have been suffering a touch of fever himself, he thought now. Whatever the cause, memories of the fire loomed large. Every time he dozed off, he again faced the horror, usually awakening when the beam crashed onto his arm. How had he heaved it off? He could remember nothing between then and his arrogant outburst in the stable yard.

A dozen people had perished in the blaze, and two heroic figures emerged as tales spread from those who had escaped. The first was Fitch. He had been asleep when someone pounded on his door, shouting warnings. He immediately fled to the floor where his employer slept. It was he who had awakened Norwood from his slumbers and allowed him to escape. Fitch had not been so lucky. He helped an elderly dowager and her unconscious companion downstairs, then returned to make sure Norwood got out. But by then, the hall was engulfed in flames. The roof collapse caught him as he raced back to the stairs.

But the greatest heroine of the night was that widow. She had roused everyone in the other wing as well as those on Fitch's floor before setting herself to treat the injured. Without her efforts, the death toll would have been much higher. Against those actions, he could only place his insis-

tence that his title demanded special treatment. He shuddered.

Had he really grown so arrogant? It was hardly surprising, he admitted. His mother was as coldly contemptuous
as any dowager in the *ton*. Her life and teachings revolved
around propriety and duty. She employed two facial expressions—haughty disdain toward anyone whose position
fell below her own, and a patently false smile when with
her social equals. He had discovered a shining example of
her priorities the day he arrived back at Norwood Castle.

The duchess had happened across the scene of an accident. Several days of rain had swollen streams and turned
roads into quagmires. A carriage had slipped as it approached the bridge a quarter mile from the Castle gates,
plunging into the racing torrent. Though the coach was
wedged firmly between rocks, the passengers were too injured to escape by themselves and were in danger of
drowning. Lady Norwood ordered her coachman to press
on, stopping only to send the gatekeeper and his son to
help. One of the victims drowned.

The question had teased Norwood since he first heard the
tale: If she had asked her coachman and groom to rescue
the passengers, would both have survived? There was no
answer, but the conundrum prompted him to evaluate both
his position as duke and his responsibilities to others. Always in the past, he had adhered to his training, setting
good stewards over his properties who hired competent employees so that everything ran smoothly. He did nothing
himself. His mother had done the same that day—ordering
the nearest available servants to assist. But her coachman
and groom were unavailable. Her welfare demanded that
they see her safely and comfortably home. She was more
important than a pair of unfortunate strangers.

Two months ago he would have agreed without thought.
Now he was not so sure. What was wrong with him?

Pushing memory aside, he turned his attention to the future. He was too old to change his ways. Issuing the necessary instructions for an early departure, he spent the
remainder of the evening disposing of estate business.

The duke glanced idly through the window as his car-

riage rumbled up the drive at Thornridge Court. The house
was large, expanded and gifted with a Palladian facade a
century earlier. Formal gardens extended beyond the struc-
ture; only the edges were visible from his vantage point,
but the hand of a perfectionist master was clearly dis-
cernible. Not a blade of grass was out of place.

His baggage coach drew up as he descended from his
carriage. A butler was already hurrying down the steps.
Through the open front door he could see the marquess, a
smile engulfing the man's face.

"Welcome to the Court, your grace," said Thorne, almost
fawning with unaccustomed good humor. "I trust you are
fully recovered."

A thread of uncertainty underlay these last words, leaving Norwood with the distinct impression that Thorne had
not believed the hasty note he had dispatched from the Blue
Boar.

"Quite," he replied without explanation.

"You will wish to refresh yourself," continued Thorne.
"Frank will show you to your rooms."

"Thank you."

"The other guests will be gathering in the drawing room
in about an hour. We dine at six."

"I will see them then."

It required several more meaningless exchanges before
he was finally able to escape upstairs. He was housed in the
royal suite, with a bedroom done up in crimson silk and a
sitting room in gold. Servants were already delivering hot
water. In just over an hour he was clean, relaxed, and
dressed in impeccable evening clothes—a wine-colored
jacket trimmed in black, dove gray pantaloons, and snowy
white linen. Half-past five. He stowed his watch, grimaced
at his mirrored image, and dismissed Winter.

The drawing room was already buzzing with voices. It
did not take him long to understand that everyone expected
an imminent offer for Lady Emily. The gathering might be
termed a shooting party in deference to the season, but he
could not avoid a declaration. Not that he minded; he
needed an heir. But it was annoying to realize that every
move he made would be watched.

Lady Emily met him at the door. Her smile lent her face

an impish look, belying her normally serious character, but her brown eyes remained bored, and he relaxed in relief. The smile was the same false social expression his mother used.

"Your grace," she said, allowing him to take her hand for a brief moment before she reclaimed it to lay on his arm.

"Lady Emily, you are looking as beautiful as ever," he replied, making no attempt to smile. His face refused to do so. The gallantry would have to stand or fall on its own.

"I presume you know everyone, but allow me to refresh your memory," she offered, ignoring his words.

He did indeed know the other guests. The Earl of Craven and his wife were cousins of Lord Thorne. The Earl of Bradford was also connected, his wife being the late Lady Thorne's sister. They were accompanied by their daughters, Lady Sarah and Lady Anne. Lady Havershoal was with her daughter Miss Victoria Havershoal, who was Lady Emily's closest friend. The rest were gentlemen invited to make up the numbers, but also intended to force Norwood up to scratch. Two were members of Lady Emily's court, Lord Geoffrey Babcock and Mr. Oliver Stevens. The other was young Stevens's father, Sir Harold. Englewood had been delayed, but was expected by the end of the week.

The Duke of Norwood knew his duty. He would make the offer. But he did not like being forced. Between his mother and Thorne, he was feeling very pressured.

He disengaged himself from Lady Emily's escort and inquired of Lord Geoffrey about the prospects for partridge.

Part of his mind carried on the discussion of shooting, but most of it insisted on comparing his very correct courtship of Lady Emily to his far more emotional encounters with Annabelle. He had not had trouble smiling in those days. In fact, he rarely did anything else. How had it felt that Season? After all the years of adhering to his father's restrictions, he had finally been on his own in London for the first time, having just come down from Oxford. Life was exciting for any young man newly on the town, but his position as Norwood's heir meant he could do anything he pleased with impunity. Gaming hells, men's clubs, cock fights, greenrooms, sparring, shooting, fencing . . . He had done it all. Prinny's friends took him under their wings,

introducing him to all manner of pastimes, some of which
made him shudder in memory.

His father had tried to direct him onto a more sober path,
but despite Nicholas's sudden wildness, the man had understood. Strange to remember that now. What had the ninth
duke been like as a young man? It was difficult to imagine
him celebrating his arrival in the adult world in a similar
manner. To keep the peace with his family, Nicholas had
also attended many social gatherings. It was at one of these
that he met Miss Annabelle Crompton. She was merely the
daughter of a viscount, but what attracted him was her
sparkling presence. Blonde, vivacious, and beautiful, she
brightened any company, drawing the eyes of everyone in
the room. Within a week, he was hopelessly in love with
her. And she returned his regard, flirting shamelessly with
him, affording him the maximum attention allowed by custom.

They had laughed so often—at the silly affectations of
others, at their disapproving parents, at the ridiculous rules
society decreed and the equally ridiculous attention they all
paid to fashion. He drove her in Hyde Park, danced her
through balls, attended opera and theater, and discussed her
wish that her mother had not died so young. They agreed
on everything. Never had he known anyone whose mind
meshed so well with his own.

Enough! he ordered his head as Lord Geoffrey switched
from shooting prospects to the upcoming races. Annabelle
was dead these ten years. He would never fall in love again.
Deep, abiding love came along but once in a lifetime, if
that. He had used his quota on Annabelle. Lady Emily was
the wife he wanted now. He needed an heir and a hostess.
She would do well. One eye watched as she moved about
the room, setting people at their ease and drawing everyone
into conversation. She had doubtless absorbed good taste
during her growing years. Lady Thorne's touch was exquisite.

The drawing room was formally decorated in an unusual
mixture of green, blue, and gold. Despite all logic, it
worked. And despite an elaborate ceiling whose design was
repeated in the carpet, it did not appear cluttered. The fur-
nishings were quietly elegant, providing ample seating

without crowding the space. The gilded silk-clad walls served as the ideal backdrop for judiciously selected paintings, statues, vases, and bowls. Adam had obviously had a hand in the styling.

Lady Emily was engaged in a lively exchange with Mr. Stevens, flirting mildly with the man, though never passing beyond acceptable boundaries. Norwood paid little attention to their conversation until Emily's voice changed to displeasure.

"But what can one expect of her?" she demanded sharply. "After all, she's hardly top drawer. Her only claim to respectability is her grandmother, who was the youngest daughter of a viscount. Her father is only two generations away from trade."

"You are cruel, Lady Emily," Stevens chided softly. "Miss Emerson is an unexceptionable young lady with a delightful sense of humor. I am surprised at your intolerance. Surely someone in your exalted position can afford a little magnanimity."

She sniffed. "If those in high positions lowered their standards to that extent, what would be the purpose of proper breeding?"

"It is better to enjoy life than endure the loneliness of hauteur," pronounced Stevens, moving on to join another conversation.

Norwood pondered the boy's cryptic statement as he continued his discussion with Lord Geoffrey. Optimistic youth. Stevens would soon learn the lessons he himself had already mastered. He had enjoyed life as a young man, harboring all of that optimism and more. It had prompted him to disregard vast differences in station, to ignore the duty he owed his title, and to repudiate his father's wisdom. And where had it led him? Straight to hell. At least embracing propriety protected him from making the same mistakes again.

Chapter Five

Norwood's mood was sour. Despite the pretense that the gathering was a shooting party, they were finding precious little game. Thorne's coverts were practically barren of partridge.

"He needs a new gamekeeper," grumbled Lord Geoffrey, tramping along at Norwood's side. In two hours the two had managed but four birds between them. The other gentlemen fared no better.

"I'd have a full bag by now in Scot—" Norwood abruptly halted as one of the dogs froze. The beaters flushed a dozen partridges into the air. Seven guns fired simultaneously.

"Got one," said Norwood in satisfaction, pausing to reload.

"Damnation," swore Lord Geoffrey. "I only winged mine."

The talk turned to horses as they circled a craggy outcrop. Despite dangling after the same lady during the previous Season, the men were friends, Geoffrey's estate running with Norwood Castle. His lordship was several years younger than his grace and possessed two brothers and four nephews to protect him from any titles, so he was under no pressure. He had not yet seriously considered marrying, content to wait until he found a lady he truly cared about.

Frustration mounted, finally prompting the party to split up. Thorne, Craven, and Bradford worked their way through a stand of trees while the others veered around the flank of the hill. The heavy overcast that had produced overnight showers was dissipating, allowing sunbeams to fleetingly spotlight a hilltop or stream or jutting rock.

The accident occurred so suddenly that Norwood had no time to think. The dogs had flushed another covey of partridge, along with a pheasant. Choosing the elusive partridge as being more worthy of his skill, he allowed Geoffrey to bring down the larger bird. But he was so intent on tracking his game that he paid little heed to the terrain. As he fired, the recoil drove his weight against his back foot, which promptly collapsed when the ground gave way beneath it. Tumbling down a steep hill, he fetched up against a rock at the bottom.

"Are you all right?" gasped Geoffrey after an undignified race down an easier slope.

"I think so." Norwood shook his head to clear the dizziness and stood up. His right knee collapsed, depositing him back on the ground.

"You don't look it," observed his friend.

Norwood took a moment to glance around. No one but Geoffrey seemed aware of his fall. They had lagged behind the Stevenses, who doubtless believed they had now stopped to reload. He was lucky. His only injuries were a gash on the thigh and a wrenched knee.

"It is nothing," he disclaimed, removing his neckcloth to wrap the thigh. "But I had best return to the house and change." His breeches were torn and the rest of his clothing muddy.

"I will collect our horses," his friend offered.

"Get mine, if you will, but you must stay with the others. I would rather not make anything of this. If anyone asks, I grew weary of the paucity of game."

Geoffrey stared for several seconds before nodding in agreement.

Norwood berated himself as he rode slowly back toward the Court. How had he allowed his attention to wander so badly? He was always cautious, especially when shooting over unfamiliar ground. But today he had paid no attention to his surroundings. Despite maintaining the usual conversation, his mind had been uselessly pondering his upcoming betrothal. Why? Five months of thought had examined every benefit and pitfall many times over. The decision was made. His courtship was too advanced to set aside. And why would he want to? Lady Emily's expectations were identical to his own. She wanted only the social cachet she would have as the Duchess of Norwood. Neither enjoyed emotional scenes. Both looked for a marriage of convenience. It was perfect.

He must speak to Thorne and get the formalities out of the way. There was no reason to feel nervous about it. He had been through the process before. And this time he was worldly enough to make no mistakes. He shuddered as another picture leaked out of his memory.

An imposing butler had ushered him into Crompton's library, where Annabelle's father greeted him warmly and pressed an excellent French brandy on him.

"I wish to pay my addresses to Miss Crompton, my lord," he had blurted out once the necessary comments on health and weather were out of the way, nerves making his voice crack as it had not done in years.

Crompton had beamed and refilled his glass. "You will suit admirably," he agreed. "Annabelle is worthy of the highest in the land, but of course, you already know that. I trust you will care for her as she deserves." And without giving the then Marquess of Medford time to respond, he had immediately launched a discussion of settlements and plans that ended an hour later with signatures affixed to the marriage contract. Nicholas had been wildly in love with Annabelle, willing to offer anything that would make her happy.

The duke's head shook in despair over that callow youth. It had never occurred to him that he should speak with Annabelle before settling with her father. Nor had he questioned whether Crompton truly understood Annabelle's needs. He had not even thought to include his solicitor in the discussion. In one bemused hour, he had placed his life and fortune in the hands of another.

He shuddered, as he always did when he remembered that day. He had been intoxicated—with love for the most beautiful, vibrant girl in the world; with exhilaration over winning her hand; with impatience at the month's delay before he could possess her; and with pride at stepping into the adult world and charting his own destiny. And so he had negotiated the settlements, set the wedding date, and sent the announcement to the papers before informing his family of his decision.

That blunder had been his first lesson in the dark side of

his position. He had long been accustomed to people fawning over him. After all, he was both wealthy and the heir to a dukedom. But his parents had protected him from the maliciously greedy. That was not a mistake he would ever make with his own heir. There had been others since then who thought to use him. He had become adept at spotting such pariahs. In fact, he had grown quite cynical in the ten years since Annabelle's death. And he congratulated himself on it. A healthy dose of cynicism was necessary if he was to protect himself. One was never too young to learn that lesson. There was a good reason for limiting his contacts to people near his own station.

He turned his horse aside to skirt a tract of oak and pollarded hornbeam, his leg protesting the movement. It throbbed painfully, blood seeping through his makeshift bandage. He wanted nothing more than to lie down for an hour or two, but he could not increase his pace. Posting to a trot was the last thing he needed.

There would be no settlements signed on this visit. Once Lady Emily accepted his suit, he would set his solicitor to the task of negotiating an agreement. Thorne was a hard bargainer, by all accounts. It might take six months or more before they were in accord. The wedding would likely be scheduled for the end of the following Season. And that was fine with him. There was plenty—

Lost in his reverie, Norwood had not headed the sound of distant barking. A stag suddenly broke from the forest, startling his horse. Under normal circumstances, he would have controlled the beast with ease, but his injured thigh was unable to grip tightly enough to avert disaster. Time seemed suspended as he sailed slowly through the air—very like his fall from the Blue Boar into the ravine. If only he could twist his feet under him . . . Pain exploded through his shoulder and everything went black.

Amanda drove her gig along a narrow country lane, skirting the boundaries of Thornridge Court. Life had settled into a pleasant routine. Her cottage was comfortable. Several area families had hired her to teach their daughters. She was also much in demand as a healer, though she seldom accepted payment for that work. Between her allowance and her earnings, she needed no additional income.

The area residents knew her well. She had often helped them in her youth, both as Granny's assistant and as a lady of the manor looking out for her tenants. Her first action on returning from London had been to seek out Granny's secret grave to mourn over it. When word of that swept round the area, people welcomed her back with open arms.

But even beyond her earlier assistance, they knew Thorne and had watched for years as the man mistreated his eldest daughter. Few approved of that situation. When Amanda quietly returned as Mrs. Morrison and made no attempt to visit the Court or discuss its residents, the people knew that nothing had changed. They rallied behind her both in support and to repudiate Thorne, who was highly unpopular. And not just by turning to her for lessons and healing. To prevent any embarrassment, they closed ranks to protect her, refusing to discuss her background with anyone. She was Granny's pupil. That was enough. As a result, those who were new to the area knew her only as a war widow who supported herself by teaching and who was knowledgeable about herbs.

Her closest friends fell into this last category. She knew Major and Mrs. Humphries from the Peninsula. The major had retired at the end of that campaign, buying a modest manor in Middleford though he had no previous ties to the area. Their pleasure at meeting Mrs. Morrison again was a balm after Thorne's cold antagonism.

Another friend was Mrs. Edwards. She was also a war widow, her husband having grown up in Middleford. She had lived with his mother while he served on the Peninsula, remaining there after her mother-in-law's death in 1811 and her husband's death at Vittoria.

But Amanda was not thinking of friends just now. Her mind was mired in frustration over Elizabeth Reeves. She had spent the morning at the squire's house, teaching the pianoforte to his three daughters. The younger girls would probably become adequate musicians in time, but the eldest was hopeless. Already seventeen, Elizabeth lacked both talent and desire. It was unlikely that she would continue instruction once she left home. Rumors circulated that a betrothal was in the offing between her and Sir Michael's youngest son. In the meantime, Amanda had accepted the challenge of improving the girl's performance. And it was a challenge. Elizabeth reminded her too much of herself as a rebellious youth.

The lane twisted sharply, topping a hill. As Amanda rounded the corner, she smiled. A patchwork of pastures, fields, and woods spread below her admiring gaze. It had always been a favorite view. The nearest meadow was a carpet of emerald that contrasted strongly with flanking stands of forest and the golden stubble of the newly harvested field beyond. Today it was even lovelier than usual. A shaft of sunlight stabbed through a break in the clouds to bathe only the greensward where a stag gracefully bounded, coat shining like flame as he raced toward the beechwood. A beautiful sight, but her admiration was immediately tempered by the riderless horse that followed in his wake. A patch of scarlet drew her eyes to the edge of the oak forest, the color quickly resolving into a motionless figure in a red hunting jacket. She thrust aside her first fear. There had been distant barking several minutes earlier but no gunshots that might hint at poachers. Yet the man did not move.

It took but a minute to reach the bottom of the hill. Snubbing the ribbons, she jumped down. The victim had landed hard, his head hitting a rock before he rolled onto his stomach. His hat had lodged in a clump of gorse, mud now caking his black hair. A large knot was visible on one temple, though it was not bleeding. The rough, blood-soaked bandage on his right thigh explained how he came to be thrown.

Satisfying herself that he still lived and that nothing was broken, she rolled him over so she could revive him. Her sudden gasp drowned out the soft sounds of the September morning as she recognized him. The Duke of Norwood. And his face was nearly as pale as the night he held down Fitch.

He groaned.

"Steady, your grace," she admonished him, pressing his shoulders into the ground when he tried to rise. "Do not move. Is there any damage aside from your head and thigh?"

Opening his eyes, he winced. "You!"

"Yes. We meet again. Have you always been so accident prone?"

"Never," he denied weakly.

"What happened to your leg?" She was removing the bandage, which had slipped, allowing mud into the wound.

"I fell."

"Obviously. And cracked your head. What about this?" She touched the bandage.

"I fell down a hill." He sounded sheepishly sullen.

"Men! Why did someone not accompany you back to the house?" Without water, there was not much she could do, but she wiped away the worst of the mud and blood.

"It is not that bad," he protested.

"Stubborn, aren't you?" she observed caustically. "It is severe enough that you could not control your horse. Men routinely forget that riding astride requires strength in the thighs. I knew at least four who perished because they lost control of their mounts after returning to battle with just such a wound."

Norwood closed his eyes, refusing to comment on her words.

The gash was bleeding only slightly, so Amanda left it open for the moment. "Can you sit up?" she asked.

"Of course." He glared.

"There is no 'of course' about it. You were unconscious when I found you. Move slowly or you risk nausea."

He flushed, obviously recalling the last time they had met, and undoubtedly ashamed of losing control of himself that night. But this time he managed it. His face paled alarmingly and she could see him swallowing hard several times, but he finally lurched to his feet and stayed there.

"Excellent, your grace," she murmured. "Now we walk."

"Where?"

"My gig is on the road." She nodded toward her horse, grazing about three hundred feet away. "You might as well swallow your pride and lean on me. It is less embarrassing than falling."

"Forthright, aren't you?" he muttered, reluctantly draping an arm across her shoulders when his knee again threatened to collapse.

"If one wishes to survive a military campaign, one learns to be practical," she countered.

"How do you come to be here?" he asked when they finally reached the road.

"I live in Middleford. Stay there," she ordered when he would have climbed into the gig. She pulled a bag from under the seat and rummaged inside.

"What are you doing?"

"That leg needs attention."

"Do you always carry medical supplies around with you?"

"Of course. Many people come to me for help. I never know when I might need something." Widening the tear in his fawn breeches, she poured brandy onto a cloth and washed away the last of the mud.

"Devil take it, woman!" he growled, flinching. "That is deuced uncomfortable! Leave it be."

"You haven't changed much," she observed tartly, drenching the cut with wine. "Still as ornery and arrogant as ever."

"Nor have you," he responded shortly. "Still as dictatorial and unreasonable as before."

"Unreasonable, your grace? Neither propriety nor toadeating is of any use when lives are at stake."

He had the grace to look ashamed. "Are you deliberately irritating that leg to pay me back for my arrogance?"

"Never! But mud never did any wound much good. I must clean this gash and I have no water. Brandy seems to work better, anyway. There. We'll leave the remains of these breeches in place to protect your modesty. Your valet can replace the bandage when you get home." Dusting the cut with basilicum powder, she wrapped a strip of linen around the thigh.

"You seem to be making a habit of patching me up," he groused.

"Be grateful you are not now trying to walk home. And you should also thank the Lord that nothing is broken—like your stiff neck."

He made a sound that could have been anything from a snort to agreement.

Norwood settled into the gig, his head in confusion. He felt like he had stepped into a dream. The fire had continued to haunt his sleep, the recurring nightmare awakening him just before dawn that very morning. Or had it? This outspoken, managing woman could not possibly be here. Was he trapped in the otherworld? His head swirled from the effects of the blow. Every movement sent sparks of pain knifing into his eyes and down his neck. He couldn't seem to think straight, and was not even sure if he was still conscious.

"Where am I?" he murmured as the horse jolted into motion.

She looked at him sharply, then relaxed. "Where do you think you are, your grace?"

"In a dream."

"Why?"

"Nothing seems real."

"You are perfectly fine," she assured him. "And you are wide awake."

"Then what are you doing here?" he asked again, shaking his head to try to clear it and only making the pain worse. It was difficult to believe he was awake, yet the woman did not look the same as he recalled. She seemed better fed, with a higher color. Or was that due to sunlight and a soot-free face?

"I live here," she explained patiently.

"But you were at the Blue Boar."

"Like you, I was a guest that night."

"I know, but—"

"I had been in London since leaving Belgium, but finally decided to return home. I grew up around here."

He raised a shaky hand to his head, trying fruitlessly to ease its pounding. "I've forgotten your name."

"Mrs. Morrison, your grace. How is Mr. Fitch?"

"He died."

"I am sorry, though I feared it. I have seen too many like him."

"It was his own fault. He was safely outside, having escorted an elderly lady from the inn, but he chose to return."

"An admirable man. How dare you blame him for dying! Or are you piqued that his selflessness deprived you of his services?"

"Devil take it! You are both impertinent and misguided, to say nothing of insulting. I am perfectly capable of taking care of myself. Fitch had no business coming back inside."

"Ah," she said in sudden understanding. "Guilt. He went back for you, didn't he? *Greater love hath no man, that he would lay down his life for a friend.* Even more so for an arrogant employer. And now you must live with that burden, whether you deserved such devotion or not."

"Not in the least," he growled, infuriated by her observation and unsure why. "I am merely saddened at an unnecessary death."

"Was it the other leg? Dr. Matthews tries to save as much as possible, but sometimes he is wrong."

Norwood grimaced. "My London physician said it was fever. He agreed the leg might heal, but we couldn't get his fever down."

"Putrefaction in the burns, most likely. It's common enough. Dr. Matthews must have been run off his legs with all the fire victims."

"No. He died that night."

Amanda choked in horror, involuntarily jerking the horse toward the ditch. Norwood grasped the ribbons and pulled them to a halt.

"How?" she asked, staring at him with pain in her eyes.

Norwood was shivering from the memory. "A man was trapped under debris and could only be extricated by removing his crushed leg." His voice broke. "A wall came down during the surgery, killing everyone."

"Don't blame yourself, your grace," she murmured, understanding the self-reproach in his voice even through her own grief for yet another friend now dead. "You were in no condition to help, having suffered too much already that night." She flicked the horse into motion, eyes again facing forward to hide their sheen of tears.

"You were very heroic from what I have heard," Norwood continued in a different vein, unable to agree with her, yet unwilling to argue the matter. "They say you woke most of the guests, allowing at least a score to escape unharmed who might not have gotten out at all."

"It was nothing," she demurred. "Anyone would have done the same."

"I doubt that."

"Cynical man. While there are a few who are too selfish, most would."

"You are wrong, of course, but I am not in the mood for a debate."

"You might wish to reread the parable of the Good Samaritan, your grace." She sighed. "I am only sorry that the fire prevented me from getting into most of the other wing."

"You woke Fitch and he alerted those on my floor." His voice cracked.

Amanda shook her head in sorrow. After several minutes of silence, she turned through the gates of Thornridge Court, drawing a look of surprise from Norwood.

"You know where I am staying?" he asked, only just realizing that he had provided no direction.

"Of course. Everyone in the neighborhood knows about this house party. Surely you expected that."

"I've never really thought about it." He shrugged, drawing a stare from his companion.

"How sad that you withdraw from life. You might also benefit from reading John Donne. *No man is an island, entire of itself.*"

He made no response, sinking into a near-stupor, rousing only when she reached the front entrance. Norwood was dizzily aware of how weak he was feeling, but he was not so removed from reality that he missed the footman's reaction to Mrs. Morrison's knock. The man froze at the sight of her, becoming even stiffer when he identified her passenger.

Lady Emily appeared before anyone said a word.

"How dare you call here?" she demanded coldly.

"I am returning one of your guests who suffered an accident," Mrs. Morrison replied calmly. "He will need assistance."

Emily looked beyond Amanda, her eyes widening when she identified Norwood. "Frank, help his grace to his room," she ordered. "Does he need a doctor?"

"It would not hurt," said Amanda.

"Fustian!" snorted Norwood, unwilling to admit to any serious injury and reluctant to face some country sawbones who would only bleed him. "I will be fine. It is nought but a scrape."

"I will summon his valet then," decided Emily, turning away from the door.

"Thank you, ma'am," Norwood formally addressed Amanda as Frank helped him into the house.

"You will recover quickly," she responded. "The housekeeper should have basilicum powder for when you change that bandage. If not, the apothecary in Middleford can supply it." Without further ado, she climbed back into her gig and headed down the drive.

"So Mrs. Miller will recover?" asked Lady Thorne, setting her cup onto a nearby table.

"I expect so," Amanda assured her, "though it was a close-run thing. The midwife is trying to convince her that there can be no more children."

"Mr. Miller won't like that much."

"He needn't abstain entirely as long as he is prudent. If he cares for her at all, he will agree."

Lady Thorne reddened, but seemed to suddenly recall that Amanda had been married for eight years. She frowned. "What is the tale I heard about you and Norwood?"

"Is rumor already making something of that?" asked Amanda in surprise. "Good heavens, it has barely been four hours."

"There is a story that he was injured."

"True, though I suspect he would rather no one knew of it. He slipped while out shooting, and gashed his thigh. In trying to hide the extent of the injury, he insisted on returning to the Court alone. But a stag startled his horse and it threw him. I happened on the scene just afterward, patched him up, and gave him a ride back to the Court."

"You seem to be making a habit of that."

"His words exactly. But think how efficient this is. He need avoid only one person to escape reminders of all his embarrassments."

Lady Thorne raised a questioning brow, but her comment remained unspoken as Emily appeared in the drawing room door and gasped. "I am sorry, Grandmama," she said stonily. "I will return when you are free to receive proper company."

Lady Thorne drew herself up, eyes flashing fire. "You will come in here this instant, young lady," she snapped.

Emily's eyes widened. "You can hardly force me to associate with a person whom Father has forbidden the estate. She has no business even being here."

"Enough, Emily. My son has no control over who I choose to entertain. Your own behavior is sadly lacking. This ridiculous intransigence has gone on long enough. Now greet your sister and join us for tea."

Conflict clearly showed in Emily's eyes, but she reluctantly entered the room. "Good day, ma'am," she said chillingly.

"You are looking lovely today, Lady Emily," Amanda responded, keeping to the formal address though her voice was warm. She had no real quarrels with Emily.

"Thank you." Emily turned to her grandmother. "I do not wish to begin an argument, but you must know that Papa will be most upset to discover that I have been exposed to Mrs. Morrison. Aside from all else, she was running around the neighborhood with Norwood, alone."

"Would you rather I had left him where I found him?" asked Amanda.

"It would have been more seemly to fetch help," stated Emily primly.

"And might have cost him his life," snapped Amanda.

Both Emily and Lady Thorne stared.

Amanda set her cup firmly on a table. "He was unconscious when I happened along. There was considerable mud ground into a deep cut on his thigh. I've seen men die from such wounds more than once. It is imperative that the injury be cleaned as soon as possible. Giving him a ride home was only what any decent person would have done."

"He claimed the injury was minor," protested Emily.

"You have a lot to learn about men," said Amanda with a sigh. "They fall into two categories. There are whiners who turn the most minor events into life-threatening crises, requiring constant attention and making the most irritating demands. That sort has vapors as easily as the giddiest female. But most men are stoics, minimizing any problem, refusing to discuss it, and spurning all assistance. They are the kind who describe a slash to the bone as a scratch and who pass off a bullet in the shoulder as a bit of a nuisance."

"She is right," confirmed Lady Thorne, seeing the disbelief in Emily's eyes. "And they make very bad patients. I've yet to meet a gentleman who can handle illness with aplomb."

"Being confined to bed destroys their image of invincibility. Plus they despise finding themselves beholden to anyone. Trying to mother them makes them worse." Amanda shrugged. "But enough of gentlemen's foibles. I must return home. You have grown into a lovely lady," she said, turning to Emily. "And despite what you might think, I have no quarrel with you. I am quite happy with my life and have no desire to return to a place where I have never been welcome. It would be nice if we could demonstrate proper manners when we meet, which we invariably must as we both live in the same area. Are you aware that I am here only because our mutual father decreed that I must stay here? Personally, I would rather have returned to London."

Emily had flushed at the words. "I did not know," she admitted. "But how can I be polite to someone who must be ostracized for eloping, among other shameful deeds?"

Amanda sighed. "Lady Emily, it would be better for all concerned if you see me as another member of the gentry class, a widow who is living quietly. I have no wish to join society, so the *ton's* opinion matters not."

"Even the gentry would not accept your behavior," scoffed Emily. "How could you be so stupid as to be taken in by a handsome face in a uniform who only wanted a big dowry?"

Unable to help herself, Amanda laughed. "Where did you get such an absurd idea? No, don't bother to answer. It can only have come from Father. You are wrong, Emily. Jack was not handsome, and though we were only friends when we married, we grew to love each other deeply. He cared nothing for money. Not only did he not ask for a shilling, we took great pains to hide his identity lest Father make trouble for him."

"Then why did you elope?" asked a puzzled Emily.

"Father refused to take me to London for the Season, instead selling me to a brutal wastrel who would have abused me horribly."

Emily blanched.

"You needn't worry for your own future," said Amanda dismissively. "Unlike me, you have always been a dutiful daughter. I only hope duty demands that you behave civilly when we chance to meet."

"I will try," she murmured finally.

Driving back to town, Amanda frowned over the meeting

with her sister. She had not been completely truthful. Though never part of the *ton*, she had enjoyed the socializing in Vienna more than she wanted to admit. But that life was closed to her, and would have been even if she had not married Jack. Her father had seen to that.

Norwood gingerly explored the knot on his head. It was much smaller than it had been earlier. Two hours of sleep had also diminished the pain. Unfortunately, the nap did nothing to restore his memories to their hiding place.

He still had trouble believing that the outspoken Mrs. Morrison lived nearby. Again he had made a cake of himself, and again she had been there to castigate him and to challenge him.

Fitch. She had put into words his own nebulous thoughts. He did indeed feel guilty. He demanded respect, loyalty, and quality service from his employees, but laying one's life on the line had never been part of the bargain. Why had Fitch done it? Several people had tried to dissuade him from returning to the inn. He must have believed it to be part of his duties. There was no reason to expect affection to play a role. Norwood was a remote, humorless man incapable of inspiring such an emotion in his servants.

But perhaps it was a broader dedication to mankind. Mrs. Morrison had quoted several writings that extolled the idea. Norwood did not espouse it himself—it was a philosophy better suited to the lower classes and the very young—but Fitch might have. He actually knew almost nothing about the valet, despite having employed the man for fifteen years. He had never entertained any interest in his servants.

Greater love hath no man. . . . It haunted him.

Chapter Six

After a day and night of rest, Norwood resumed his activities. He despised weakness. Besides, lying in bed was boring. He had brought no books and Winter had found nothing of interest in Thorne's library.

"Good morning, Lady Emily," he murmured when he arrived downstairs for a late breakfast.

"I trust you are recovered, your grace," replied Emily.

"Quite."

Conversation lagged while a footman filled Norwood's plate. The silence was not strained, but neither was it comfortable.

"Do you miss London?" he asked at last.

"Town offers more activities than the country, but both have their merits," she responded politely.

Another silence stretched.

"I hope you do not mind attending dinner at the Grange with Squire Reeves tonight, your grace," said Emily eventually. "I am not sure how Father came to accept the invitation."

"Not at all," he disclaimed, though he wondered what he would find to discuss with the man. He rarely associated with the gentry.

"I suppose it is necessary to remain on good terms with one's neighbors, regardless of rank." She sighed. "Is that how it is at Norwood Castle?"

"I seldom bother with entertaining," Norwood admitted. He saw her eyes widen and continued, "though that will change in the future. Now that I am involved with Parliament, I must spend more time in town."

"Entertaining adds interest to life," pronounced Emily. "I

have been in charge of ours since my mother died nearly two years ago."

She was well trained, Norwood admitted, nodding absently in her direction. The house party was proceeding smoothly. But he refrained from complimenting her expertise. It was ridiculous to draw attention to the obvious. If she had not been adept at this necessary skill, he would not have chosen to court her.

Again the silence stretched.

Emily finally excused herself from the breakfast room. "I must convey the ladies to Middleford to look at the shops."

Norwood merely nodded.

All in all, breakfast had gone quite well, he reflected as a footman jumped to bring him another slice of toast which he absently slathered with marmalade. His own thoughts were usually preferable to conversation with others. It would seem that Lady Emily was not a chatterbox in the mornings.

Annabelle had posed no problem over breakfast either. She invariably ate it alone in her room. But her continuous prattle over other meals wore on his patience. Not in the beginning, of course. He had been delighted that she found him so easy to talk to. Few people did. Only after they were wed did he discover that her volubility was a screen that covered nervousness and fear. The more those feelings grew, the more she talked until he cringed at the sound of her voice, hating himself even as he did so.

Suppressing a shudder, he rose from the table, deliberately turning his mind to the question of whether to ride out with the gentlemen. It would be prudent to wait another day to allow his leg to recover its strength. There would be dancing at the squire's that night. If he were limping, he would have to supply an explanation of his accident—his two accidents. He shivered. Neither reflected well on him.

Squire Reeves was an influential man locally. Despite lacking a title of his own—Thorne had pointedly informed Norwood that one of the man's ancestors had refused a barony several generations earlier, having fallen out of charity with the monarch who offered it—he was welcomed in the highest circles. His dinner party included the area nobility as well as the upper reaches of the gentry.

Norwood adopted a pleasant, though unsmiling, face, willingly exchanging remarks in the drawing room before dinner. He owed it to his position to behave as a model guest even toward those with whom he would not ordinarily associate. The company was typical of a country gathering. Besides the party from the Court, it included the dowager marchioness, a local viscount, two baronets, some retired military officers, and a smattering of others.

Not having met Lady Thorne before, Norwood gravitated to her side. "I understand you were close to my grandmother," he commented.

"You make her sound dead," she chided him gently. "We still write regularly. Catherine is delighted that you decided to visit us."

He knew why. His grandmother was another who fretted about the succession. "It is too bad that she could not accompany me," he said. "She would have enjoyed seeing you again, but her health has not been good for several years."

"So I understand. Her last few letters have rambled quite badly."

"Her good days are becoming less common," he admitted.

"That is sad. She was so full of life when she first came to London, with a spark that attracted the attention of everyone she met, and not just the gentlemen. She had an equal number of female friends. I was surprised when she chose your grandfather, for he was a bit of a dry stick and older than some of her other admirers."

"Perhaps the choice was not hers," he commented cynically. Who would bypass the heir to a duke?

"Hardly. Her father was pushing her to accept the Marquess of Woodcross. He doted on his daughter and wanted a gentler husband, begging your pardon."

"Not at all," he disclaimed, fascinated by her words. He had never met his grandfather. "Why did she choose Medford then?"

"She loved him." A snort and shake of the head told him that she disagreed with the criterion her friend had used.

"And he was as mooncalf over her as a giddy young girl. It was positively embarrassing to see them looking at each other."

Norwood stifled a pang of envy, but his customary cynicism quickly returned. "I doubt it lasted."

Lady Thorne frowned. "It did, actually. When he died fifteen years later, she was devastated, withdrawing from everything for nearly three years. Her grief intensified her regrets that there had been only one child. She and your father had never been close."

"I know, though no one ever explained why."

"They were too different," said Lady Thorne. "There was never any particular incident to divide them—at least not that I ever heard. But your father was a cold, stern child who was uncomfortable around warmth. In that regard, he was a throwback to his grandfather. Catherine was unhappy over it, doing her best to teach him to care—she would have been pleased if he had developed an attachment to a horse or a toy even. But he never did. The only emotion he showed was cold fury at any slight to his consequence. Yet it was not until he married your mother that he and Lady Medford became truly estranged. The new duchess encouraged his most unfeeling traits and deplored Lady Medford's open friendliness."

"That is why she moved to London?"

"Precisely, though she was sorry to have given in. It meant that she rarely saw you. That wrenched at her heart for she recognized in you many of the characteristics she had loved in her husband."

"Thank you for sharing that," he said, bowing his head in acknowledgement. "It is a tale I had not heard."

"I suspected as much. But how is she?"

Norwood answered questions about his grandmother's health and prospects, but his mind was no longer engaged in the exercise. What traits could his grandmother have noted that differed from his father? Unless it was his childhood tendency to rebel against his father's teachings, having to learn the hard way that his parent knew best. His intransigence had led him into several scrapes. He seemed to harbor a streak of madness that occasionally burst out to overwhelm all rational thought, leading him to behave as unreasonably as those born in the lower orders. Thank heaven he had finally outgrown that youthful quirk.

He terminated his remarks about Lady Medford and moved on to exchange a word with Lord Quinn. They were discussing the continuing unrest over food prices when a nearby conversation attracted his attention.

"Why was Mrs. Morrison not invited?" demanded Major Humphries, his voice carrying as if he were still on a battle-field. Several people turned their eyes toward him, including a glowering Thorne, an icy Lady Emily, and Lady Thorne, whose eyes unexpectedly twinkled.

"She was," Mrs. Reeves assured him. "I would never dream of excluding her. I am so very grateful that she condescended to help Elizabeth and my other girls improve their pianoforte skills. But she declined, claiming a prior engagement."

"Fustian!" exploded the major. "Who would demand she bypass a gathering like this?"

"She did not say, but you must know that one cannot constrain her to do something she does not want to do." The words were lightly barbed and accompanied by a swift glance toward the group that included Bradford, Craven, and Thorne.

What was that all about? wondered Norwood as he concluded his discussion with Lord Quinn and moved on to talk to Sir Timothy and his son, James Taylor. His impression of Mrs. Morrison had placed her in the ranks of the merchant class, though now that he thought about it, her accent was genteel. But she was the wife of a soldier and had followed the drum, if his memory was correct. She still involved herself with nursing—an activity no one of quality would approve—being at home with the most gruesome sights. Why would Mrs. Reeves feel obligated to invite her to dine with a marquess and a duke? And why would she decline such an honor? The one comment that he understood was the last one. He recalled all too well how impossible it was to force Mrs. Morrison into diverging from her chosen course.

Dinner was delicious—Squire Reeves employed an excellent cook—but the duke spent the meal trying to repress memories of the Blue Boar. They kept intruding at the odd-

est moments—the flame-filled hallway resurrected when a
candle suddenly flared; Fitch's surgery recalled as the
squire carved into the baron of beef; the scent of well-
larded mutton dredged up a picture of Mrs. Morrison
spreading lard on his burns. He was thankful when the meal
finally concluded and they could commence dancing.

The servants had taken up the carpets in both the drawing room and the adjacent morning room, moving all furniture against the walls to allow space for sets to form. The
vicar's wife took the first turn at providing music.

Norwood was in a strange mood. Perhaps it was due to
his upcoming declaration. He had never enjoyed coercion.
And he could feel the pressure building. Everyone gathered
at Thornridge Court knew why he was there. Lady Emily
was working hard to bring him up to scratch, flirting with
the highest-ranking young men in attendance. Thorne
seemed piqued that Norwood had yet made no overtures.
But some buried remnant of the youthful Nicholas Blaire
had deliberately refrained from doing so. He harbored a
stubborn streak nearly as strong as that of Mrs. Morrison.

Not that he was having second thoughts. It was a deliberate ploy to set the tone for their marriage. He would be
firmly in charge, for he had no intention of living under the
cat's paw. The Duchess of Norwood must adjust without
protest to his way of living.

And so he waited. In response to her flirting, he ignored
her. She was not the sort to develop deep feelings for anyone, so he cared not that she pretended interest in other
men. She would quickly learn that such actions would not
further her cause. In the meantime, he set himself to be
pleasant to the various young ladies present. That made
Lady Emily even more flirtatious, but he refused to give in.
She could not control him. Duty did not require devotion,
only execution. He would show her all the attention her position as his wife required. But no more.

Mrs. Morrison might have declined to attend in person,
reflected Norwood two hours later, but she was present
anyway. Her name had often cropped up in overheard con-
versations, and here it was again. He had been on his way
to join Thorne and several other gentlemen in the billiard
room, but instead he paused to listen.

"I knew her quite well on the Peninsula," Major Humphries was booming at James Taylor. "As did my wife, of course. Amazing woman, Mrs. Morrison. Never saw her snappish in six years. She was caring and compassionate, yet tough as old boots. Stayed with the regiment even on campaign—crossing waterless plains in heat and dust, slogging through mud and across snowy mountains, enduring hunger when the quartermaster got lost and stranded us for three days without food. But never a complaint. She mothered us all, though not annoyingly, tending sores, illnesses, and battle wounds, and listening to our problems."

"I can believe that," murmured Mr. Taylor, his own voice almost lost in the background chatter. "She's a witch the way she can prod people into talking. I stopped to chat a moment when we met down by the mill the other day and found myself unloading all my complaints onto her shoulders. Not only that, but she offered advice that was more sensible than anything my father ever said."

"She's always been known for her common sense," agreed Major Humphries. "Many's the lad who entered battle with a clear head because she had talked away his fears. I don't doubt she saved scores of lives over the years from that alone."

"Too bad Granny died when she did. She'd have enjoyed seeing her star pupil again."

"What's that?" asked the major in surprise.

"Surely you knew Mrs. Morrison grew up here," exclaimed Mr. Taylor.

"She mentioned it when she moved back."

"She used to make the rounds regular-like with old Granny Gossich, learning about remedies and healing. I was only a young lad in those days but I remember her well. She always had a kind word or a helping hand for everyone. Kept it up until she left."

"You mean that old lady in the woods who died last spring?"

"That's the one. Folks were mighty worried when Granny died. Most can't afford a doctor and the ladies of the Court are little help, but the Lord doth provide. Mrs.

Morrison came home, having learned even more than
Granny in her travels." He shrugged.

"Surely the ladies of the Court don't neglect their duty to
their tenants," protested Norwood, joining their conversation.

"I never meant to imply that," returned a shocked Mr.
Taylor. "No one connected with Thorne would ever skimp
on duty. But medical help is different. Lady Thorne wasn't
much for working in the stillroom, so her daughters know
nothing of tonics or nostrums. The old housekeeper was
well versed in healing, but she retired eight years ago and
the new one is ignorant on the subject, so Granny was all
most folk could rely on. And now Mrs. Morrison."

"Just like on the Peninsula," observed the major. "She
was always ready to help anyone, and many of the lads
willingly turned to her for minor problems that they never
would have bothered the surgeons with. It was considered
unmanly to complain, even though the ills reduced their effectiveness."

The music resumed. Norwood excused himself and led
out Mrs. Edwards, losing track of the continued discussion.
So Mrs. Morrison had been a healer even before she went to
the Peninsula. It made her odd behavior more understandable. One often ran across healers. There had been one in
the next village in his own youth. His father had decried the
woman, of course, but Nicholas saw no reason to follow
suit. If she had been a witch, it would have been different,
but she did not practice black arts, as far as he could tell,
contenting herself with dispensing healing drafts and advice.

It was odd how one never thought of such people as being
young, but they had all been young at some point. And most
had probably started like Mrs. Morrison. He wondered if
she would prove to be a witch as well as a healer. She had
certainly cast a spell on him at the Blue Boar. There was no
other explanation for his behavior that night.

Emily kept a smile pasted firmly on her face while Norwood waltzed for the second time with the lowly Mrs. Edwards. Why was he bent on embarrassing her so publicly?
Her father had been very displeased when he'd called her
into his library that afternoon.

"What have you done to annoy his grace?" he demanded

harshly. "He has been here for three days without making his offer. Did you give him a disgust of you?"

"Of course not, Father," she disclaimed, hiding her uncertainty. In all her seventeen years, Thorne had never spoken so coldly to her. "Give him time. He has only just arrived and was forced to spend yesterday in his room recovering from an injury, as you well know."

"You must bring him up to scratch," he commanded, ignoring her excuse. "He will make a perfect husband for you. His breeding is impeccable, his demeanor faultless, and his wealth unmatched by any other suitor. All of society expects this match. Your credit will be permanently diminished if you let him get away. I expect this situation to be resolved immediately. Otherwise, I shall be forced to confront him myself. This teasing is unworthy of both of you."

"Yes, Father," she replied, unsure just what she could do to hurry the duke. It was doubtful she could pressure him into doing anything he did not want to do.

Mr. Stevens led her into the waltz, allowing her to relax a little. Oliver was one of her most persistent admirers, though wholly ineligible, as they both knew. As the younger son of a baronet, his prospects were limited. He had inherited enough from an uncle to support himself, and he owned a small estate, but he made no pretense to wealth. At his age there was no pressure to acquire a bride, so they had become good friends during the course of the last Season. He was one of the few people that she allowed to question her behavior.

"You seem dispirited," he said now, twirling her through a complex series of steps.

"I hoped it would not show." She cringed at what her father would say.

"Of course not," he replied at once. "I doubt anyone suspects, unless they know you as well as I do. But what is wrong?"

"Father is pressing, demanding that I bring Norwood up to scratch, but I don't know how. If only Mother were still alive."

"You won't accomplish anything by flirting with everyone in sight," he scoffed. "Norwood is too old and too proper to play such games. He is not a frivolous youth like myself."

"How can you condemn me for flirting when you do it yourself?"

"I do not condemn. I merely point out that the duke will not succumb to juvenile attempts to arouse his jealousy. As for me, I flirt with you because you enjoy it," he said, grinning at her discomfort. "It is time to ask yourself what kind of life you want, my lady. If you dutifully drift along a course prescribed by others, you may wake up some fine morning and discover that you are miserable. Norwood is just like your father."

"Are you insulting them or me by such an observation?"

"Neither. But think on this—traits that are tolerable in a parent might not be so in a spouse. You are not the cold, unfeeling daughter Thorne has demanded you play."

"Nonsense! Father would never push me into a bad match."

"I see I've said too much," he responded stiffly. "Let us talk of something else."

"Not yet," pleaded Emily. "What can I do about Norwood? Father is becoming quite angry at the delay. It was bad enough that the duke cried off visiting last summer, though I understand that his reasons were real enough."

"Just be yourself." He shrugged. "Norwood is not a man you can rush into anything. He is dour, staid, and very independent—the last man to respond to pressure. If you try to force him, he is likely to look for a wife elsewhere."

Emily gasped. "But that would tarnish his reputation. Everyone in society expects him to offer for me."

"When you are duke, it takes more than terminating a courtship to draw censure." He grimaced. "Why am I telling you this, anyway? I cannot like the idea of you wedding the man. You are too young to settle down. Having been under the thumb of such demanding parents for so long, I wonder if you really know what you want out of life."

"Enough, Oliver," she reprimanded him. "I cannot shirk duty. You know that as well as I. Now speak of something pleasant."

He reluctantly complied.

Chapter Seven

Amanda strolled alongside the stream that separated the dower house grounds from the rest of Thornridge Court. Her usual good spirits had fled, though she did not really understand why. If only Jack had not died. Her days had little purpose now. Usually she managed to stay busy enough to ignore that continuing emptiness, but when she ran out of activities, loneliness and desolation were always waiting to overwhelm her.

Dearest Jack. He had been her life for eight years. She suppressed all memory of Waterloo, instead pushing her mind back to the beginning. They had not been in love then, of course, but friendship kept them both content. Though already three-and-twenty with six years of army service under his belt, Jack retained a childlike enthusiasm for life that made him seem the same age as herself. His strength was still middling, but he had recovered from the worst of his injuries and was only waiting word from his regiment before rejoining them.

Those early months were the most relaxed they had shared, even though Jack was fretting to get back into uniform. They had lived with his great-uncle after their visit to Gretna Green. The old gentleman welcomed them, grateful for their company. She and Jack spent their time wandering the countryside and reading large portions of Uncle George's extensive library. The three passed evenings in lively discussions of books and ideas. Despite her inadequate education, they expected her to hold her own in debates on any number of subjects from literature and the nature of the world to politics and philosophy. She had reveled in new concepts and also in her new freedom.

Love had evolved from friendship during that period.

When word arrived that the Light Bobs would form part of the Peninsular expeditionary force, Jack arranged for her to accompany him. And she was glad. Fear for his safety would have landed her in Bedlam had they been separated.

But Jack was now gone.

She wandered into a clearing and sat down on the grass, taking a moment to admire the beginnings of color on the trees as the season changed to autumn, and to note that the afternoon sun slanted beautifully through breaks in the leafy canopy of the forest. It was not the sort of day one expected to spend on dispirited reflection.

What was she to do with the rest of her life? It was a question she had never asked before. After Jack's death, she had stayed in Belgium, burying her grief in endless work lest she break down. By the time she returned to England, her mind was numbed, unable to look beyond the next day, or at most the next week. She had pursued activities that kept food on the table and a roof over her head, but she had never considered the future.

Moving back to Middleford put her in a familiar place among friends, both new and old. She enjoyed teaching, deriving pleasure from her students' excitement over learning a new fact or mastering a new skill. Her allowance finally put her in a position where she need no longer worry about money. So why was she suddenly restless and unhappy?

Perhaps it was the security—a paradoxical idea, but one she could not ignore. She and Jack had never had any spare cash. In fact, they often had no cash at all. Pay was perpetually in arrears. It had been worse in Paris and Vienna. Not only were their pockets to let, but the demands of appearing in polite society led them well into the River Tick. And so a growing amount of her time had gone into worry. Now that she was comfortably circumstanced, there was a void in her days. Yet it was unlike her to fill the vacancy with melancholy.

Perhaps it was the place. For the first seventeen years of her life she had been immured here, never traveling beyond Middleford, not even to attend school. Lord Thorne was convinced that she would call censure down on his head if he allowed her out of his sight, so her education was imparted at home—very spottily. The governess mimicked every other member of the household and scorned her.

She frowned. Most of her learning had occurred during the months they had lived with Uncle George. She shook her head in sudden sadness. Not once had she ever thanked either of them for broadening her mind and stimulating new ideas. George was as responsible for the woman she had become as Jack was. And it was too late to rectify her negligence.

So what was she to do with her life? She already suspected that living close to Thornridge was a bad idea. It was only a matter of time before she came into conflict with the family. Despite her warning, she doubted that Thorne understood how many people knew her background and criticized his actions. Some of them were members of the aristocracy. When he learned the truth, fur would fly. He could never remain silent in the face of ridicule from his peers. And he would blame her, convincing himself that she was spreading scurrilous stories.

Yet how could she leave? Her financial situation was unchanged. She could not afford to set herself up elsewhere on what she could earn by teaching. There was no use denying that her birth and breeding were responsible for many of the students she now had. If she went back to being the anonymous widow of a soldier, she would lose that advantage. She was investing the bulk of her allowance in Consols, but it would be years before those investments returned enough to support her.

Her mind circled uselessly. There was no other widow who might welcome her as a housemate. Nor could she seek a traditional post as governess or companion, for no one would hire her without knowing her background. She had given her word to forget all connections to Thorne. Her relationship with both Jack and the army left her dangling near several worlds while belonging to none. She could not live like the officers' wives—their backgrounds were similar to her own but her unconventional interests barred her from their circle. Nor could she fit in with the camp followers. Harry Smith's wife had been her closest friend on the Peninsula, being similarly trapped between worlds, but Harry was still very much alive, so she could not intrude there. Besides, when he was around, Juana saw no one else. Eloping with Jack had severed her ties to the nobility, working for a living made even Jack's peers in the upper reaches of the gentry look at her askance. As did her work with the army surgeons.

She shifted position to lean against a boulder. She needed a plan, a comprehensive one that would map out her future. There had to be something she had not yet considered. She tried to drive all thought away for a moment so she could start with a clean slate. Her eyes drifted closed as the warmth of the sun relaxed her tense shoulders, and she slept.

"You will need to hurry if you plan to change before the picnic, your grace," warned Emily when she discovered Norwood idly perusing a newspaper in the library. Four days had passed since the squire's dinner, yet nothing had changed. Thorne was again castigating her.

"I will not be accompanying you this afternoon," announced Norwood.

"You jest, I perceive," she said lightly, almost desperate over his continued indifference. "It is a beautiful day and the view from Sutter's Ridge is delightful."

"I never jest, Lady Emily."

"Is your injury still bothering you?"

He looked at her brown eyes and read her anxiety. But the prick of conscience was gone almost before he recognized it. "I suppose I could claim that as an excuse, but it would be false," he stated coldly. "The truth is that I deplore picnics, and I never do anything I dislike."

"Nor should you, your grace," she quickly agreed, slipping silently from the room.

Norwood stared at his paper without seeing it. He was behaving disgracefully, but he couldn't seem to help himself. It was perfectly true that he disliked picnics, but it was also true that a houseguest was duty bound to participate in the activities arranged by his hosts, especially when he was the guest of honor. Yet he had done very little with the company. Why? He had come to Thornridge to settle his betrothal. Yet after a week in residence, he had not done so. He might not enjoy feeling pressured, but digging in his

heels and ignoring his duty was just as bad. He was allowing outside events and lesser people to dictate his behavior.
And that was not what his birth and position demanded.

The sooner he got this over with, the sooner he could return to Norwood Castle and the estate business that always
awaited him. Harvest was under way, and though he never
participated in person, he preferred to keep a close eye on
things through his bailiff. Then there was the hunting season. He would be spending it at a friend's box near Melton
this year rather than at his own and was due there within
the month.

Laughter echoed in the hall as the guests departed. His
guilt grew over remaining behind. Setting aside the paper,
he ordered a horse and went to change into riding clothes.
But he did not, after all, follow the rest of the party. Aim-
lessly trotting in quite the opposite direction, he again recounted his need for marriage and his reasons for choosing
Lady Emily Sterne.

Half an hour later, his contemplations were interrupted
by a horror-filled scream. Pushing his horse to a gallop, he
headed toward the river. What disaster had befallen now?
He had never experienced such an ill-wished summer.

Sobs punctuated continued screaming, drawing him to a
clearing. Mrs. Morrison writhed on the ground, her face
twisted in agony. It took him a moment to realize that she
was neither ill nor injured, but was dreaming. An unaccustomed wave of commiseration washed over him as he dismounted and knelt beside her. He had suffered nightmares
regularly after Annabelle's death and again since the fire.

"Wake up, Mrs. Morrison," he ordered softly, shaking
her shoulder.

"No!" she screamed again. "Jack!"

He shook harder. "You are dreaming. Wake up."

She shuddered a moment, then warily opened her eyes.
Never had he witnessed such terror and pain. "What happened?"

"You were dreaming. It sounded an unpleasant experience."

Shakily sitting up, she battled to pull herself together. "I
am all right now, your grace. You needn't concern your-

self." She looked around as if to identify her surroundings. "I must return home. This is not a place I should be."

He pulled her to her feet, then moved aside to seat himself on a boulder. "Surely you can stay a moment. What troubles you so? Nightmares are seldom pleasant, but they can often be eased by sharing."

"No, they are not," she agreed, staring blankly across the stream.

"I have no wish to force you," he continued calmly. "But I owe you much, both in gratitude for your medical attentions and in apology for my arrogance on the occasion of our first meeting."

"It did not bother me for long. Stress often affects people in strange ways," she observed softly.

"I cannot claim that excuse," insisted Norwood. "I had fallen into the habit of considering myself omnipotent. You had every right to remind me that the assumption was false."

She smiled. "I should also apologize for coercing you. I fear that arrogance makes me dig in my heels and fight. It was unconscionable to force you into so gruesome a task."

"You are forgiven."

"I trust you have recovered from both the fire and your mishap of last week."

"Completely, save for a slight scar on my left hand." He drew off his glove to gaze at the puckered skin.

Amanda walked over to glance at it and nodded. "It looks better than I expected and should fade almost completely in time."

"I use it as a reminder to think before I speak," he murmured. "But enough of my problems. What is troubling you today?"

"The usual." She shrugged. "I made the mistake of looking for my husband's body after Waterloo, not wanting the inevitable looters to desecrate him. It was stupid, of course. Jack had warned me never to do so. But I was not particularly rational that day. The memories remain."

Norwood stared. "Did you find him?" The question was out before he had time to think.

She nodded. "At least it was quick. Those who died in

the hospital over the following weeks had a much harsher time of it."

"What happened?"

Amanda had dropped onto another boulder several feet away and turned to stare across the river. Her words were quiet, almost emotionless.

"The battle was the worst we had ever encountered," she said slowly. "Three days of hell, though the first two proved to be merely a prelude. I rarely stayed with the baggage train at such a time, usually positioning myself with the spare horses so I could be available to bind up wounds that were not severe enough to require a surgeon. Waterloo was terrible—far worse than Badajoz, which was awful enough itself. There was a time about mid-afternoon when we honestly thought all was lost. Many of the Belgian troops had long since fled the field, the French kept coming, and there were no reserves to throw into the fray. Thank God Blücher finally arrived."

Norwood remained silent, though his attention was riveted on her words. Who would allow a woman so close to a battle? Her husband must have been crazy.

Amanda's voice caught. "The worst aspect of combat was the paucity of news. We got only the briefest reports as grooms exchanged horses or the wounded moved past. Time always crept slowly during battle, the wavering between hope and fear overshadowed by screaming boredom because there was so little a woman could do. Waterloo was the worst of all. The battlefront stretched for miles so it was impossible to see anything. Just after the Germans arrived Major Collins limped in for a new mount and mentioned that he had not seen Jack in some time. I knew then that he was gone. As soon as the French retreated, I brushed off Burt's objections and went to look for his body. By that time I would have heard if he had been injured, so I knew he was out there somewhere. I can't explain it even now, but I had to find him."

"I understand," he murmured when she stopped to regain her composure. "You had to see for yourself exactly what had happened."

She glanced at him in surprise before again turning her eyes away. "Yes. As I said, it was quick."

"And so you threw your energies into nursing the wounded?" he asked softly.

She nodded. "It was the only way I could retain any semblance of sanity. There was nowhere else I could go. And the doctors were so overwhelmed with our massive casualties, they welcomed any assistance. I spent four months in Brussels, working in the hospitals. When the last contingent came home, I did, too."

"The nightmare includes that? Or is it just the battlefield?"

"The battlefield. I heard what Wellington wrote in his dispatch—*Nothing except a battle lost can be half so melancholy as a battle won*. And he was right. So many friends died that day. The carnage was unbelievable. Tony. Robin. Eddie, whose wife had just written to tell him that she was increasing. Philip, who had joined the army only a month before with no idea of what war was really like. And they weren't clean deaths. Ned was the worst. I have no idea where his body was. There was only his head . . ."

Norwood swallowed bile, feeling suddenly inadequate to this situation.

"Poor Jack," she continued woodenly, caught up again in the nightmare so that she forgot the duke's presence. "He lost an arm and half of his face. I could identify him only by the scars on the remaining cheek. Most of him was hidden beneath his horse. I'm not sure how much of the blood was Jack's and how much was Charger's."

Norwood gagged, controlling himself with great difficulty.

Amanda suddenly came to herself, horrified that she was relating appalling tales to a near stranger. "I am sorry, your grace," she stated firmly, rising to leave. "I must have lingered in the dream world. You have no need to hear such gruesome stories."

"I can understand why such sights would trigger nightmares, but surely they will fade in time," he suggested. "As you said, it was quick. He could have felt nothing."

"True, but I will never know whether I caused his death." Her voice was the merest whisper.

"How could you possibly be responsible for a soldier's death in battle?" he demanded incredulously.

She shrugged. "One has to remain alert at all times. We had parted in anger three days before."

She stopped talking, but Norwood had no trouble completing the thought. She feared that he might have been distracted by memories of an argument. If he could ease her mind, perhaps it would repay some of what he owed her.

"I did not know your husband," he began slowly. "How long had he been a soldier?"

"We were on the Peninsula from the first expedition to Portugal in 1808, but he had been in the army for six years before our marriage. He was home recovering from the South American campaign when we met."

He nodded. "He had survived many engagements, then. A professional soldier is not likely to allow errant thoughts into his head when in the heat of battle."

She frowned, but finally nodded. "That is true. Jack enjoyed a challenge. He was never so alive as after a fight. The army was his life."

"What was it like on the Peninsula?" he asked softly, hoping to turn her mind to happier times.

"Boring," she replied without thought before straightening in surprise. "Actually, no more so than any other life. Winter quarters were the worst because there was so little to do. We organized dances and theatricals and any other events we could think of to stay busy. Jack and his friends spent the days coursing hares—Harry Smith kept a pack of Spanish greyhounds. It was always nice to supplement rations with rabbit. Pay was so badly in arrears that we never had any money."

"I would think that summers would have been worse with the army off on campaign."

She turned to stare in astonishment. "I was always with them. Who else was available to see after blisters and boils and burns? The surgeons had enough to do."

Norwood felt a fool. Major Humphries had mentioned her nursing only four nights before. He turned the talk to the sights she had seen and the local customs of Spain and Portugal. With the shift to lighter subjects, she relaxed, proving to be a witty conversationalist and astute observer. As her humor improved, he could see the shadows departing from her brown eyes.

"I think the funniest thing I ever saw was on march one summer," she offered some time later. "John Kincaid had been on picket duty much of the previous night. By the time we made camp that afternoon, he was dropping in his boots, not even bothering with dinner before falling asleep. But not half an hour later a pair of frisky donkeys romped through, tangling themselves in his tent ropes. The tent rolled up with him inside, the whole writhing mass of them tumbling down the hill. John was swearing luridly enough to burn even Burt's ears so we knew he was unhurt, but everyone was laughing too hard to help the poor man."

Norwood's dark eyes twinkled, but he only managed a slight lifting of one corner of his mouth.

"That reminds me of an incident from my schooldays," he offered. "I had an amazingly pompous classmate at Eton who alternated between looking down a patrician nose at the entire universe and bragging about how much better he was at any activity than the rest of us. My own arrogance is paltry in comparison."

Amanda shook her head in mock despair.

Norwood continued. "Wrexham challenged his claims one day. He was a year behind us but had more standing, being a real lord while the rest of us were merely heirs or younger sons. But he was also an inveterate prankster."

She giggled. "What did he do?"

"Wrexham's groom had brought up his curricle as we were all headed home for long break. Even at fifteen, he was an outstanding whip who always drove very spirited cattle. Nolly went into his usual routine, claiming he could drive anything, so Wrexham dared him to prove it. I don't know how he managed it, but the next thing we knew, a terrified Nolly was caught behind two galloping horses, curricle nowhere in sight as he bumped across the commons on his *derrière*."

Amanda burst into laughter. "I trust no one was hurt."

"Nothing but his sensibilities. Nolly had always been roly-poly and is now downright corpulent. When I saw him last spring, he rivaled the Regent in girth."

"Dear Lord, you aren't referring to Lord Wedgeburn, are you?"

"Do you know him?" he asked in surprise.

"Hardly. I don't move in those circles, but I met him in Paris after Napoleon's abdication. His braggadocio was excessively annoying. A more odious toad cannot possibly exist, begging your pardon. I should not insult one of your friends, I suppose."

"Not a friend, I assure you. And he has indeed grown despicably obnoxious."

"That's all right, then," she said, gathering her shawl close and turning her feet toward the road.

"May I escort you home?" he asked, noting that the afternoon was waning. The picnickers would be returning soon.

Her good humor vanished. "There is no need, your grace," she said. "I should not even be here, but I had to stop briefly at the dower house and succumbed to temptation by taking the shortcut back to town. It is a pretty walk, though not a public thoroughfare, I fear. I trust you won't report me."

"Not at all." He accepted her refusal with relief, already wondering what had prompted him to make the offer. She bade him farewell and strode briskly away.

Why had he stayed to talk to the woman after discovering that she was unharmed? Such conduct was beneath the dignity of the Duke of Norwood. An examination of his motives shocked him. He had succumbed to curiosity and then been touched by her story. It had elicited emotion in his heart for the first time in years. And he could not remember when he had held such an open conversation with anyone. The man who had sat in that clearing offering comfort to a commoner was little different than the frivolous youth he had once been, that absurd creature who had led him down the path to disaster.

It did not help that he found the woman attractive. And that was another thing he could not explain. She was nothing out of the ordinary—brown hair, brown eyes, unfashionably tall, nondescript features—and could never be touted as a beauty. Yet she drew him. She radiated a force that evoked unnatural behavior even in him, pulling him away from more than thirty years of training in propriety. Memories of the fire returned. She was definitely a witch.

He shivered.

It was time he quit shilly-shallying and completed his business at Thornridge Court. It was unconscionable that he should feel attracted to a soldier's widow who had spent years doing things no respectable female would even consider.

By the time the picnickers returned, Norwood and Thorne had come to an amicable agreement. If Emily accepted him, the betrothal would be officially announced at a grand ball a fortnight hence. As expected, the wedding would take place following the next Season.

Amanda walked home almost in a trance. Her conversation with Norwood was shocking at the very least. She had told him things she had never divulged to another living soul. Why?

The question bedeviled her. There was something about the man that demanded confidences. Only one other person had ever exerted that effect on her—Jack. She remembered how Jack had elicited her tale that long-ago morning when her father's announcement shattered her life. And now Norwood had done the same. It must never happen again. It was bad enough to even talk about her unladylike experiences, but to a duke of the realm? She could never face the man again. Yet there was little chance of avoiding it. Her father had decreed that she remain in Middleford. Norwood intended to marry her sister. Even without an official family tie, they were bound to meet many times in the course of their lives.

The duke's own behavior had been unlike his usual demeanor, she realized suddenly. Where was the arrogance and disdain to which she was now accustomed? He had started by waking her from a nightmare when he could easily have passed her by, and had then stayed to offer solace and talk her black mood away. Neither action accorded with his customary conduct, returning to mind her earlier impression of a quite different man lurking beneath the surface.

A picture of Reginald Potter suddenly floated before her eyes. Goodness! She hadn't thought of the boy in years. He had been a young ensign when they first landed in Portugal, as arrogant a lad as she had ever met. It wasn't until

Vimeiro that she discovered that he used the arrogance to cloak fear, both of battle and of failing to acquit himself in the tradition of a long line of military Potters. Reginald had done well that day, though he later died in the retreat to Corunna.

Norwood might also be hiding behind arrogance, not that she could imagine from what. Interest piqued, she decided to learn more about the haughty duke. Lady Thorne was acquainted with his grandmother.

Norwood stood rigidly before the chimneypiece in the vacant morning room, waiting for Lady Emily. There was no reason to feel nervous, he reminded himself. Thorne had no vices that needed a wealthy, high-ranking son-in-law to rectify. Emily should be under no pressure. There was also no reason to think about his inappropriate chat with Mrs. Morrison. The widow was a minuscule snag in the fabric of his life and would disappear entirely when he moved on. He stifled the thought that he would continue to run into her whenever he visited Thornridge Court.

To deflect his attention, he examined the room in which he stood. Located on the east side of the Court, it was always bright and cheerful on sunny mornings. But in late afternoon, like now, it was gloomy—not the most auspicious location for proposing. But perhaps it was an appropriate setting for initiating a marriage of convenience. Clouds eclipsed the setting sun, throwing his surroundings into deeper shadow.

"You wished to speak with me, your grace?" said Lady Emily coolly.

"Yes, I did," he replied. "We both know why we are here. I will be blunt, my lady, for I want there to be no pretense between us. I am in need of an heir. To get one, I must marry. You are a comely young lady of good family whose training accords with my own. I cannot claim to love you, nor do I believe you love me, but I think we could rub along quite well together if we choose to do so. I shall expect you to behave with all propriety and to conform to my wishes. In return, you will have my respect and a free rein to run the household as you see fit, though I expect to be consulted about large expenditures. There would be limited entertaining necessary when we are in London for Parliament. Beyond that, I have no interest in the giddy social whirl, but you are welcome to participate as much as you like. I make the rounds of my estates once a year. You would be free to accompany me or not. Will you do me the honor of accepting my hand in marriage?"

"You have stated the situation very well, your grace," she responded calmly. "And your offer is most generous. I accept."

"Thank you. You have made me the happiest of men," he intoned dutifully, placing a chaste kiss on her gloved hand. "Shall we join your guests for dinner?"

Chapter Eight

The Marquess of Thorne looked up in surprise when Jameson appeared in the library doorway.

"The Duke of Wellington to see you, my lord," the butler announced woodenly.

"What brings you to Thornridge Court, your grace?" Thorne asked several minutes later when the two men were sipping excellent brandy, seated on either side of the window that overlooked the formal gardens.

"I was in the neighborhood and thought to sound you out about some bills that will be coming up before Parliament next session. One would provide pensions for the lads who fought so well on the Peninsula. But even more important, the Whigs are pushing harder than ever to scrap a system that has stood us in good stead for centuries."

"Not another reform measure," groaned Thorne.

They settled in for a lengthy discussion of politics.

Wellington's arrival caused a stir throughout the district. Major Humphries immediately scheduled a dinner party that would include all of Thorne's guests. He also coerced Amanda into attending.

"I cannot put myself forward in such exalted company," she demurred when he first tendered the invitation.

"Fustian, Mrs. Morrison," he countered. "You know very well Old Hookey will be upset that you declined to join him for dinner. What would Jack have said?"

She knew very well what Jack would have said, and not just about the duke. He would have castigated her roundly for allowing Thorne to dictate either her friends or her social calendar. She had done so once already by crying off the squire's party. A second time would establish a pattern that would give Thorne control of her life. Impossible.

And so she had accepted, using the occasion to put off mourning. It had been well over a year since Jack's death, and society no longer demanded the outward show. Not that she had ceased to miss him. A dozen times a day she wished she could share a thought or sight with him, or longed to feel his arms around her. But he had had little patience with pious affectations. What one wore was irrelevant. It was the contents of the heart that mattered. And so he would understand. She had nothing in mourning that was suitable for a formal dinner party.

Sighing, she pulled out the nicest of her evening gowns, a favorite creation in Brussels lace over a deep rose slip that she had purchased in Paris. What matter if she dressed in the fashion of two years earlier? She had no aspirations to society, but Wellington deserved her best efforts. With it she wore her mother's pearls that she had managed to keep through all the years of tenuous living. They had often been her solace. No matter how bad things were, there was one last option before they must starve.

She shuddered with nervous fear as she completed her *toilette*. What would Thorne say to find her rubbing elbows with the area gentry? There was every possibility that he would explode in anger. Not even his very stiff-rumped propriety could be counted on to contain his fury. No one had dared counter his wishes in the years she had been away. With no reason to control his countenance, he had forgotten how. Or perhaps he had merely grown testier with age. But the upcoming confrontation promised embarrassment, if not outright mortification.

Setting aside the problem of her father, she considered the other guests. She had not seen the Cravens since her sixth year, so they were unlikely to recognize her. The Bradfords might, though she had been kept firmly in the schoolroom during their visits, even when her half-siblings were presented to their aunt and uncle. Lady Thorne would welcome her attendance without mentioning their relationship. Emily was another question mark. Would her continuing antagonism raise questions from the other guests? She hoped not. Everyone else either accepted her as Mrs. Morrison or was a stranger.

Wellington was one who knew her, of course. They had first met in Portugal after Vimeiro. She shook her head, recalling the last time she had seen him. Whatever else happened, the evening was going to reopen a lot of wounds. Brussels. He had found her in a makeshift hospital, nearly dropping from exhaustion after two days of continuous nursing.

"I might have known you would be here," he commented softly as he drew her into the only corner that was not littered with casualties.

"Life must go on."

"Yes, it must. But I will miss Jack," he said steadily.

It was too much. She burst into tears which he muffled against his shoulder. They were the first she had been able to shed and seemed unstoppable, great rending sobs that threatened to tear her apart. Even the embarrassment of place and company made no difference. Not until tremors ran through Wellington's arms was she able to regain her control. If she caused the Iron Duke to lose his composure, she would never forgive herself. Especially in front of so many of his troops.

"I heard Morgan is also gone," she murmured. "How is Somerset?"

"Learning to write left-handed. He will rejoin me as soon as possible. I leave for Paris at dawn."

"I appreciate you taking the time to come, then."

"My condolences, my dear," he replied, "but you will manage. There is nothing you cannot do. You have suffered a great personal loss, but I want to leave you with something to think about in the days ahead—how would Jack have adjusted to peace?"

Recalling that meeting, Amanda for the first time considered Wellington's parting words. How *would* Jack have adjusted to peace? He had always been brave to the point of recklessness, and she had to admit that perhaps it was due to a love of danger rather than the heedlessness she had always assumed. Would he have been happy living in tranquility?

But there was no time to explore the question. She must leave.

*   *   *

She was sipping sherry in Major Humphries's drawing room, chatting quietly with Mrs. Edwards, when the party from the Court arrived. The first to enter was Thorne himself. His face turned white.

"What are you doing here?" he hissed the moment he had frowned Mrs. Edwards away. "And dressed like that!"

"I admit the gown is two years old," she replied calmly. "But it is not unsuitable to the occasion."

"You look just like your mother. I might have known you would flaunt yourself all over the neighborhood."

"I was invited, my lord. Even the great Marquess of Thorne cannot dictate other people's guest lists."

"You vowed not to trade on your connection," he reminded her with a sneer. "But I suppose I can expect no less from so unnatural a child. I was a fool to allow you to stay here."

"Enough!" she snapped. "You are a fool indeed to twist your own dictatorial demands. Save your accusations for someone deserving of them. I would not dream of presuming on any connection to so unfeeling a man, but I met Major Humphries in Spain, and Wellington as well. His grace would be appalled if I refused an invitation to dine with him."

Thorne's response was forestalled when Wellington himself appeared in the doorway, his face lighting as he strode across the room.

Anyone not knowing him could be forgiven for initially overlooking the man. He was neither tall nor handsome, possessing mousy hair and a high-boned, hooked nose. But one look into his chilly blue eyes and no man could ever forget him. He exuded a presence that dominated any gathering he graced.

"My dear Amanda," he exclaimed in his battlefield voice. "I had no idea you lived in this area. You are looking lovelier than ever."

Amanda ignored her father, who appeared on the verge of apoplexy. "Thank you, your grace. Peace seems to be agreeing with you. I've never seen you look so distinguished. Or so relaxed."

"If true, it is of very recent origin."

"Did the talks not go well?" she asked. "I thought nearly everything had been settled at the Congress." She watched the barest hint of a shudder cross his face.

"I wish you had been there," he said. "Much as I applaud your accomplishments in Brussels, I should have dragged you off to Paris with me. Plots and counterplots for months. It was almost as bad as Vienna, what with the Prussians baying for revenge, the Poles demanding new borders, the Russians scurrying around in ineffectual diplomacy, and every other faction in Europe pushing its own interests at the expense of the common good."

"But the treaties were signed in the end," she commented.

Thorne had been fighting to control his temper, finally turning to the duke. "You know each other?"

"Of course," replied Wellington. "Colonel Morrison was one of my best staff officers. I never saw a better soldier, not only because of his own brilliance, but because he inspired similar efforts from those around him. His loss was tragic. And Mrs. Morrison has been of invaluable assistance over the years. In addition to patching up so many of my men, she proved to have an uncanny ability to unearth conspiracies while we were in Vienna. I wish there was some way to honor your service, my dear," he finished, turning back to Amanda.

"Fustian," she demurred. "You must cease this ridiculous flummery else you will put me to the blush. Besides, you know very well that spying is not considered an acceptable profession, no matter how much we needed the information."

"I had no idea you had worked as a spy," exclaimed the major, overhearing the end of this exchange as he approached the group. "Is there anything you cannot do, my dear?"

"It is not something one advertises," Wellington reminded him. "Even Jack did not know about it."

"And here I thought your calm good sense and timely advice were your greatest contributions," joked the major.

"Not to demean her career as a confidante, but her highest achievements are a toss-up between spying and nursing. I swear she treated more wounds than some of the surgeons."

"Enough, gentlemen," begged Amanda with a laugh. "Your accolades threaten to turn me into an overweening prig. I pray you, let us discuss something more interesting.

Is it true, your grace, that a bill might soon pass to provide pensions for those who served with us?"

They lapsed into politics.

Norwood and Emily were the last to enter the drawing room.

"How dare she show up here?" hissed a seething Emily.

"Who?"

"Amanda. Papa ordered her to stay away from decent folk when he kicked her out of the family," she replied without considering the effect of her words.

Norwood examined the group across the room. Mrs. Morrison was a surprisingly beautiful woman without mourning. The face that had always looked wan now glowed like ivory above the rose silk and lace of her gown. And the combination of low bodice and high-dressed hair bared a slender neck and delightfully soft shoulders. She and Wellington seemed on the best of terms. Major Humphries's face wore a look of surprise. Thorne appeared on the verge of explosion, as though only Wellington's presence kept him in check. Was the enigmatic Mrs. Morrison really one of his relatives? There was one easy way to find out.

He joined the group by the fireplace, waiting until a lively discussion of a proposed pension bill reached a conclusion. "I have not yet had the opportunity to thank you for rescuing me last week," he lied, raising Mrs. Morrison's hand to his lips.

"What was that?" demanded Thorne.

"The day I was injured, it was Mrs. Morrison who discovered me."

"As caring as always," commented Wellington. "Many a man made it home from Waterloo only because of her ministrations. Dr. Hume sang her praises for weeks afterward." He smiled at Amanda.

"You're doing it again, your grace. I never thought to hear such careless exaggeration from the lips of so cautious a commander."

Wellington's neighing laugh blanketed the drawing room.

"What is this that Lady Emily tells me?" Norwood turned to Thorne. "Is Mrs. Morrison really related to you?"

Wellington raised his brows at Amanda. "You never mentioned high connections. I thought Jack was the aristocrat of youÏr family."

Amanda saw the shock in Thorne's eyes. He must not have looked up her husband even after she revealed his name. At the very least, he should know that Wellington's protégés always had noble connections. What would he do now? She had never seen him less sure of himself.

A noticeable shudder traversed the marquess's face as he inhaled deeply, his expression set in resignation. "Your grace of Norwood, your grace of Wellington, may I present my eldest daughter, Lady Amanda?"

Gasps filled the drawing room. Wellington recovered first.

"That explains how you fit into every circle I introduced you to." He chuckled. "How could you tolerate that obnoxious Lady Tidwell? She was constantly lording it over you because her husband was a baronet and yours was merely the grandson of a viscount."

"But one can hardly blame her for trying to build up her credit," she countered, eyes twinkling. "Her own father was a butcher."

He laughed and Amanda found herself relaxing in the familiar atmosphere as she had not done since Jack's death.

"I never knew that," Wellington admitted. "No wonder you were so marvelous a spy."

Emily had turned sharply away as soon as Norwood joined Amanda's group, and was pointedly conversing with Mr. Stevens. She heard the duke's comment and sniffed. "I might have known someone so disgraceful would stoop to such low behavior."

"Show a little charity," urged Oliver. "I see nothing to condemn in the lady. And it would seem that she is your sister."

"Half-sister," snorted Emily. "Even Father deplores the necessity of claiming her."

"What did she do to draw such censure?"

"Her behavior has always been unseemly, though I recall few details as I was only eight when she eloped. But she spent much of her time with the lower orders. My parents were appalled."

"What do you think constitutes improper behavior with those lower than yourself?" Oliver asked stonily. "Granted I do not know Lady Amanda, but she seems to be all that is proper."

"Why, she laughs and jokes with them, caring for their ill-

nesses with her own hands, and giving them food and clothing and blankets good enough to grace her own home. How
can she lower herself to sit down at filthy tables and touch
pest-infested bodies?"

"You are higher in the instep than I ever suspected," he
countered sharply. "You describe a loving, caring lady who
pursues the duties of a landowner in the same way that any
progressive person does in these enlightened times. I suggest
that you take a close look at yourself, Lady Emily. You sound
like the most odious of prigs."

Wellington and Thorne had drawn aside to talk, leaving
Amanda and Norwood facing each other.

"Why did you never mention your relationship to Thorne?"
he asked in amazement.

"Why should I? It is not necessary to have noble connections in order to be a worthwhile person. I severed all ties
when I left home."

"You did or he did?"

"It was mutual. I chose the life I wanted to lead and have
never regretted it."

"Then why did you return to live so close at hand?"

"That was Father's idea. He wanted me where he could
keep an eye on me."

"I don't understand," he murmured.

"There is no need for you to do so, your grace. I trust you
are enjoying your visit," she continued, deliberately changing
the subject.

"As much as I enjoy anything." He shrugged. "I have offered for Lady Emily, who I now gather is your sister."

"I know." At his look of surprise, she continued. "The entire
neighborhood is aware of why you are here, your grace. And
Emily is my half-sister. My mother died when I was born."

"Ah. So you are also Englewood's half-sister?"

"Yes. He arrives home tomorrow, I understand. I've not
seen him in ten years. He was at school when I left."

"Forgive me for prying, Lady Amanda, but I am trying to
understand the family into which I will be marrying. What is
really going on here? Thorne looks furious."

She sighed. "It is quite simple, your grace. You have set
the cat among the pigeons with a vengeance. Not that I didn't
warn him what would happen."

"What are you talking about?"

"My father. We are permanently estranged, which must be obvious to even the dullest observer. He never approved of me. I was a wild child who refused to adhere to his standards. Ultimately, I could stand the confrontations no longer and eloped. He responded by cutting me from the family. Frankly, I rejoiced. But after my husband died, I found that I could not support myself as merely one of thousands of war widows. There came a point when I faced the choice of trading on family connections that I had long since abandoned or begging an allowance to supplement my earnings. In a gesture of fair play, I offered him the decision. He chose the allowance, with the stipulation that I remain in the neighborhood without making further demands on the family. But you needn't fear the connection, your grace. I have no interest in exploiting it, so you can forget my existence without fear that I will suddenly pop up to embarrass you."

He ignored her last comment. "You were on your way home the night we met?"

She nodded.

"I missed Wellington's greeting. Did you know him well?"

"My husband was on his staff."

"Good God! He was *that* Morrison? The man was mentioned in dispatches after every battle."

She nodded again.

"And you were one of Wellington's spies?"

"In Vienna."

Norwood shook his head. She was turning all his ideas topsy-turvy. He would never have imagined a marquess's daughter running off to follow the drum, working side by side with the surgeons, and inhabiting the shadowy world of spying. Yet she appeared so ordinary.

Dinner found Amanda pressed for stories about her army life and her days in Vienna and Brussels. Wellington was similarly deluged. She parried as many questions as she could, finally managing to start Colonel Potter on his own reminiscences. He had been involved in the American conflict in his distant youth and later served in India, where he met the young Arthur Wellesley.

Oliver Stevens appropriated her company as the guests settled in for cards, drawing her into a hand of piquet as an excuse to talk.

"Ever since I heard that you were in Brussels, I have wanted to ask whether you might have met my brother, Philip."

"Philip Stevens." Her voice broke. "Yes, I knew him. He was so young and so eager. There were many like him, boys who hadn't the least idea of the realities of war."

"Have you heard any details of how he died? The letter was infuriatingly vague."

She stared at him, but he appeared to have both feet firmly planted on the ground. Though younger than his brother, he seemed the elder, his lighthearted manner covering a core of seriousness. "I know just how he died. I found his body while I was searching for my husband."

He paled, but refused to break the silence as she paused to push her own ghosts away.

"Do you really want the details, or is it enough to know that he died quickly, without suffering?"

"Tell me."

She sighed. "He was in one of Picton's squares. At some point he had been wounded in the leg, for it was bound, but the gash was not bad enough to warrant retiring from the field. He had also received several lesser cuts to his arms. The blow that killed him sliced deeply into his neck, nearly severing the head. It appeared to be a saber wound rather than from cannon fire and must have occurred late in the day, for the body had not been moved from the spot where he fell."

"Oh, my God," Oliver choked.

"War is hell," she observed succinctly. "At least he felt nothing at the end. I could not begin to count the number of men who died days or weeks later after untold agony. And others die every day from starvation or disease because their injuries left them unfit for labor."

They played several desultory hands of piquet while Oliver quizzed her on battles and campaigns she had witnessed. In a way, talking with him helped her relax. She had not realized how weighed down she had felt from the waste of it all.

Norwood and Wellington were also engaged in piquet, continuing a congenial discussion of politics that had begun over billiards that afternoon.

"I have trouble believing Mrs. Morrison's exploits," said Norwood out of the blue. "She does not seem real."

"Oh, she's real enough." Wellington chuckled. "But she is as eccentric as they come, meaning no disrespect to the lady."

"You were not exaggerating, then?"

"Never. I met her shortly after we landed in Portugal. Jack had distinguished himself at Vimeiro—as he did in every battle we fought. The first time I saw Amanda, she was binding up a gash on a Portuguese child who had been caught in the fight. I think we were in Paris after the abdication before she managed to pass an entire waking hour without helping someone. It was at a ball." He shook his head. "I may be wrong about that. She was probably eliciting life stories and offering advice to half of her dance partners."

Norwood sighed. "I first met her last summer. We were both guests at an inn that burned down. She roused most of us, then set up a first-aid post outside."

"Typical." And he recounted some of Amanda's Spanish exploits.

Late in the evening Lady Thorne encountered her son alone in the hallway.

"Such ill-bred behavior before dinner!" she chided him coldly.

"Are you standing up for her?"

"My personal feelings are irrelevant. Think well on your actions, Thorne. You came close to making a complete cake of yourself. Too often have you jumped to hasty conclusions, acting without checking the facts. Neither Norwood nor Wellington was impressed. With two such formidable champions in her corner, you can hardly ignore her."

"You did not seem surprised by the duke's words," he snapped in irritation. "I suppose she has already bragged of her feats."

"Again you assume wrongly. Her only mention of the war was admitting that her husband died at Waterloo. If I appeared unsurprised, it is due to properly controlling my face, a lesson you should review. You might also consider your father's dictums on duty. No matter what your feelings, you have a responsibility to your daughter. It is unseemly to continue this feud, as everyone in the area knows the connection and derides your intransigence."

"Enough, Mother," he growled. "I am head of this family and will choose my own course."

"Think on it," she suggested.

Emily lay awake long into the night, reviewing Major Humphries's dinner party. Despite everything that she had been taught, Oliver's challenge had caught her attention. Was she really insufferably toplofty? She knew that the lady of the manor had a duty to care for the tenants. Did using warmth and kindness detract from her position? Perhaps the cold dislike she had always detected in Thorne's dependents was in response to her own haughty condescension. The thought was not comfortable since she had always patterned her behavior on her mother's teachings. But she had to admit that many well-born girls followed different precepts.

Then there was Amanda. She actually remembered very little of her sister. Amanda had avoided the schoolroom whenever possible, and who could blame her? Both the governess and her brothers had tormented her unceasingly. She herself had followed suit, knowing that her parents would approve.

For years she had believed that Amanda had run off with a half-pay soldier, the implication being that no wedding had taken place and that the man was worthless. She now had to admit that her father had either fabricated the story or had deliberately embellished a tale of which he knew few facts. Wellington's accolades had shaken her badly, as had Colonel Morrison's aristocratic connections. Oliver had spent over an hour with Amanda. Lord and Lady Craven had been delighted to see her again. Everyone else had applauded her activities, despite their unconventional character. Only Thorne continued his icy disdain. Why? Had he deliberately lied about Amanda's departure, or had he not known the truth? It made her wonder if his other pronouncements were half-truths. Was his judgment flawed?

Chapter Nine

The Duke of Norwood rode alone across the moor above Thornridge Court, pondering recent revelations. All his ideas of propriety were being challenged, and he was not sure why.

Mrs. Morrison was as odd a lady as he had ever met. How could the daughter of a marquess tolerate life as the wife of a soldier? It did not matter that the soldier had risen to become one of Wellington's aides. Society ladies were taught to avoid vulgar company, making such a life anathema. He thought of the young ladies he had met in town the previous Season. Lady Emily was the most proper—which was why he had chosen her—but she was not very different from the others. Few would lift a finger to do anything that could be done by a servant. If one of them had been trapped in that inn fire, she would have gone into strong hysterics. Faced with a crowd of wounded strangers, none would have rushed to help. While he was not proud of his own behavior, it was typical of his class. How had Lady Amanda become so different?

He should follow the lead of his host and deplore her. Thorne had been deeply embarrassed at being maneuvered into acknowledging the woman. His own part in forcing the disclosure brought a blush to his cheeks. And Mrs. Morrison's claim of lifelong antagonism was not exaggerated. His mother had not known of her existence, despite a long acquaintance with Thorne's wife. She had strongly championed Lady Emily as a suitable spouse, frequently referring to her as Thorne's oldest daughter. Would she have considered the family in such a positive light had she known that it contained a Lady Amanda?

Yet something prevented him from condemning her.

Granted, she was not typical of aristocratic ladies. But her efforts always seemed effective and appropriate to the situation. If she had not taken charge in the stable yard, the fire would have been even more destructive. More than once he had heard praise for the bucket brigade that had saved the stables. Mrs. Morrison had ordered that action. Her soothing presence kept panic from spreading. Her organization allowed medical care to reach everyone. She had probably learned much of her command in the army, but that did not detract from its effectiveness. And she had controlled his own tantrum by employing the very haughtiness she would have learned from Thorne.

Would Annabelle have shown to such an advantage? She had never been prone to hysterics, but he doubted she would have been useful. His mother was something else again. He shuddered. Her outburst would have made his own seem paltry. It was not an image he could point to with pride. On the other hand, he suspected that Mrs. Morrison would have handled the duchess with ease. The picture raised a spurt of amusement. Despite her breeding, he still suspected she was a witch.

Wellington's disclosures had shocked him deeply. From the tales the military leader had told and others extracted from the major, Norwood had pieced together a fairly clear picture of her career with the army. Captain Jack Morrison had first come to Wellesley's attention in 1808. When Wellesley returned to the Peninsula the following year, he kept an eye on Morrison, promoting him regularly as he did with several other protégés. Mrs. Morrison had rapidly gained renown as both a healer and a confidante. By the time Colonel Morrison transferred to Wellington's staff after Vittoria, Lady Amanda had established herself as an assistant to the surgeons. When they reached Vienna, the duke enlisted her to work as a spy.

Norwood shook his head. Every bit of gentleman's training abhorred the very idea of spying, but he had to admit that in wartime—and the Congress was simply an extension of the war—information was vital to the national interests. But spying was a dirty, dangerous business. How could anyone assign a lady to the task? Yet Wellington had praised her more than once for her successes and for the importance of the information she acquired.

It all seemed so alien to his world. So why was he thinking about it? Thorne had made it clear that Lady Amanda was no longer part of his family, by mutual agreement. She had said the same. But Norwood was not so sure. Even though she had voluntarily cut the connection, it would be impossible to sweep the whole business under the carpet. Now that Wellington was aware of her origins, he would push even harder to see that her deeds were recognized. Whatever the family thought of the situation, people were going to learn the truth. And so he must determine his own position.

He sighed. The last thing he needed was scandal. Yet if he could not condemn her, he must support her. The idea was not as repugnant as it should have been. She had disputed the need for recognition, so there might not be any official accolades. In that case, perhaps he could minimize her activities by explaining that she had stumbled across some information that Wellington would be interested in and, as a good citizen, reported it. Her medical work could be likened to a lady's duty to see after the tenants. There was a considerable gulf between the two, but he already knew that Lady Amanda would never aggrandize her own achievements.

His wanderings had brought him back to cultivated areas. The sun was unusually warm for September, burning uncomfortably into his back. It was more than time that he returned to the Court for breakfast. He was rounding a blind corner when a branch snapped just ahead. His horse shied. Something yelped, landing squarely in front of him in a shower of leaves. Swearing, he jerked his frightened mount aside. Not until he had pulled to a stop did he identify the miscreant as a boy of about four.

"Are you all right?" he demanded, kneeling beside the lad. Bright blue eyes set in a grubby face held surprise, but there was no sign of pain.

"Ben!" A second lad of about seven pushed through a hedge, fear evident in his voice.

"He seems to be fine," reported Norwood. Ben was already struggling to his feet.

"You should know better than to bother a Swell," hissed the newcomer, grabbing his brother by the sleeve. "And stay away from horses."

"I fell," Ben stated without contrition.

"Forgive him, sir," begged the older boy.

"Of course. Are you sure you were not hurt?" Norwood asked Ben.

He nodded, even as his brother murmured into his ear. "I'm sorry," he added, blue eyes staring guilelessly into Norwood's dark ones.

The duke watched as Ben was unceremoniously led away to the accompaniment of a furious scolding. A tenant farm was visible in the distance. Shaking his head, he turned to his horse.

Amanda turned her gig into a new lane and gasped. Norwood was standing in the center of the road, his buff breeches and shining topboots liberally streaked with dust, a broken branch lying at his feet. Two of the Wilson boys were trudging away, Tom reading Ben a scathing lecture. A restive horse rolled its eyes in nervous fear.

"Are you all right, your grace?" she asked, jerking her own horse to a stop.

"Of course." He seemed to read her mind, for he hastened to reassure her. "There was no accident, just a minor mishap. Ben tumbled in front of my horse, but seems unharmed."

She grinned. "That boy is a sad trial—too adventurous by half. You would not believe some of his escapades. I suppose he slipped out during the confusion."

Norwood remounted. "Confusion?"

"His mother just delivered another son."

"That explains your presence."

"The midwife was engaged elsewhere, arriving only near the end. I could hardly leave Mrs. Wilson to suffer alone."

"Of course not," he murmured, then shook his head. "I am not used to taking action myself. All my training was in giving orders, though you are making me wonder if self-reliance might have some advantages." He described his mother's reaction to the carriage accident near the Castle.

"She is hardly unique," pointed out Amanda. "Such arrogance is typical amongst the nobility. Thorne would do the same and my stepmother would not even have ordered the gatekeeper to help."

He rode beside her in silence for several minutes. "Did you challenge me to read the parable of the Good Samaritan the day you found me in the field, or was that part of some delirious vision?"

"You were not delirious."

"Are you sure? Sometimes I think I still am. You are turning out my head as determinedly as my housekeeper turns out my study each spring."

"Perhaps it was a trifle dusty."

"How did you become so different from ordinary ladies?"

"Rebellion." She shrugged and her horse twitched his ears. "Thorne had only to forbid something to make me do it. I was a despicably undutiful child, deserving a reputation as the family black sheep."

"Don't belittle your worth," he urged her. "I would be honored to count you among my friends."

Reality dumped ice on Amanda's spirits. The duke did not understand that friendship was impossible. "If you wish for a peaceful future, you had best ignore me, your grace. Thorne will not welcome such sentiments. Persisting will create a permanent rift between you. The one to suffer would be Emily, who will deplore being cut off from her father. This is my turn."

Mute, he watched as she negotiated a corner. Her words made him furious, yet he had been unable to respond. The message was clear—he must choose between her and Thorne. How could anyone treat a daughter so shabbily? But he knew her warning was true. Cultivating her friendship would adversely affect his wife—unless he could induce a reconciliation between those two.

Thorne poured a glass of good French brandy for Wellington and another for himself, holding onto his temper with difficulty.

"You are going to seriously erode your credit if you continue to ostracize Amanda," continued the duke. "She is a remarkable lady who cannot possibly succeed in hiding her light under a basket for the rest of her life. When she comes to the attention of society, the first question will be why you have locked her away all these years."

"But how can I possibly claim a woman who flouts authority and ignores her duties?"

"Flouts authority?" Wellington repeated in astonishment. "If my regular troops had followed orders so well, we'd have finished the war a year earlier. And I've never seen her shirk a duty, even when it placed stress on her marriage. If you mean that she is different from yourself, I would agree. But where is the harm in that?"

"Are you actually condoning her unladylike behavior?"

"How can I not? But I would never call her unladylike. Take a look around you, my lord! It would be a real tragedy if all people were alike. Consider soldiering, for example. Jack Morrison was an able officer. He demonstrated more skill and bravery than any two ordinary men. But if he had had to manage an estate, he would have landed in Bedlam within the month. Now Lord Englewood seems just the opposite. I don't know him well, but I wager he is an able manager. Yet he would have succumbed in his first battle had he joined us on the Peninsula. I've seen too many like him. They are slow, deliberate thinkers who are still mulling over options when the enemy cuts them down."

"Are you implying that Amanda is like her husband?"

"Indubitably. If she had been a man, she might have made an even better soldier than he. And she has the advantage of fitting into many worlds, so she is at home in both war and peace."

Thorne turned the talk away from his daughter, but Wellington's comments remained in his mind.

"Emily has not been herself the last few days," complained Lady Thorne when Amanda came to call. They had already disposed of several tenant problems and indulged in a lengthy discussion of the major's dinner party.

"In what way?"

"I do not know exactly, for she rarely talks about herself." She frowned. "She has always been cool and collected, as one would expect of Thorne's child. You are the only one who defies his edicts. But a mask of propriety makes it difficult to discover what she is thinking."

"Then why do you believe that something is wrong?"

"Perhaps it is her face. There is the faintest hint of a pucker in her forehead, as if she is anxious about something. Or perhaps thinking deeply about something. But why should that be? She is safely betrothed. It is a match she was very excited about when she returned from town last summer. Norwood was the premier catch of the Season—or of the last half-dozen Seasons."

"I cannot think why she would have any problem there," countered Amanda. "He is much like Father. She has always gotten along well with Thorne. And she can hardly be fearful about her duties as his duchess. She has been running the Court since her mother died."

"As you say. Perhaps my imagination is running away with me."

The subject lapsed, but Amanda wondered about it. On second thought, only Norwood's facade was like Thorne. Underneath dwelt a much different man. She could not imagine Thorne helping with an amputation. It was true that she had coerced the duke into doing so, but Thorne would not have succumbed. Perhaps Emily had discovered that same difference and did not know what to think of it. Or maybe the problem had nothing to do with her betrothal. She gave it up and turned her attention elsewhere.

But Lady Thorne was not the only one to wonder at Emily's odd demeanor. Norwood had also noticed it. Since accepting his suit, she had spent almost no time with him, preferring to flirt with the other gentlemen and escort the ladies around the neighborhood.

Why? Was she satisfied now that the betrothal was fixed? He had chosen her for a marriage of convenience, knowing that she wanted only his title and wealth, and admitting that his own attraction did not extend beyond her birth and training. There was no pretense of affection on either side. Yet he now had reservations about her coldness. Was this really how he wanted to spend the rest of his life?

It was a little late to be second-guessing himself, he decided as he listened to Lady Havershoal in the drawing room before dinner. The woman was relating some tale involving society figures he could hardly place. For better or worse, his future was settled.

Perhaps he was overreacting. Emily was the official hostess of this house party. She could not devote her time to a single guest at the expense of the others. But he was receiving less attention than any of them, and it irritated him. He finally decided to mention it.

"Have I done something to annoy you, Lady Emily?" he asked, moving his horse close to hers when the company was riding the next afternoon.

"Of course not, your grace," she responded, sounding surprised at the question. "Why would you think such a thing?"

"You seem to be avoiding me. Surely as your betrothed, I am worthy of more than a simple greeting." Good Lord, he almost sounded petulant, he scolded himself.

"I assure you that you are imagining things," she demurred, suddenly pulling her horse slower so his seemed to forge ahead. Within moments, she had moved to the rear of the group. He could not follow without making a scene. Mentally shrugging, he joined in conversation with Lady Sarah, cutting out Mr. Stevens, who had been attending her.

Emily chided herself for her reaction. Norwood was right. She had been avoiding him, but she could not help it. Despite rigorous training in manners and flirting, she could never think of a word to say to him. He never smiled and was always coldly disapproving. Not that she had allowed that to alter her acceptance of his suit. They would eventually become accustomed to each other. She had a duty to marry well, and there was no better match than the Duke of Norwood. She would be one of the highest-ranking ladies in the realm, the envy of everyone she knew. So why was she not ecstatic over her prospects?

Her horse lagged behind the other riders as she pondered this question. There had to be something wrong with her, for the thought of marriage filled her with trepidation. If only her mother were still alive. The lady might have been able to explain away her fears. It was not something she could discuss with her grandmother. The woman was too far removed from modern society, and her views never quite accorded with those espoused by Emily's parents.

Surely this was only wedding jitters. She would have nine months to adjust herself to the situation. And what was it that bothered her? Norwood would be an unexceptionable husband. He was looking for a well-trained and well-bred wife to provide an heir, plan his entertainments, and see after his household. His proposal offered her a wider degree of freedom to pursue her own interests than she had ever anticipated. It would seem the man was a veritable paragon. He would never expect her to show affection for him, just as he would never feel affection for her. It was alien to both of their natures.

Or was it? Perhaps that was what was bothering her. It was certainly alien to his. She shuddered to recall the icy *ennui* that had permeated his proposal. Just so would he offer a contract to install a stove in his kitchen or reroof his stable. Surely even a marriage of convenience should involve at least friendship. The future stretched as a lonely eternity.

But there was nothing she could do about it except pray that he would be less aloof once they were wed. Had her father been wrong to command that she attach the duke? She had automatically obeyed the order, but now she wondered if there wasn't more to life than duty.

She had never questioned her father's edicts in the past, but Amanda had revealed that she had grown to love her own husband. And the emotion evident in her voice as she uttered the words had haunted Emily ever since. Perhaps it was possible for those in her position to experience love, though she had no idea what such an emotion felt like.

Her parents decried romanticism, describing it as a myth of the lower orders. Emily had spent only one year in a select academy for high-born young ladies. Though several of the girls had giggled over gothic novels and sighed over the fictional heroes, she had never joined them. It was much too improper. But that meant that she had never even read a description of love.

She had slipped into the library the previous evening, hoping to find a book that might explain the concept, but the room contained little but collections of sermons. Recalling the Sunday homilies offered by the local vicar—as rigid a man as Thorne himself—she doubted they would help. Nor did a perusal of her Bible. She found comments like *love is the fulfilling of the law* and *love covereth all sins,* but nothing to explain either what love was or how it felt.

Her thoughts abruptly ceased when her horse neighed loudly and lurched into an uncontrolled gallop. She was thrown off balance, the reins pulled from her hands by the unexpected motion. Screaming, she grabbed for the beast's mane.

The other riders had disappeared into the forest some minutes earlier. Caught up in her reverie, Emily had fallen nearly a quarter mile behind. Fortunately, Mr. Stevens had noted her lagging progress and had dropped back to find her. When she screamed, he pressed his mount into a canter. Bursting from the forest, he spied her difficulties and cut across a field to intercept her.

"What happened?" he demanded when he had pulled her to a halt.

"Gabriel suddenly bolted. He's never done that before."

The horse continued to tremble, even after Emily had dismounted.

"Hold them," he ordered, shoving the reins of both their mounts into her hands. He ran his gloved hands over Gabriel's coat, suddenly stopping and peering closely at the horse's neck. "A bee," he announced, pulling out the remains of the stinger.

"Will he be all right?" asked Emily.

"He should be. See? He is already calming." He offered her a leg up, then remounted his own horse.

"Thank you, sir," she said, smiling gratefully at her friend.

"It was nothing," he disclaimed. "But you should not have dropped so far back."

"I was thinking and not paying attention," she admitted in chagrin.

"Problems?" he asked.

"Nothing serious. I must refrain from doing so again while riding." She smiled and turned the conversation to more pleasant topics, but her questions refused to depart, plaguing her with increasing frequency as the days passed.

And friends or no, this was not something she could discuss with either Oliver or Victoria.

Amanda glanced up in surprise when Ellen appeared in the doorway of her sitting room.

"The Duke of Wellington, ma'am," announced the maid, awe clear in her voice.

"Show him in."

Though her countenance remained unchanged, the duke's call was unexpected. She glanced quickly around the room, seeing it through different eyes. It was hardly worthy of hosting a duke. The walls were painted a dark green that she had tried to lighten by installing gold silk draperies and striped covers on the chairs and couch. Her pianoforte occupied a disproportionate amount of space, though she had never minded on her own account. But now she decided the room looked cluttered and gloomy. She should at least have replaced the drooping flowers that decorated a corner of her writing table. But it was too late to repine. The duke's firm tread had already stopped before her chair.

"Good morning, Lady Amanda," Wellington murmured, taking her hand in greeting.

"Your grace." She nodded. "But it is just Amanda. I have used no title since marrying Jack."

"As you will."

"I should have expected you. 'Tis Wellington weather," she teased, referring to the night's torrential rain. "Are we in for a battle?"

The duke chuckled. "Not to my knowledge. I know it is early for calls, but I am on my way to another house party and wished to speak with you for a few minutes before I go. We had little time to talk at dinner, and you have attended no festivities at the Court."

"You are astute enough to realize that I am estranged from my family. But I have done little socializing since Jack died in any event. I have only just put off my blacks."

"He was a remarkable man," agreed the duke. "And a damned good officer. All who knew him must miss him, but do not allow that to blight your future, Mrs. Morrison. You are quite remarkable on your own account."

"Such flummery. And most unnecessary. I am reconciled to his death. Given his recklessness, it was bound to happen sooner or later. And now that I realize how silly it was to blame myself, I am doing much better."

"Blame yourself? How did you arrive at that absurdity?"

"As if you needed to ask. I know very well that you disapproved of wives on campaign, for domestic problems invariably affect performance. I took great care on the Peninsula to prevent any discord. But we fell into increasing strife in Vienna that continued in Brussels. There was a bitter argument that final day, which is why I missed the Duchess of Richmond's ball. It was the last time I saw him. He cannot have liked parting on such a note. I had feared that it distracted him from his duty until a friend recently pointed out that a professional like Jack would have considered nothing but the job at hand." Tears threatened, but she managed to blink them away. She had cried on Wellington's shoulder once before and could not do so again.

"And quite rightly so. I had no idea you were harboring such ideas, or I would have disabused you of this nonsense in Brussels," he said with a shake of his head. "Not to minimize Jack's affections, but he was only truly alive when in battle. You were well acquainted with his normal verve and energy. In the heat of combat, that was doubled. His mind worked twice as fast and his strength grew to Herculean levels. But beyond that, his concentration was total."

"Is that why you asked how he would have adjusted to peace?"

"Yes, I often thought he would have made the perfect knight-errant, prowling the land to dispatch villains, rescue damsels in distress, and accomplish deeds of skill and valor. Mundane chores pressed heavily on his shoulders. Anything smacking of routine left him restless. Surely you saw how unhappy he was growing in Vienna with nothing to do but copy reports and placate politicians."

"I'm not sure that his job was responsible for that," she countered. "Much of it was my own fault. Not being privy to my activities, he was impatient with the amount of socializing I was doing. In some respects, I think he felt inferior, given my parentage. Watching me throw myself into the giddy social whirl activated guilt for removing me from those circles. I wanted to tell him it was all for duty—I have no real interest in such a life—but you had forbidden me to reveal that assignment even to Jack."

"And for good reason. His jealousy over the attention you received was necessary to hide your purpose. Even had I known of your origins, it would have changed nothing. We needed the information you uncovered and there was little hope of obtaining it elsewhere. You've an uncanny gift for inspiring people to talk. But do not blame yourself for Jack's unhappiness. I swear that most of it grew from his own frustrations. And that would have worsened as time passed. I suspect I did him a disservice when I transferred him to my staff, for he was always happier in the field. He was a different man after we left Brussels."

Amanda nodded, accepting his statement. It was depressing to know that she had been unable to offer her husband contentment, but she was not inclined to argue with Wellington. They chatted a few minutes longer, the duke reiterating his appreciation for her contributions in the late war. Then he took his leave.

It was going to be a very long day. Not only were her emotions in turmoil, but Wellington's visit had shattered her armor, leaving her powerless to evade the memories. Her teasing comment had been prophetic. She was in for a battle, though of the mind rather than of the body.

The perfect knight-errant . . . With his usual acuity, Wellington had captured Jack's spirit in that one phrase. Challenges were as necessary to him as breathing. What would they have done if Jack had lived? The duke had retired once the treaties were signed. There was already talk of a position for him in the government. Jack would have rejoined his old regiment. But they were doing nothing of interest, nor was there a chance of new wars now that Napoleon was so far away. Jack's vivacity would have withered and died under such circumstances. Not even love could have sustained them. He would probably have turned to some other dangerous occupation to fill the void in his life.

How sad that she had never understood his basic nature. Despite her vaunted perspicacity, she had been ignorant of so central a truth, misjudging his relationship with the army. For eight years she had ascribed his devotion to duty as a temporary measure demanded by the grim reality they all faced as Napoleon methodically wrested control of Europe from its rightful governments. Now she realized how blind she had been. He was not fighting for peace. He was battling evil for its own sake, charging into the fray because he delighted in pitting himself against others.

The only other activity that made him truly happy was helping people—finding a home for a family of orphaned Spanish children, rescuing a fellow soldier who had fallen over a cliff and was trapped on a ledge, fishing a pair of peasant lads out of a rain-swollen stream at great risk to himself—the list went on and on. It was one of the things she loved about him, this willingness to ignore his own safety and comfort when someone was in trouble. She was only beginning to understand that his actions were not purely selfless, that he nurtured his own needs by such conduct. Could she have made him happier if she had known that from the beginning?

They had often talked of her childhood and of her pain from the constant rejection and hatred. Jack was so very understanding. He must have experienced similar situations himself. The realization hurt. She had taken so much from him—safety, support, love, comfort—but she had given little in return, not even the sympathetic ear that she offered to every other man in the regiment. Tears stung the backs of her eyes. *Forgive me, Jack,* she mouthed silently. *I hadn't the experience to know that you needed more.*

Chapter Ten

Norwood stared at the letter, a frown driving furrows across his forehead. The missive was either a glaring example of his grandmother's deteriorating mental faculties or it contained an intriguing mystery he would have to solve, for his peace of mind if nothing else.

Congratulations on your impending betrothal, she had written in the flowing script that had characterized her younger days. That made him think she might be improving. *I am sure that you will be pleased with your wife. Her mother was one of my goddaughters, you might recall, a loving, caring girl with a vivacious temperament and a delightful sense of humor. I was devastated by her death.*

Emily's mother was Lady Medford's goddaughter? He recalled no such thing, but he knew little about his grandmother, especially her early life. Yet Lady Thorne had not mentioned so interesting a connection at dinner that night, and she surely would have known.

His mother, the dowager duchess, had long been acquainted with Thorne's wife and had waxed almost poetic over her friend when pressing him to attach Lady Emily's regard. He could translate the accolades well enough—her ladyship was exactly like her grace: cold, haughty, high in the instep, and undoubtedly selfish and vain as well. His grandmother could never describe the same woman as loving and caring, with a delightful sense of humor. But it was unlikely that her memory was faulty. Though she often forgot present events, her recollections of long ago were clear.

So his grandmother must be referring to the first Lady Thorne, to Lady Amanda's mother. It made sense. Lady Amanda was so different from the rest of her family that her character must come from her mother. Lady Medford's description fit her quite well. And he had noted no agitation in his grandmother after Lady Thorne's death. Thus the professed devastation must have occurred many years before.

He would have to write immediately and straighten out the misunderstanding before false rumors appeared in town. But before setting pen to paper, he collected Debrett's *Peerage* from Thorne's library, wanting to verify his assumptions.

He was right. Thorne's first wife had been Lady Amanda Holburn, second daughter of the Duke of Shumwell. The lady had died delivering a daughter, and Thorne had remarried immediately. That in itself generated a host of new questions, but Norwood pushed them aside. Shumwell's duchess was the eldest daughter of the Earl of Westcote, whose principal seat ran with Broadbanks, seat of the Marquess of Idlebury, who was Lady Medford's father. The two girls were the same age.

Norwood shook his head. He could see how the confusion had arisen. The second Lady Thorne had routinely referred to Lady Emily as her oldest daughter. If she had ignored the existence of Lady Amanda, his mother would never have heard of the earlier birth. And he had contributed to the confusion. In all his communications with both parent and grandparent, he had never referred to Emily by name, instead calling her Thorne's eldest chit. He frowned. The girl had never been real enough to accord her a name, remaining even now a nebulous concept of suitability rather than a living human being. That would have to change. But at least he could rest easy. His grandmother's faculties were not as impaired as he had feared.

Unbidden memories deepened his frown as he rose to replace the book. It had been an unmistakable flash of attraction he had felt for Mrs. Morrison that day by the stream. He had recognized it at the time and recoiled from it, adhering to duty by offering for Lady Emily lest he be tempted by a low-born commoner. He had buried the feeling under a mountain of self-reproach but it had now worked its way back into the light of day.

He castigated himself roundly. A flash of lust for a

widow was bad enough, but he could not entertain warm thoughts for his future sister-in-law! Propriety must be outraged. She was ineligible for a mistress and impossible for a spouse. Her conduct was unconventional, exhibiting few of the traits one expected of a lady. She was outspoken to the point of rudeness. Yet both Humphries and Wellington described her as a good listener. Perhaps it was that quality that he responded to. It was not attraction but comfort. After dealing with his rigid mother for so many years, it was not surprising that he would have confused the two emotions. Lady Amanda would make an interesting relative.

In the meantime, he must tackle the job of getting to know his betrothed. No matter how dutiful the girl was, she could not be happy spending her life with an aloof stranger. The thought sent his mind off in a new direction. Why was he concerned whether she was happy? He had deliberately chosen a woman who would not interfere with his routine. She had asked him for nothing, yet here he was, wondering how to make her life enjoyable. It was Lady Amanda's fault. She had awakened a concern for others that he had discarded years before, but he doubted if he could lay it to rest any time soon. And so he must find a way to satisfy his wife. Perhaps they could become friends.

Having reached that decision, he turned his thoughts to the morrow. Geoffrey might be interested in shooting over a piece of moor that Thorne claimed was loaded with partridge.

Amanda was walking home from visiting a tenant child who was suffering from a chill when Thorne caught up to her. To her surprise, he dismounted and mutely fell into step beside her.

She had not seen him since the major's dinner party and had no desire to face him again. Their meetings had never been congenial. Yet she held her tongue. He seemed different—almost uncertain. An odd wave of sympathy swept through her and she stifled a gasp. Spending his life in constant disapproval could not have been pleasant. The only kindred spirit in his world had been his second wife. Was he lonely? But she immediately scoffed at so ridiculous a notion. The Marquess of Thorne needed no one. The only characteristic he had shared with his wife was icy aloof-ness.

"Good afternoon, Amanda," he said after five minutes had passed in silence.

"Father," she responded. Until she knew what had prompted this odd behavior, she was determined to remain detached.

"It occurred to me at dinner the other night that perhaps I misjudged your departure." His voice revealed a continuing struggle between honesty and stubborn pride.

She glanced at his impassive face but made no reply. What could she say? If he was looking for an argument, let him start it.

"Why did you leave?" he asked at last.

"I refused to wed a brutal man who would have beaten me every day of my life whether I deserved it or not."

"Fontbury?" He sounded surprised.

"Surely you knew that much about him," she scoffed, then brought her tone under control again. "The one time he visited here, he struck down and permanently crippled the stable boy for allowing his horse to sidle while he was mounting, ran Ned Taylor into the ditch for not removing himself from the road when Fontbury approached, and rav-ished Mrs. Sutler—you might remember how pretty she was."

Thorne blanched, but it was not his nature to admit either ignorance or fault. "So you eloped with a half-pay soldier. Did he expect to acquire a large dowry?"

"An unworthy question," she said, not adding *even for you,* though the words hung in the air between them. "You know he never asked you for so much as a penny-piece. We were friends. He could not stomach consigning me to so evil a man, so he offered to take care of me himself. And he did."

"What was he doing here?"

"Recovering from injuries. He had been gravely wounded in Buenos Aires. After we married, we spent sev-eral months with his great-uncle while he regained the rest of his strength." She shrugged.

Another silence stretched. Thorne's horse clopped along behind them, its hooves the only sound in the still air. Not a whisper of a breeze ruffled the leaves. It seemed the entire world held its breath, amazed at the marquess's unusual behavior. Amanda glanced toward the woods and distant stream. Neither bird nor bee fanned the air. Time hung suspended as if they had stumbled into a dream. She returned her eyes to the road, negotiating a corner and starting downhill.

"Was he unable to provide a home for you here while he was in Spain?" Thorne asked at last, censure threading the words though he was noticeably trying to control it.

"The question never arose. Jack's life was the army. Either I could remain behind, lonely and fearful for his life and health, or I could join him. I chose the latter."

"Did Wellington exaggerate your own activities?" he asked after another pause.

"He made them sound more glamorous than they really were," she said with a shrug. "I knew quite a bit about healing even before I married Jack. It was better for everyone if I bound up simple injuries immediately after battles instead of forcing the men to wait hours—or even days—until the surgeons had seen to the serious wounds. Not until Waterloo did I work directly with the doctors. But the number of casualties that day was so high that they drafted anyone with even modest skills. Society ladies who would normally faint at the sight of blood were treating the wounded on the streets of Brussels."

Silence returned. Amanda dared not say anything. Thorne had never spoken to her this way in her life. He usually harangued her for faults and misdeeds before ordering punishment. Now he was not only asking questions, he seemed to be listening to her answers, even taking the time to absorb them.

"What about Vienna?" he said at last. "Did Wellington throw you into society so he could trade on your birth?"

"He did not know of my connections until dinner the other night. As the wife of one of his staff officers, I was invited everywhere. He had already observed my ability to fit into any crowd. And he knew that people routinely came to me for advice, often pouring their life stories into my ears. I've a knack for listening. So he asked if I would look for particular bits of information. I was hardly alone in that regard. Every third person at the Congress was spying, often for more than one master. It was an unusual situation." Again she shrugged.

"Wellington made your husband sound almost acceptable."

Amanda bristled, not only at the words, but at the sarcastic, disbelieving tone. "You needn't stretch your principles too far. You would not have liked him. Jack was larger than life in many ways. He was very energetic, always busy doing things. If he wasn't on duty, you would usually find him coursing hares, organizing races, or throwing his heart into some other physical activity. He frequently scrambled to help others, even peasants, often at great risk to himself. He also deplored arrogance and delighted in discomforting the pretentious. I suspect that was at the root of his estrangement from his own family. But he had no use for fools and would certainly have called you on the carpet for the life I lived before we wed."

Thorne glared. "Enough of this nonsense. I have work to do." Mounting his horse, he headed for the Court.

Fool! she cursed herself as Thorne disappeared. Despite her resolution, she had insulted him. Not that the words were false. Jack had been appalled at her ignorance, her isolation, and her family's antagonism. She had sometimes wondered what would happen when they returned to England. It would have been just like Jack to confront her father. With her new understanding of his character, the possibility was even more likely. Bored and frustrated, he would have welcomed a fight, and the marquess would have offered one. She shivered.

She was still mulling over the meeting with her father the next morning. After a largely sleepless night spent trying to deduce what had prompted his unusual behavior and castigating herself for driving him away, her mind was so preoccupied that she cannonaded into a gentleman as she exited the bookseller's.

"Excuse me, sir," she said automatically as he bent to retrieve her package.

Dark brows jutted alarmingly. "Trying to drum up a new patient, Mrs. Morrison?"

"Never, your grace!" she gasped before spotting the sparkle deep in his eyes. Heavens! The man had a sense of humor. She lightened her tone. "Merely testing your reflexes. You failed. I trust I haven't damaged you too badly."

"Only my dignity. You may repair it by joining me for cakes. That shop looks inviting, but it is gauche to gobble gooey pastries alone."

"Thank you, your grace."

"What problem is so distressing as to make you oblivious?" he asked idly once they had been served. Scooping up a dollop of icing with one finger, he licked it off, something he had not done since childhood.

"I was recalling a conversation. Ridiculous place to do so, I agree."

Even his silliness had not eased the furrows in her forehead. Norwood looked at her face with its obvious signs of sleeplessness and felt an uncharacteristic urge to pry. "Is someone ill?"

She glanced up, and their gazes locked. "No, it was merely a meeting with my father." Shock flooded her face with the words. "Forgive me, your grace. I should not be prattling on so."

"Why not? We will be brother and sister in a few months. Is Thorne cutting up rough again? He looked ready to strangle you at dinner that night." He had a sudden memory of her strained face as she admitted the lifelong estrangement with her father, and wondered if she realized how much the situation still hurt her. Probably. She had already warned him that he must choose between her and Thorne.

"No. That's too normal to even notice." She hardly knew what she was saying. There was something about the duke that pulled words out of her mouth before she had a chance to examine them. "I met him unexpectedly. Not only did he ask questions about Jack, he seemed to be listening to the answers. There is no explaining such odd behavior."

"Perhaps he is trying to make up your quarrel."

"How does one undo a lifetime of hatred?" she asked bitterly. "In the end, nothing has changed. I infuriated him, as usual."

"I doubt it lasted long."

"You do not understand, your grace. The unbreachable barrier will always remain. I share those traits that he abhorred in my mother, for I am undutiful, undignified, improper, and unworthy of my breeding."

"Not everyone views those as detriments," Norwood assured her, surprising himself with a statement that stood at odds with his own oft-stated views. "I received a letter from my grandmother yesterday in which she described your mother as loving, caring, vivacious, and possessed of a delightful sense of humor."

"She knew her?" Amanda's face lit up, changing her into the same beauty who had laughed with Wellington.

"She stood godmother to your mother." He spoke with deliberation to hide a sudden touch of very unducal indigestion.

"I never knew the duchess had any connection."

"She is styled Lady Medford, as her husband died before inheriting."

"Ah." Amanda relaxed. "So Lady Medford is your grandmother."

"Do you know her?"

"No, but my grandmother does. It is odd that she never mentioned that there was a further connection to my mother. But perhaps it was out of courtesy to Thorne's second wife. I don't suppose you ever met my mother."

"Not to my knowledge. Aside from rare visits to Lady Medford, I never left home before going off to school."

"She did not live in the dower house?"

"No. There was little attachment between her and my parents, so she chose to live in London."

"What caused such a rift?" she murmured softly, sensing pain.

"Nothing in particular. Just different ideas—much like you and your father, I expect. My great-grandmother had died with her sixth child, so when Medford married, Grandmama assumed running the Castle, retaining that position even after her husband died. My father had already achieved the title before he married, so my mother naturally assumed control."

"But surely Lady Medford would not object to that."

"Of course not. But my father had long disapproved of

Grandmama's softness in dealing with tenants and servants. His wife was even less tolerant. They also disagreed on how I should be raised. Ultimately, Lady Medford decided to avoid frustration by living in town."

That explained some of Norwood's arrogance, decided Amanda as she followed his lead into neutral topics. His parents were just as cold and haughty as hers, but he had not rebelled. Did he regret discussing himself? His manner had stiffened again.

That afternoon Amanda took tea with Lady Thorne. Having disposed of the neighbors, the progress of Mrs. Miller's newest infant, and Ben Wilson's dive off the barn roof that broke his leg, they were discussing Wellington's brief visit when Emily arrived. The girl had been coolly polite since Thorne's acknowledgement of Amanda.

"How are things at the Court?" asked Lady Thorne when they finished greetings and Emily was sipping a cup of tea.

"Hectic. There are a thousand things that must be done before the ball if it is to proceed smoothly."

"You will manage," murmured Amanda. "Grandmama tells me you are a wizard at organization."

Emily smiled, obviously surprised by the compliment. "Thank you, but the credit must go to Grandmama. That was never one of Mama's strengths."

Amanda raised her brows. She had not known that, but then she had never been included in either planning or attending Thorne's entertainments before she left home. One of the books she had read while staying with Uncle George had been Samber's translation of a French volume subtitled *Mother Goose's Tales,* which contained a story about Cinderella, a girl whose stepmother barred her from her rightful place in society. Amanda had felt a certain kinship with the mistreated girl. Now that feeling had returned, but she quickly suppressed it. Her situation had never been the same, for her father had been the force behind her own ostracism. Besides, both her stepmother and her Prince Charming were now dead. Life was not a fairy tale.

They chatted half an hour about the activities Emily had planned for the house party. She was getting ready to leave

when the housekeeper burst into the room, so agitated that
she ignored custom, propriety, and the presence of guests.

"My lady, I was never so shocked!" she exclaimed in
horror. "The housemaid is in a family way! She must be
dismissed instantly!"

"Mrs. Dawkins, control yourself!" commanded an impe-
rious Lady Thorne. "I am occupied with guests just now.
We will discuss this at a more appropriate time when you
have recovered your manners."

Mrs. Dawkins reddened and retreated, mumbling an
apology.

"Forgive her," said Lady Thorne. "She is new to the position, and a Methodist to boot, so has not dealt with flighty
maids before. But she is too good at her job to dismiss her."

"She has every right to be shocked," stated Emily.
"Surely you do not condone such improper behavior! You
must get rid of the girl at once. Her influence has probably
ruined your entire staff."

"You would throw her out without even discovering the
circumstances?" asked Amanda. What a stupid question.
Thorne's dutiful daughter could do nothing else.

"Of course. She should be made an example of."

"An example of what? There are numerous situations that
could result in her condition. Few of them require censure."

"You are being deliberately obtuse," complained Emily.

"Hardly unexpected considering your youth and innocence," Lady Thorne reminded her.

"I had not intended to be obtuse," retorted Amanda. "I
had forgotten that she would know nothing of the world.
But since Emily is to be wed soon, she may as well learn."
She turned her attention to her sister. "Servants are routinely
preyed upon by unscrupulous sprigs of the aristocracy. Despite what pious ladies decree, I have seen no evidence that
they invite such advances. Indeed, after years of living with
all manner of men, I have learned that the upper classes believe that servants exist solely to serve in any way their mas-
ters decree. Footmen are not much better. Many unwanted
pregnancies have resulted from such ravishments."

"You cannot believe that anyone from the house is responsible for the girl's condition," choked Emily.

"Not in this case, for I spoke with her this morning and

know the father. But to continue your education, there are a few girls in the servant classes who lack morals. It would be simplistic to blame all situations on arrogant lords and importuning footmen. There are also many girls who are genuinely in love and succumb to a moment's temptation when they find themselves alone with their beaux. That occurs in all classes, including the highest. When you are in charge of your own house, I would hope that you would try to discover the truth before meting out punishment. A sharp eye quickly discerns which maids invite advances."

"Do you really expect me to lower myself by accepting the very odd ideas you picked up living among the scaff and raff on the Peninsula?" demanded Emily in amazement.

Amanda drew in a deep breath to steady her temper before replying. "I would hope that your behavior would always reflect both Christian compassion and British fair play. But neither is possible unless you first discover the facts of a situation."

"What is Lucy's story?" interrupted Lady Thorne as Emily's face twisted into fury. "And why have you not told me this earlier?"

"That was the reason for my call," admitted Amanda. "The girl is in love with the son of one of the tenants. I do not believe he has been teasing her, but he is not in a position to marry at this time, a fact both know full well. It is unfortunate that they allowed their passions to run away with them, but I cannot see that turning Lucy off will accomplish anything beyond throwing both her and the child onto the questionable mercy of the workhouse."

"You cannot be suggesting that she stay!" Emily burst out in surprise.

"Of course not. It would be fair neither to her nor to the other servants. A better course would be to speak to the young man and discover whether he has any prospects. His family cannot support another mouth, but there may be other options."

"Has he not discussed it with her?" asked Lady Thorne in surprise.

"Lucy has not yet told him of her condition. She is scarcely two months along. Mrs. Dawkins probably tumbled to the truth because the girl has been suffering morning sickness. If her beau wishes to marry her, then we must contrive some way of bringing it about. They will need a place to live, and he must find some kind of job."

"You are actually going to mollycoddle those sinners?" asked Emily.

"You are harsh," commented Lady Thorne coolly. "Life is rarely black and white. I must learn the facts before passing judgment."

"Discovering the facts is a useful first step to solving any problem," agreed Amanda, looking pointedly at Emily. "But that can only occur if you keep an open mind and control these emotional outbursts. And the facts often differ from first impressions. There was a case like that on the Peninsula some years ago. Two officers were talking one night in company with several others. I will call them Tom and Dick. Tom suddenly began insulting Dick, deriding his courage, his leadership, and his honesty. Dick tried to pass the comments off as drunken fustian. But when Tom resorted to physical blows despite everyone's attempts to draw him off, Dick challenged him."

"Of course," agreed Emily. "No gentleman could take such ridicule and abuse. I am amazed he showed as much reticence as he did. None of those I met in London last spring would have done so."

"What really happened?" asked Lady Thorne. "Since you raised this as an example, I presume appearances lied."

"Precisely." Amanda nodded. "Dick deliberately goaded Tom into provoking an argument so that his own honor would not be stained by the challenge. He wished to dispatch him and hoped the obvious provocation would stave off surrendering his commission. Tom was avid for a fight so he could kill Dick without incurring a charge of murder. None of the allegations were true, a fact both men knew from the outset."

"But why?"

"Dick had been carrying on an affair with Tom's wife, which had resulted in her conceiving a child. He deplored allowing his offspring to carry Tom's name. Tom had just discovered both the connection and his wife's interesting condition. Instead of challenging Dick for his dalliance— which would have tarnished his wife—he chose to take the blame by provoking a fight over some other cause, for he still cared for her."

"What happened?" asked Emily.

"Both gentlemen died in combat before the duel could take place."

Silence reigned while all three ladies considered the story. What Amanda had not mentioned was that the wife had remarried only two months later. The child resembled none of the three men suspected of fathering it. Her new husband was forced to uphold her nonexistent honor in several duels before being cut down at Vittoria.

"But what is to know in this case?" asked Emily. "The maid is increasing, yet is unmarried. The Bible labels that as sin."

"You had best reread that book," suggested Amanda. "Scripture is not at all consistent on that point. Are we to condemn Mary because Jesus was conceived out of wedlock?"

"Blasphemous!" sputtered Emily. "That is not the same thing at all."

"No, it is not, but I am delighted to see you judge it on the merits. Try to do the same here. Compassion is a wonderful concept," she added thoughtfully. "It lies at the root of the religion we all espouse. Do not be too quick to assign blame, Emily. God will do so soon enough. And that is His prerogative."

"Am I to condone her behavior, then?"

"Not at all. It is unfortunate, at best. But there are degrees of guilt and ranges of punishment. Sometimes it is better to help someone work through a problem rather than apply a harsh penalty that simply makes matters worse."

Emily subsided. She had not fully accepted Amanda's comments, but if Lady Thorne chose not to condemn them, Emily could not. She took her leave and departed.

"Who is Lucy's young man?" asked Lady Thorne when she and Amanda were again alone.

"Tom Pilcher."

The dowager raised her brows. As the youngest son of the poorest tenant family, it was obvious why he could not offer marriage. "Is there anything he can do to support Lucy?"

"Not at the Court, certainly. But Lucy claims he is a wizard with his hands. There is a tinker in Middleford who is said to indulge in inventing. He seems wealthy enough to afford an assistant."

"Mr. Summerton?"

"Yes. I do not know if it will work, but it is worth considering."

Lady Thorne agreed, so Amanda bade her farewell, leaving her grandmother the unpleasant task of soothing the ruffled feathers of the righteously indignant Mrs. Dawkins.

Emily was waiting for her outside. "I must apologize for my comments just now. I was being a hopeless prig."

"Not surprising in one raised at Thornridge," said Amanda. She motioned Emily into her gig and set her horse in motion.

"I am not usually this testy," murmured Emily. "I don't know what is wrong with me lately."

"You aren't regretting your betrothal, are you?" Emily did not look like a happy bride. No one knew better than Amanda how inappropriate Thorne's choice of spouse could be.

"Of course not!" Emily sputtered. "It is an excellent match, better than anyone else can hope to achieve."

Amanda said nothing. The silence stretched until Emily felt compelled to fill it.

"I do occasionally wonder how we will suit," she murmured, almost to herself. "He is so cold. And he never smiles."

"I have only met him a few times, but he seems to be a very contained individual," Amanda agreed. "I understand he was married before. Do you know anything of his first wife?"

"Nothing. He never mentions her. In fact, I did not even know of her existence until the duke cried off the house party last summer. Papa mentioned his widowed state but did not elaborate."

"I would hardly call it *crying off,*" Amanda chided her. "A broken arm must be carefully tended if it is to heal properly."

"I didn't mean it that way. But how am I to live with so aloof a man? He refuses to have anything to do with the household, or entertainments, or anything else that I can see."

"How do you know?"

"To start with, he does nothing but play at cards and billiards, or go out shooting. He shuns games, charades, musical evenings, and even conversation. He told me some time ago that he deplored society and will not participate beyond a bit of entertaining necessary to politics."

"That is not unusual," stated Amanda firmly. "Many gentlemen dislike the shallowness of the polite world."

"Perhaps. But he was horrid to me yesterday," she admitted. "I asked him whether he would object to waltzes at the ball—Papa deplores them, even though they have been allowed at Almack's for years, and I hoped that Norwood's sanction would ease the restriction."

"Did he object?"

"He said nothing. Just castigated me for bothering him with silly details. I swear, his haughtiness was worse even than Papa's. I wish Mama were still alive. Her help would make this easier."

Amanda caught a plaintive note in Emily's voice and realized something she should have known long ago. She had always lumped her siblings together with Lord and Lady Thorne, assuming that they shared every trait. They were a family to which she did not belong. But she had failed to consider the Thornes' temperaments. Both were cold individuals who loved only duty. Their children would have suffered the same lack of affection that she herself had lived with. Emily was looking for warmth. And she would not find it in Norwood.

"I do not know the duke well, but my impression is that he is much like Father in that he will expect the same adherence to his wishes that Thorne demanded from your mother. If you recall, she never asked him for anything, carrying out his orders without question, seeing that meals and household routine reflected his tastes, and making his life as easy as possible without ever subjecting him to female megrims or uncertainties."

Emily shuddered. "I had forgotten."

"What else does devotion to duty allow?" asked Amanda. "If you wish for companionship, you must make an effort to know the real man. I suspect that a warmer individual might be lurking beneath his cold facade, but you will have to look for it on your own. He will not willingly expose himself to the world. Gentlemen never do."

"But how can I?" she countered in despair. "He has made it clear that he wants no close connection between us.

Trying to push for more than he is willing to give is both forward and undutiful."

"It will take time. But that is one thing you will have in abundance—your whole life, in fact."

"I suppose we are bound to grow closer eventually," observed Emily.

"Perhaps he also wishes for a companion but is uncertain how to achieve that," suggested Amanda.

"That might be possible." She paused and Amanda could feel her tension. Emily finally sighed and plunged ahead. "You mentioned that you were not in love when you wed but came to be so. Is it really possible for well-bred people to experience such a plebeian emotion?"

Amanda glanced at her sister, but Emily was staring at the hedgerow they were passing. "Absolutely," she answered. "Love is not restricted to any particular class. Those who claim it does not exist have simply not met a person whom they could love."

"What is it like?" asked Emily hesitantly. Her neck indicated that she was blushing.

Amanda felt a wave of compassion for her sister. The poor girl knew nothing of the world and faced being passed along from one cold lord to another, with no more control of her destiny than a family heirloom or the prize in a game of chance. Personally, she doubted that Emily could ever love Norwood. But odder matches had worked, so perhaps she was wrong. "Love is difficult to describe and nearly impossible to define," she said matter-of-factly. "Every person experiences something different. The more common descriptions include an accelerated heartbeat when the loved one enters the room, chills and goosebumps from each touch, and an aching longing whenever you are apart. But the same feelings also describe infatuation. Telling the difference between the two can be difficult. For example, I always believed that love grew slowly—probably because that is how it was with me—but Jack's friend Harry Smith fell in love in less than a minute and remains so to this day. There are questions that can help clarify your thinking, however. *Do you put his interests first or yours?* Do not confuse that with duty, by the way. This concerns honest desire. *Can you see and accept his faults?* It is not love if you think he is perfect. *Do you*

care as much when you are together as when you are apart?
If your feelings are stronger when you are together, they are
probably rooted in lust. If they are stronger apart, you are
using him to escape some unpleasant situation."

"It all sounds so confusing," complained Emily.

"True. But you alone can define your feelings. I hope
you can someday love your husband, Emily. It leaves you
open to pain, yet the joy more than makes up for that. But
do not expect miracles. In my experience, love grows from
friendship. To become friends, you must first find some
common interest that you can develop together."

Amanda dropped the subject. Whatever had triggered
these questions, she did not believe that Emily and Norwood
would be happy. They were too different, and neither resembled their public facades. Her sister was not the dutiful, emotionless miss that Thorne had decreed she portray, though
she was still too uncertain of her own needs to step out from
behind that mask. Norwood, on the other hand, seemed set in
his ways, firmly ensconced behind the facade of the cold, humorless duke. A strong-willed person could pull him out of
that shell, but Emily was not forceful. Compounding the
problem was the vast gulf that separated the two—in experience, in temperament, in age. Emily lacked the confidence
and Norwood the motivation that might bridge it.

But it was too late to change anything. The betrothal was
fixed. Though it had not been publicly announced, too
many people knew of it. And she could never counsel another girl to rebel as she herself had done. It had been right
for her, but elopement and life in the army had severed her
from society. Emily could never accept that. No matter how
many second thoughts she entertained, jilting a duke would
cast too big a shadow on her reputation to allow her to return to town. And there was no one with whom she could
elope. Simply repudiating her betrothal would be even
worse, leaving her virtually unmarriageable.

Chapter Eleven

"Will you be accompanying us to Fountains Abbey, your grace?" asked Emily hesitantly as the duke accepted breakfast from a footman.

"I believe so," he replied, though he had no particular desire to go. But he had decided to spend more time with his betrothed in hopes that they might become friends. Since she spent most of her time with the guests, he would have to follow suit.

They ate in silence for some minutes.

"Have you seen Fountains before, your grace? I presume it is the abbey itself that attracts you, since you've no interest in picnics."

"I have no particular liking for ruins, having lived with them. One of my estates contains an old abbey, though not so well preserved as Fountains. But it is a pleasant day for a drive."

A spark lit her eyes at the mention of his ruins, but it disappeared immediately. Five minutes later she excused herself from the breakfast room, not having uttered another word. Norwood sighed.

It definitely was a beautiful day, he decided as they began the two-hour trek to Fountains Abbey, though he would have been happier spending it shooting with Geoffrey. The gentlemen were riding while the ladies sat docilely in carriages. He was making no progress with Emily. She avidly conversed with her friends, paying no attention to the men. And before long, the road narrowed so they could not ride alongside. He must wait until they arrived.

But that did not work either. He exchanged a few words with Lady Bradford while Emily instructed the servants and spoke with the guide. Before he could disengage himself and join her, she had accepted Geoffrey's escort and was already moving away. Mentally shrugging, Norwood offered his arm to Miss Havershoal and followed.

"Have you known Lady Emily long?" he inquired idly, more for something to say than from any real interest.

"We were at school together three years ago, though she did not return after her mother died."

"Because she was in mourning?"

"Not really. There were often students in mourning. But Thorne demanded she stay home and oversee the household. Marianne will be expected to do the same once Emily marries." She blushed.

"Did she not protest leaving school so suddenly?"

"Of course not. Her father expects absolute obedience to his every request. She would not have been at school at all if Lady Thorne had not been dying. But Thorne wished her to acquire some polish before assuming control of the Court."

"You sound disapproving."

"Forgive me, your grace. I was not raised to such standards and often find things to criticize. I meant no disrespect."

"I took none, Miss Havershoal. But do I understand that you condemn duty?"

"Not at all. But one should ask if the duty is both necessary and desirable. If I had been in Emily's position, I would have demanded that I spend my mother's last months with her before starting school. A competent housekeeper needs minimal oversight."

"But your mother seems loving and kind—not at all like Lady Thorne, from all accounts," he commented.

"True, but Emily was very attached to her. Only Thorne's autocratic commands tore them apart. But she lacked the courage to oppose him."

Norwood turned the talk to the abbey, adding to the guide's comments from time to time. He was developing an uneasy feeling about Emily. If she could not oppose Thorne's edicts even when they ran counter to her wishes, how could he be sure she desired this match? She had definitely been avoiding him.

Amanda walked past a row of shops, paying little attention to the window displays. Her concentration was focused on the continuing problems of Lucy, her grandmother's housemaid. The girl needed to marry as soon as possible, yet Mr. Summerton understandably wanted to give Tom Pilcher a month's trial before accepting him as an assistant.

"Good afternoon, Lady Amanda." The unfamiliar voice pulled her out of her reverie and she recognized Philip's younger brother. Though he was handsome, with blond hair cut in the very fashionable Brutus, he exhibited none of the airs she had noted in the dandies of London. Both shirt-points and cravat were modest. His pantaloons fit comfortably, allowing him to walk with a masculine stride rather than a delicate mince. And his coat could doubtless be donned without assistance.

"Good afternoon, Mr. Stevens," she responded with a smile. "Is the party in town today?"

"No, they went off to visit Fountains Abbey. I am not enamored of such things, so I came to see you."

"Why?" she asked in considerable surprise.

"I am in need of information and hoped you could help me. Can you tell me more of army life? Philip had no time to learn much. I hate to ask Major Humphries, as his opinion will be biased."

"Certainly," she agreed. Was he looking for additional information about his brother, or did something else underlie this request? His shoulders were rigid and his eyes seemed strained. She had seen that look on others, usually before a first battle. "Are you thinking of buying colors?"

He nodded, leading her into the confectioner's shop where they could enjoy a quiet chat over tea and cakes. It was the same place she had visited with Norwood the day before.

"Why do you wish to begin a military career now?" she asked, once they had been served.

"Are you implying that I am too old?" he returned.

"No, nor am I impugning your courage just because the war is over," she added as his eyes flashed. "But you cannot deny that you are older than most gentlemen who buy colors." She stared at him in question.

"I am two-and-twenty," he muttered at last. It was the same age as Philip had been.

"Are you your father's heir now that Philip is gone?"

"I am the third son."

"Then why did you not join earlier?"

He frowned. "I suppose I was enjoying town too much. I have an inheritance from my grandmother that allows me to live as I choose."

"And you now choose the army?"

"It seems as good a way as any to get away."

There was a problem behind his sudden decision, decided Amanda. But until she knew what it was, she could not help him. She doubted if the army would be a solution. Buying colors to escape life seldom worked, especially in peacetime.

"Now that the war is over, military life can be exceedingly dull," she said calmly. "You would probably be posted to India. I have heard stories of that area, from Wellington, among others. It is very hot and very primitive." She expanded upon the themes of boredom and discomfort for some time, wanting him to be prepared for the worst that he might encounter. Staying in England was unlikely for one in his position. His family had neither the consequence nor the connections to get him a commission in one of the elite regiments posted around London. When his expression indicated that running away seemed less glamorous, she set herself to discovering his real problem.

"Are you enamored with the idea of faraway places?" His sudden interest might arise from *ennui* and a desire for adventure. She could understand that. She had suffered such yearnings herself in her younger days.

"I need to escape society for a while," he said with a sigh.

"Can you not simply rusticate until the problem resolves itself?" She set her face in the expression of understanding she had often used with young men.

"It wouldn't work. I've made a mess of my life and need to get away," he mumbled.

"It sometimes helps to talk," she murmured soothingly. "You needn't worry that the story will become an *on-dit* in town."

He stared at her for a minute, eventually accepting her statement. "I fell in love last Season with the most beautiful girl in the world, but any future together is hopeless. Her position is too high for me to be an acceptable suitor. I knew that from the beginning, but I thought I could become her friend and adviser while hiding all personal feelings."

He paused to swallow hard. Amanda found that her head was shaking over his naiveté. Poor boy.

He sighed. "I was a fool, of course. It all worked as I had foreseen except that continually meeting her is causing me too much pain. You've no idea how hard it is to keep from dragging her into my arms. Even worse, she will have no choice but to marry someone else. I do not think I could tolerate seeing them together. There is little chance I can continue to behave like a gentleman. The only solution is to leave."

Lady Sarah? wondered Amanda. Mr. Stevens had spent much of the dinner party at her side. And he had been riding with her when she spotted the party several days earlier. But he was right. The daughter of an earl was considerably above the younger son of a baronet, even one of means. The Earl of Bradford was nearly as toplofty as Thorne. On the other hand, Bradford doted on his daughters. If the girl truly loved Mr. Stevens, he might consider it.

"Does she return your affections?" she asked softly.

"I do not know," he admitted. "We are friends, but it would be unconscionable to press for more. I could not so dishonor her."

"Fustian! You ought to at least discover her feelings. If she loves you, running away will leave you both miserable. And you need to know the truth. If you leave now, doubts will plague you until it becomes impossible to find happiness elsewhere."

"It is impossible anyway."

"Nonsense. If you are such a poor specimen that you cannot face the truth, then you will not be an asset to even a peacetime army."

He flushed.

Amanda continued. "If your love is not returned, there will be considerable pain, but it will eventually wane. You will know that your attachment was only an intense infatuation. But if your love is returned, then you must fight for the happiness you deserve. Despite the difference in station, your birth is not base. What father can condemn a daughter to misery?" She refrained from mentioning that her own father was such a one. There was no point in scaring the boy.

"But how can I approach her?"

"You will have to decide that for yourself. No one can do it for you. My husband often compared life to war. One of his favorite adages was, 'An army that never takes the field wins no battles.' That is an important lesson in any endeavor."

"I will think about it."

"If you try and fail, your position remains unchanged. But think on this, Mr. Stevens—any difference must thus be an improvement."

He nodded.

Amanda turned the conversation to the weather and soon took her leave. What would he decide? On such short acquaintance, she could not tell if he was truly in love or was merely infatuated with the Season's incomparable—though she would hardly describe Lady Sarah as a diamond. But the girl had a pert prettiness that would appeal to some gentlemen. And perhaps his devotion to someone less than a diamond was a gauge to the strength of his feelings.

Norwood and Lord Geoffrey were unable to go shooting the morning after the abbey trip. The heavens opened, then settled in for a long, drenching rain. Confinement left the company increasingly grumpy—or at least the male contingent: the women were content with their needlework and their plans. There was a move afoot for a mummery at the end of the week. Norwood declined to participate, citing a lack of ability. Not even the decision to spend more time with Emily could overcome his antipathy to parlor games. He had already ducked a musical evening and liked acting even less. In like manner, he avoided charades and other activities. Playing piquet with Geoffrey or billiards with Lord Englewood was far more entertaining. He pulled his eyes from Mr. Stevens's attempts to mime some asinine phrase in company with Lady Sarah, and began to shuffle the cards.

But it wasn't just confinement that bedeviled the duke. Memory was playing havoc with his sensibilities. He was

getting nowhere trying to befriend Emily. They had exchanged no more than a dozen words at the abbey. His betrothed rarely joined him in the drawing room before
dinner, nor did she remain by his side when they were in
company together. He could not help comparing her demeanor with Annabelle.

During that long-ago Season, he had been too caught up
in happiness and the frenetic social rounds to notice the
changes in Annabelle's behavior. He later berated himself
for his stupidity, but at the time life had been too good to
consider any possibility of disaster. Yet it should have been
glaringly obvious. Once Crompton had accepted his proposal and arranged the settlements, he had dismissed
Nicholas, claiming that Annabelle was out making calls.
And so he had not seen her again until the Debenham ball
that night. She smiled, as usual, and danced with him twice,
as usual, but there had been no flirtation. That alone should
have warned him that all was not well. But it had not.

The month leading up to their wedding had been the
most hectic of his life. It was easy to impute Annabelle's
growing coolness to exhaustion. He was ready to drop as
well. Both grew stiffer as the days passed. It required a
greater effort to be congenial in public. The constant accolades became burdensome. Though there were moments
when he wished they had eloped, Nicholas bore it without
complaint, believing that all would be well as soon as they
were able to be alone together. He even counted the days
until that magical time.

The duke snorted, banishing the memories. But he could
not banish the worry. Why was Lady Emily so reluctant to
spend time with him? The situation was not at all the same.
He had been open and honest when he proposed. She had
been the same when she accepted. Neither pretended affection for the other. He did not expect false adoration, but
neither did he approve of disdain. As hostess, it was her
duty to at least afford him the same attention she bestowed
on others. That she did not was noticeable, though so far,
he was the only one to remark it. But it did not bode well
for the future. Even a business arrangement needed continuing attention if it was to run smoothly. They must have a
serious talk before the ball.

Chapter Twelve

Norwood slumped into the corner of his carriage, oblivious to the passing scenery as blue devils chased around his head. Even billiards and cards had palled until he found himself more restless than ever before. At least if he were at home, he could read or study reports from his various estates.

Not until the fourth day had the downpour finally waned. He was driving in to Middleford, hoping the local bookseller might offer something interesting—Thorne's library contained only collections of sermons. It was discouraging to discover that the man set no store by education, and daunting to realize that Lady Emily's insipid ignorance was not merely a fashionable facade.

Startled, he considered that last thought. Why would it matter? Father-in-law or not, Thorne would rarely be in his company. Lady Emily was a paragon of correct behavior, for society decried intellectualism in females. Ladies thought of nothing weightier than fashion, gossip, and the latest novels. His expression darkened as he realized that his purpose had changed over the past six months. Instead of reluctantly bowing to duty, he now welcomed the idea of marriage. Why?

Ennui. That explained his sudden urge to make a friend of his wife. Time hung heavy on his hands. For all his dislike of the shallow social chatter of a London Season, he had enjoyed conversing with other gentlemen and had even warmed to some of the activities. The summer back at Norwood Castle had been lonely. Not that he had admitted it at the time, attributing his increasing melancholy to the limitations posed by his broken arm. But in retrospect it was obvious. He needed someone he could talk to, who could sustain a serious discussion.

A wife could make a perfect companion, provided she did not indulge in the empty prattle common among society ladies. Annabelle had destroyed any tolerance for that. In fact, instead of an ornament or a dutiful vassal, what he needed was that dreaded breed, the bluestocking.

Devil take it, why was he ranting on like this? The thought itself was bad enough, but his timing was abominable. He had carefully chosen his wife to fit his ideals, and intelligence had not been one of them. At best, Lady Emily had the most conventional of educations, with less than one year spent at a school for young ladies. She was not even the sort of spend her time on gothic novels, and would doubtless condemn their impropriety. Nor was she capable of sustaining a true discussion, for that would involve stating her own ideas even if they disagreed with his. But a comfortable miss would never dare counter him, and conformability was why he had chosen her.

He ran his hands through his hair. What was happening to him? He was suddenly doubting not only his decisions, but his most basic ideas. It was all the fault of that damnable Mrs. Morrison. She had swept into his life like an avenging fury and was maliciously overturning all his perceptions. He had indulged in more uncharacteristic behavior since meeting her than he had in years. Since Annabelle's death, in fact.

But he repressed his mental tirade and forced himself to reconsider. She had not really forced him into abnormal behavior. She had merely reached past his cynical propriety to find the enthusiastic boy he had once been. Not once had she held a gun to his head.

There had been a time when he would have done all those things without thought. Lacking affection at home, he had often turned to the tenant children for companionship. His parents had paid so little attention to him that he doubted they even knew that. Having done her duty and produced an heir, his mother had gone her own way. The ninth duke cared for no one. And so Nicholas grew up alone, his tutor a lazy man who welcomed frequent days to himself.

There had been an element of wonder in the way he looked at the world at that time. The future was a marvel to be embraced and enjoyed. Each new experience triggered enthusiasm. A new day brought a smile to his face. It was hard to recall such carefree impetuosity from the perspective of a cynical, dour man of two-and-thirty. But the memories could not be denied.

That laughing boy would have readily pitched in when confronted by a crisis, doing whatever he could to help without considering either his own safety or the social standing of the victims. He felt no pride in the man he had become, having adopted the worst traits of his parents in an effort to protect himself from another painful interlude like his reckless marriage. But that facade was not Nicholas Blaire. No wonder his life contained no joy.

He climbed down to visit the bookshop, pleased to discover a Fielding novel he had never read. As an afterthought, he added the works of John Donne. As he headed back to the Court, he tried to concentrate on his purchases, but his mind would not cooperate. Sighing, he turned his attention back to his problems. What was he to do? The course he had so carefully charted was impossible. He could not tolerate another forty years trapped in the joyless existence of the last ten. The only solution was to develop affection for Lady Emily. They needed to feel close if they were to benefit from their marriage. And he must encourage her to speak her mind. It would take time to move her away from Thorne's expectations, but he must try.

A crash of thunder drew his gaze to the window. The storm had returned. Rain poured down in sheets, accompanied by gusty winds and more lightning. The coach lurched, skidding slightly on the corner. He rapped firmly on the panel that separated him from the box.

"Slow down and take it carefully," he called to Carson. "We don't want to risk a ditching."

"Very good, your grace," the man responded.

The elderly Carson undoubtedly wanted to get back as soon as possible, but he was a conscientious coachman and would understand the need for care. Norwood sighed. The road had already been muddy. He could feel it worsening under the sudden onslaught.

Ten minutes later, the carriage rocked to a sudden stop. One of the horses screamed in protest.

"What is the matter?" demanded Norwood, opening the window that was away from the wind.

"Accident, your grace. Looks like someone went off the bridge."

Norwood realized that they had passed the estate gates while he was lost in thought. The main drive crossed a stream on an arched stone bridge a mile from the house.

"Who is it?" he asked, shocking his driver by jumping down from the coach.

"Dunno." Carson shrugged.

It was raining heavily, with a high wind screaming through the trees. Wheels had plowed deep tracks through the mire that disappeared upon reaching the wood planking, but part of a broken wheel lay against the parapet. He could see the confused hoofprints of wildly plunging horses in the roadway. Lightning had struck the ancient willow that stood sentinel at the far end of the bridge, splitting it in half.

Norwood slogged through the mud until he could see over the edge of the drive. Within seconds, his sodden coat was plastered against his back. A carriage lay on its side in the raging water, wedged almost out of sight against the center bridge support. There was no sign of either coachman or horses. Had they been swept away? More likely, everyone had escaped, leaving the empty coach abandoned until the weather improved. But it had been less than an hour since he had passed this point on his way to town and only fifteen minutes since the weather had worsened. He could not take any chances.

"Here." He thrust his jacket and waistcoat into Carson's arms and slithered down to the river bank, the rising wind whipping hair and water into his eyes.

"What are you doing?" shouted Carson.

"I must see if anyone is inside," called Norwood, testing the current and finding it even stronger than it appeared.

"Let me do it, your grace," begged Carson. He was already looking for a place where he might descend more easily.

"Stay there," ordered the duke sharply.

The carriage was half-submerged, wedged under the bridge about eight feet out from the bank. Norwood tossed a stick into the water, watching as it swirled dizzily away, whipping between the wreckage and the bank. He tossed another, farther out, then another and another. Within a minute he had a good idea of where he must go.

Taking a deep breath, he moved a few feet upstream, then flung himself into the water. Its speed terrified him. Almost before he could surface, the carriage loomed ahead. He was slightly off course, he realized, kicking strongly as his arms stretched to grasp his target. He should have removed his boots, they were dragging him down. One hand managed to grab a wheel, but he had not counted on the current slamming his body into the perch. The blow drove the air from his lungs, though he managed to hang on.

Gasping, he pulled himself up until he was able to crawl out on top. But there was not enough room to open the door more than a few inches. Twisting his head around, he finally managed to peer through the crack. The first thing he saw was an arm.

A shout raised no response, but the arm was caught in the loop of the strap, so it was possible that its owner still lived. There was no time to go for help. If there was any chance of saving the victim, he must work quickly, for the water was very cold.

Scrabbling about in the confined space, he detached a metal bar from the remains of the driver's box. Several minutes of work broke the door from its hinges and he flung it into the raging river.

Afraid of what he would find, Norwood lowered himself gingerly inside. Mr. Stevens appeared to be the only occupant. He was unconscious, but his head remained above the water, his trapped wrist supporting him only inches from death.

Norwood poked his head out the door. "Have we any rope, Carson?"

"I have it here, your grace," shouted the coachman.

"Can you pull Stevens up to the bridge with it?"

"I doubt it is that strong," he admitted.

"Then you will have to come down to the bank. There is

only an eight-foot gap. We should be able to cross that with your help."

Ten minutes later, he was ready to try it. He had hauled Stevens up through the opening and laid him out on top, sorry now that he had abandoned the door, which could have floated Stevens to safety. With the rope about the lad's chest and an end fastened to his own waist, he was ready to go. The trickiest part would be keeping Stevens's head above water. Though the river was not deep—no more than four feet—the current would make it impossible to stay on his feet.

But they managed it. Carson pulled them to shore as rapidly as he could, helped by the river that swung them toward the bank like a pendulum. Norwood kept Stevens's head on his own shoulder and even gained purchase on the streambed with one foot when halfway across.

"Let's get him to the house as quickly as you can safely manage it," ordered Norwood, tossing the unconscious boy over his shoulder to climb back up to the road. His teeth were already chattering with cold.

Their arrival caused a considerable stir. Norwood sent a footman racing for the doctor. Sir Harold Stevens was not available. He had gone riding with Thorne and the other male guests during a lull in the storm. None had returned. It was presumed that they were taking shelter until the rain slackened.

Oliver Stevens was still unconscious. Though no bones seemed to be broken, there was a large knot on his head and bruises were already forming in several places. The housekeeper fluttered around him while Norwood took himself off for a hot bath and dry clothing.

What a peculiar day, he thought as the warm water and newly kindled fire finally combined to thaw his half-frozen body. It might still be September, but the storm felt more like December, particularly when the wind cut through his dripping shirt and sodden pantaloons. He hoped young Stevens would escape contracting a chill, though submersion in an icy stream would certainly not help his constitution any. Winter poured more hot water over the duke, whose skin was beginning to resemble a boiled lobster. An hour later he had donned a dark blue jacket and fawn pantaloons and was adjusting his cravat.

Jameson met him outside Stevens's door. The gentlemen had still not returned, but the footman had, with the unwelcome news that the doctor was unavailable, having been called out in quite another direction to attend Sir Reginald's wife, who was experiencing a difficult and dangerous delivery.

"Get Mrs. Morrison, then," he ordered.

"That is impossible, your grace," said Jameson woodenly. "She is not allowed in the house."

"What?"

"There are permanent instructions barring her from Thornridge Court, your grace. Both the house and the estate."

Norwood recalled the icy stare she had received the day she brought him home after his own accident. He had known that there was no love lost between Thorne and Lady Amanda, but he had never dreamed that the situation included banishment. He had opened his mouth to protest such absurdity when Lady Emily appeared.

"What is this I hear about Mr. Stevens?" she demanded, though softly as they all stood just outside his room.

"His carriage went off the road at the bridge," said Norwood. "He is seriously injured, still unconscious when I checked on him just now."

"Surely the doctor has been summoned!"

"He is unavailable. I have been trying to call in Mrs. Morrison, who has considerable experience with the sick and injured, but Jameson informs me that she is forbidden the house."

"That is true. Father disowned her nine years ago." She frowned.

"I care nothing about your family disagreements, Lady Emily, but one of your guests is like to die without care and the best person to provide that care is your sister."

"Half-sister," she corrected absently. "Is he that bad?"

"I have no way of judging, but he remains unconscious and was submerged in cold water for some time." His voice was grim. "Are you trained to care for him?"

"No," she admitted, as he knew she must.

"Nor is Mrs. Hammond," he reminded her, watching the emotions cross her face. It was the ultimate dilemma for a conformable miss—her father and her betrothed were making conflicting demands.

Emily made her decision and straightened her back. "Jameson, you will send a footman to summon Mrs. Morrison immediately."

"I have my orders, my lady," he insisted stubbornly.

"Who is in charge of the house?" she demanded.

Uncertainty flickered in the butler's eyes. "You are, my lady."

"Then you will follow instructions. I want her here as soon as possible. It will be on your head if Mr. Stevens dies unattended."

"Yes, my lady."

Norwood was pacing the hallway outside Stevens's room when Amanda finally arrived. She seemed surprised to see him there.

"Thank heaven you were able to come," he said in relief. Just the sight of her was enough to lift his spirits. She would know what to do. And with her at hand, Oliver would not dare die.

"What happened? The footman was nearly incoherent and Jameson merely glared."

Again he explained all he knew of the accident. "As near as I can tell, his head remained above water the whole time, but he is still unconscious from a sharp blow. Nothing appears broken, though he has been rather battered about."

"What have you done for him so far?" she asked as they entered Oliver's room. He removed her cloak, noting absently that her green daydress set green glints glowing in her brown eyes.

"Mrs. Hammond has been looking after him." He nodded to the housekeeper, who was seated beside the bed.

Unlike the butler, Mrs. Hammond's eyes did not glare with disapproval. "The poor boy shows no sign of waking," she announced.

"Aside from cleaning him up, have you done anything else?"

"Just kept him as warm as possible. He won't swallow, and I've little experience with the injured."

"How cold was he when you brought him home?" She turned questioning eyes on Norwood.

"Quite. His legs felt especially icy. The stream was very cold."

She turned back the sheets and ran her hands down his limbs. "They are warming well, so that is one less concern for the moment."

Norwood raised his brows in question.

"If the legs remain cold several hours after submersion, he risks developing gangrene," she explained. "But if they warm up, that is much less likely. I would hate to see him lose anything."

He blanched and she flashed an impish grin at his discomfort.

Amanda prodded Oliver's head, gently feeling the large knot. "Good," she murmured, laying a pad over the site and wrapping it.

"What is good?" asked Norwood.

"The bone does not seem depressed under the swelling. That is another thing that often leads to serious complications." She turned to Mrs. Hammond. "I will need water, both for washing and for making tea. The latter will need to be kept hot, so make sure there is plenty of coal in here. Have one of the girls renew the warm bricks. There is nothing further that can be done until he wakes. I will sit with him. Hopefully, the doctor will call soon."

"Thank you, Mrs. Morrison," murmured Norwood when the housekeeper left.

"The footman said that you rescued him?" Her voice held a trace of surprise, though she was busy unwrapping Oliver's wrist to inspect the scrapes left by the strap.

He flushed. "Yes."

"He owes you his life, then."

"It was nothing."

"I doubt it, though I always suspected you were not the unfeeling iceberg you pretend to be. How badly were you injured?"

"Nought but cold and that is long gone."

She turned back to Norwood. "What a bouncer! Show

me your wrist." She pointed to the red spot peeping out from under his sleeve.

"It is just a scrape. I had to break off the door to enter the carriage."

"Have you dressed it properly?"

"It is nothing."

"Men! Do you remove that jacket or do I?"

He matched her glare but pulled off his coat. Blood stained his shirtsleeve. She glowered at him and jerked open his cuff.

"You are a fool, your grace," she snapped as she bandaged his arm. "And your valet is a fool for not tending you properly."

"Enough," he pleaded as she tied off a strip of linen and refastened his sleeve. "It is nothing."

"Stoicism will kill you one of these days." She sighed and returned her attention to the rescue. "But Sir Harold will be grateful for your efforts. He lost one son at Waterloo. Fate would be too cruel to take another."

"Is that what Stevens was quizzing you about so intently that night?"

"Yes. He wanted to hear any details I could provide."

"I suppose you knew the brother."

She nodded. "And found his body when I was searching for Jack." She suddenly recalled where she was and mentally shook herself. "Enough of this maudlin fustian. Go and seek your dinner, your grace. There is nothing further you can do here."

"Until later, Mrs. Morrison." He bowed and left.

But before he reached the drawing room, his attention was drawn to a strident argument in the library. Thorne was berating someone for disobeying an order. Frowning in distaste over a scene that was already attracting the servants, he was moving on when Emily's voice took over.

"You would condemn one of your houseguests to possible death just to perpetuate a nine-year-old feud?" she asked incredulously.

"I was right to disown the chit," Thorne countered. "Her disreputable ideas have already corrupted you. How dare you abandon your duty by overturning my instructions and undermining my authority?"

"There is more than one duty involved here," she all but shouted, the passion in her voice surprising Norwood, who had never heard a hint of emotion from her in the past. "Have you considered your own duty as a host? If you fail to care for an injured guest, your credit must suffer. And if the world learns—as it will—that such inadequacy arose from the misguided hatred of an unnatural father, you will be scorned by the very society you have always worshiped."

"Unnatural, am I?" sputtered Thorne, rage vibrating through the words. "The description fits you far better. Is this how an obedient daughter thanks the father whose training allowed her to capture the prize of the marriage mart?"

Norwood could hardly believe his ears, but he refused to allow the argument to continue. Without knocking, he shoved open the door.

"You are castigating the wrong party, Lord Thorne," he announced coldly. "I am the one who ordered that Mrs. Morrison be summoned to tend Mr. Stevens. The doctor is unavailable and your guest is in dire need of competent attention."

"So you are abetting my daughter's defiance," Thorne stormed, propriety forgotten in his fury.

"I suggest we both have a glass of brandy to settle our tempers and then discuss this like reasonable gentlemen," suggested Norwood through gritted teeth.

Thorne drew in a deep breath. At last he walked over to a cabinet and poured two glasses of wine.

"Sit down, Norwood, Emily," he ordered, seating himself in a nearby chair. "And then you can explain why it was necessary for a guest to counter the orders left by the estate's owner."

Norwood succinctly described the day's events.

"And his injuries are that serious?" asked Thorne.

"He is still unconscious. I have no idea when the accident occurred, but it has now been five hours since I found him."

Thorne frowned. "We will discuss your behavior when I have had time to consider it," he addressed Emily. "Perhaps you will see to our guests now."

"Thank you, Papa," she replied demurely, curtsying first to Thorne, then to Norwood. She smiled at the duke for the first time in days.

"Why was it necessary to forbid Lady Amanda the house?" asked Norwood when Emily was gone.

"I cannot have her contaminating my children with her appalling ideas and disreputable behavior," he replied shortly, his tone making it clear that questions were unwelcome.

Norwood continued anyway. "What did she do that was so bad? I have seen no evidence that she deserves censure." His old self reared up to castigate his newer self at that clanker, but he ignored it.

"She has always been an unnatural child," said Thorne with a sigh. "She took after her mother, exhibiting no respect for her position and no sign of good breeding. Despite all we could do, she ran wild, sneaking off to consort with peasants, dangling after the local witch, and displaying unseemly emotion at every turn. We tried everything we could think of to teach her proper manners, but she harbors some devil that repudiates all that is good."

Norwood was frowning, but not in commiseration. Shorn of the vitriolic tone, Lady Amanda's childhood sounded remarkably like his own. He suspected that her motives were also the same—a search for enjoyment. He could not believe that she was deserving of contempt. Nor could he forget the pain in her eyes when she spoke of her father.

"There is nothing wrong with emotion," Norwood said aloud. "Not even among the upper classes. From what I have observed of her, she is a caring, compassionate woman devoted to assisting others."

"You are hardly impartial, having met her when she gave you a ride home that day," snorted Thorne.

"It is true that she has done me some service," agreed Norwood. "More than you know. It was she who patched me up last summer when I sustained several injuries from being trapped in an inn fire. She treated many people that night. Her efforts saved more than one life. Nor do I believe that I am alone in my admiration for Mrs. Morrison. Wellington gave every impression of both gratitude and friendship."

"He is biased. So many years of war are bound to warp any man's judgment. How can anyone praise a person so lost to propriety that she stoops to spying? A more dishonorable activity I cannot imagine."

"I can think of many activities more dishonorable, including some practiced regularly by men and women high in society," countered Norwood, controlling his anger with an effort. Thorne was proving with every word that he was an unforgiving, vindictive, and rigid man whose vision of the world was so constrained that few would agree with it. Even his own father had not been openly antagonistic. Why had he never noticed this before? More importantly, what legacy had so unfeeling a parent bequeathed to his daughter? All he could do was try to temper the intransigence. "Information is vital to any war effort. Gathering it requires skill and courage. I would never slight anyone who served his country in that way. The fact that Mrs. Morrison is female makes her achievements all the more admirable. She lived in a man's world for many years, holding her own according to those who knew her, yet never abandoning her ladylike behavior."

"Are you aware that she eloped?" sneered Thorne.

"Yes. Why did you refuse her permission to marry? Granted Morrison was considerably beneath her, but not impossibly so."

"I did not know Morrison existed," said Thorne more calmly. "She was already betrothed to another."

Norwood frowned. "Perhaps I misjudged her then," he admitted. "I had not expected her to break her word in such a way."

Thorne suddenly appeared nervous. "Actually, she had never spoken with her betrothed."

"You tried to force her?" exclaimed the duke incredulously. Anger flared and his voice turned deadly. "Coercing any young lady into an unwanted match is unforgivable. And I cannot envision a more cowhanded approach to taming a spirited filly. She had no choice but to elope."

The dinner gong sounded, cutting off the marquess's sputtering response. "After you, your grace," he murmured tonelessly, seeming relieved to escape the discussion.

"Of course. But I would suggest rethinking your edicts

concerning Mrs. Morrison. She would be a credit to any family and will always be welcome at Norwood Castle."

Very impudent of him, he admitted as he escorted Lady Bradford to dinner. But what was the point of being a duke if he could not occasionally throw his weight around? And he had run across few worthier causes than encouraging a reconciliation between Lady Amanda and her family.

Oliver finally awoke late in the evening. Amanda sighed in relief when she heard the first moan. She had been worried about his continued unconsciousness. There was still no sign of the doctor.

"Where am I?" he groaned softly.

"In your room at Thornridge Court," she answered. "Your carriage tumbled off the bridge during the storm this afternoon."

"Who—" He bit off the words, his face twisted in pain.

"Don't try to move. I am Mrs. Morrison, called in to tend your injuries until the doctor returns from another call."

"I remember now," he murmured. "Lightning struck quite close as we were returning to the Court, and John had trouble bringing the team back under control. How badly was he hurt?"

"I have heard nothing of him," she admitted. "But I will inquire. How is your head?" She gently explored around the swelling with soft fingers, relieved that it seemed smaller than when she had arrived.

Oliver bit off an exclamation of pain. "It feels like an army is marching through my brain, with knives protruding from every foot."

"How about your neck?"

He experimentally moved his head a fraction. "It is fine."

"And your arms and legs?"

"A few bruises," he admitted after a limb by limb examination. "And my right wrist and shoulder seem sprained."

"Be grateful. Your hand caught in the strap when you went over the side and saved you from drowning. Now let's try some of this broth, and then I will give you something for the pain."

He sighed and opened his mouth, grimacing as he swallowed. "How did I get here?"

"Norwood rescued you, apparently at great risk to himself, though I know no details."

"That doesn't sound like him."

"Many people differ from the face they show the world. You hide behind a mask yourself."

Oliver raised questioning brows.

"Do you wear your heart on your sleeve?" she prodded him.

"Ah. Perhaps I should have joined the army after all."

"My former comments still apply, Mr. Stevens. And accidents can happen anywhere. When I was on the Peninsula, there were often problems. Lightning struck as we were trying to cross a rain-swollen stream one summer, hitting six men."

"How awful," he whispered, paler than before. "Did all die?"

"Two survived," she reported, "though both were badly burned. But you must realize that no place is safe. Death in war is common. Worse were the letters from home—a house that burned down, killing the family; a beloved brother who broke his neck while hunting; a young child drowned in a lake. It is not a perfect world. Be grateful Norwood pulled you out when he did. As for the other, running away from a problem rarely works."

Chapter Thirteen

Oliver had fallen into a natural sleep by the time his bedroom door opened, admitting Norwood.

"How is he?" he whispered.

"He should be all right," Amanda replied softly. "He woke an hour ago and took some broth."

Norwood sighed in relief, but all he said was, "Good."

"Do you know what happened to his coachman? He was asking."

The duke dropped into a chair and frowned. "He died. We sent grooms out as soon as we returned to the Court. They brought his body in two hours ago. The neck seems to be broken, but whether that happened in the accident or as a result of being tumbled about by the stream, I cannot say. Both horses also perished."

Amanda shook her head. "How tragic. If it had happened anywhere else, all would have survived. I did not question him about the details, but he mentioned a lightning strike quite close at hand."

"Then it is possible that he had only been in the water ten or fifteen minutes before I found him. There was an excessively loud crash of thunder about that time."

"Excellent. That improves his chances for a full recovery."

"Did he suffer any other injuries?"

"Nothing serious. And he was completely lucid."

They fell silent for some minutes, the only sounds an occasional creak of the house and Oliver's quiet breathing. Even the wind had disappeared as the storm moved on. The duke knew that he should return to his room now that he had assured himself that the boy was all right, but he had been unable to sleep earlier and did not believe that had changed. In here he was relaxed.

Why that should be he did not understand. Was it just because he craved company? That feeling had been growing since his arrival at the Court, though he had never experienced it in the past. But the idea did not seem right. He derived no comfort from being with Geoffrey. Comfort. Perhaps it was female company he needed. Not for intimacy, but for companionship. Since even betrothed couples were not allowed to be alone together, he had to settle for his future sister-in-law.

"I always seem to see you under dramatic circumstances," he murmured in an apparent non sequitur.

"Not always, though I can see why it might seem that way." She shrugged.

"I cannot forget that fire," he admitted even as he wondered why he was mentioning it. Perhaps it was a combination of the dark room with its single candle and the weariness of a late night after a long day. But he could not keep his mouth closed, uttering thoughts he normally bottled up in the privacy of his mind. "It haunts me."

"Nightmares?" Sympathy warmed the single word.

He nodded.

"No wonder you recognized mine so readily. Trauma frequently prompts night terrors. It is hardly surprising in your case. I doubt you are often subjected to drama. The dreams should fade in time."

"They are becoming less frequent," he admitted, leaning his head against the back of his chair and closing his eyes. "But at first it was two or three times a night."

Amanda raised her brows, for that seemed excessive even for a disaster. She hoped her own behavior was not haunting him. "What are they about?"

"Oddly, Fitch's surgery rarely appears," he answered, seeming to read her thoughts. "It is always fire—being trapped in my room; watching Fitch engulfed as he fights to rouse me; watching Matthews buried under that wall." His voice cracked.

"You needn't feel guilty about that," swore Amanda, understanding what he had not said.

"Two men died because of me."

"Fustian," she scoffed. "You are intelligent. How could you possibly believe that?"

"Fitch would be alive if he had not gone back to save my worthless hide," he insisted, staring bleakly at her. "And one of Matthew's helpers was there only because I suffered an attack of cowardice and refused." It was the first time he had voiced his shame aloud.

"Using that twisted logic, I was responsible for him myself," she countered.

Norwood gasped. "Ridiculous!"

"Not at all. If I had not forced you to help with Fitch, you would never have considered whether to volunteer, and it *was* force," she added, cutting off his protest. "Despite my denial at the time, I lost my temper that night and deliberately decided to knock you down a peg or two, knowing almost exactly what would happen."

"Almost?" he interrupted.

"I hadn't expected you to let him kick you."

"Ouch."

"I definitely owe you an apology, your grace. But beyond that, if I had not selfishly boarded the stage before the work was done, it would have been me under that wall."

"I can't deny I needed knocking down a bit, but you go too far to blame yourself for any deaths. You saved so many lives that night."

"You also go too far," she said, ignoring his last comment. "What happened was beyond either of our powers to influence. It is God who determines life and death. We should leave the second-guessing to Him as well."

Norwood nodded.

"Did they ever discover what caused the fire?"

"It might have been a candle," he suggested, "but the consensus was a careless soldier who occupied the room in which it started. He had spent the evening in the taproom, drinking heavily and smoking cheroots."

"Nasty habit," agreed Amanda, seeing Norwood shudder in distaste. "Many soldiers acquired it on the Peninsula. I was grateful that Jack never did."

"The speculation was that he fell into a wine-induced slumber with one still alight."

"I imagine so. The same thing happened in Spain to a

captain camping near us—but not of our regiment, thank God. His tent went up in flames and him with it. I still hear his screams . . ."

"Don't," he urged her sharply, then lowered his voice as Oliver stirred restlessly on the bed. "I find it hard to believe that any gently reared lady could have survived what you experienced."

"Fustian!" she scoffed, recovering her composure. "Women are not the delicate creatures that men have decreed. It is custom alone that relegates them to that position, not inherent weakness. You should have seen all the gently bred ladies succoring the dying in Brussels. I am unusual only because I refused to simper or play the coquette. I have always despised dishonesty, even when society expects it."

"I applaud you, Mrs. Morrison. The airs and affectations that most women employ are indeed deceitful." He sounded bitter.

"You must have had an unfortunate experience with someone who was less than truthful," she murmured, hoping to draw him out about his past. Perhaps that was why he hid behind hauteur so often. She had been unable to learn much about him from Lady Thorne. Her grandmother had repeated what his grandmother had written when he was a young man, but she had no idea why he was so different today.

Her warmth and sympathy worked its usual magic. Norwood answered without thinking. "My wife." A spasm of pain twisted his face.

"Tell me about her," she whispered.

"Annabelle. She was the most beautiful creature in the world—not that her looks were perfect, but vivacity animated her like no other. I fell in love with her almost at once."

"You must have been fairly young at the time," she murmured.

"Yes. Not quite one-and-twenty and just down from Oxford. But that mattered not. She was so warm, so loving, so particular in her attentions. If she had flirted with everyone, I might have been warier, but she did not. Her face would light up whenever I appeared, her entire being relaxing, almost in relief. She seemed alive only in my presence. Dear God, but I was naive."

He ran a hand through his hair in a gesture of frustration she had never seen him use. Even his voice was livelier, convincing her that he desperately needed to talk about his marriage. He had probably never done so before.

"What went wrong?" she asked softly.

"Her father accepted my offer without consulting her. I should have realized then that something was not quite right. We settled on a wedding date barely a month ahead. I did not talk to Annabelle until that night at a ball. I do not know how familiar you are with society, but there is no opportunity for private words at *ton* entertainments. And when the heir to a dukedom marries, everyone turns out to fete the couple. It is even more frenzied than the usual Season."

"So there was no chance to discuss anything with her until it was too late?" she asked, understanding where his comments were leading.

"Exactly. Nor did I have a moment to contemplate her changed demeanor. She was suddenly cold, quiet . . . almost brittle. I put it down to exhaustion, which was something I was feeling excessively myself." His hands again threaded his hair and stayed there, the weight of his head dropping his elbows onto his knees.

"Was it a case of title-seeking then?" she asked.

"Not exactly, though I entertained that notion myself for quite some time. After the wedding, I realized that she was not exhausted, but was afraid of me."

Amanda jumped in surprise. "Of you? Or just of marriage?"

"I thought at first it was marriage, and that would hardly be surprising. She was only seventeen and had never been out in the world before coming to London. It is a shocking transition, even with a spouse one cares for."

Amanda nodded, but made no comment.

"But it quickly became apparent that it was me. Her terror eventually settled into hatred." He raised his head to meet her eyes, his own as bleak as she had ever seen. Pain twisted his face.

"Dear heaven. But why would she marry someone she

despised? Even title and wealth can hardly make up for that."

He shrugged. "I pieced the story together bit by bit over the next months, but the crux of it remained a mystery until after she died. One of the mourners was Annabelle's childhood neighbor. It seems that they had fallen in love when she was barely fifteen, but her father refused to countenance the union. The lad was the younger son of a baronet, with no money and no prospects. Annabelle's father was a viscount with aspirations to higher circles. She was his only child so she represented his lone chance to improve his consequence."

"Unfortunately not an unusual situation."

"I know that now. If only I had known it then, but one of the few favors my cold parents ever did me was to protect me from the greediest of the toadeaters. I wish they had not."

"Why did they not protect you from Annabelle and her father, then?" she asked, sensing another lifetime of pain associated with his family but choosing to ignore it for the moment.

"In a burst of youthful independence and self-confidence, I arranged the whole without consulting them," he admitted in chagrin.

"Typical."

"You condemn me?"

"Never. How can I, having fallen prey to youthful indiscretion myself on more than one occasion? But what happened? If Annabelle loved another, how came she to fall in with her father's plans?"

He frowned. "She had no choice. She was not as deceitful as I initially thought. Her father brought her to town for the Season, ordering her to attach a wealthy title, and demanding at least an earl. Her beau claims that she had concocted a scheme to avoid any union."

"Ah," sighed Amanda in sudden understanding. "She probably cut every eligible gentleman who showed interest in her, but was able to flirt with you because there was no chance you would offer for her."

He raised his brows in surprise.

She smiled. "Think, your grace. How often does any

gentleman wed at so young an age? What duke would ever countenance his heir attaching a lady so far beneath him in consequence? She must have assumed that you were engaging in harmless flirtation like any other young sprig. That would account for her demeanor with you. She could relax and be herself, knowing that no other gentlemen would dare to cut you out."

"You are right, of course. I was merely surprised that you worked it out so quickly. Unfortunately, I did not do so until it was much too late. I put the poor girl through hell," he whispered, his voice cracking badly at the memory of his marriage.

"I assume that her father forced her to wed you," she stated calmly, pulling him back from the brink of collapse.

"Yes. He had already accepted my suit and agreed to settlements before she even knew that I had offered. It was one of the first things I learned after the wedding. He had threatened to incarcerate her for life if she did not comply."

"The disadvantage of being so proper. You did not discuss your feelings with her and probably did not even hint at a future together."

"Exactly. And then I defied all propriety by arranging everything myself. I was a devil of a fool."

"It is over, your grace. One cannot change the past, however much one might wish to. One can only learn from it."

"For myself, it would not matter. I deserved everything I suffered. But she was an innocent victim. There is no justice."

"Poor Annabelle. But why was her father so adamant? Was it just the vicarious power and enhanced consequence?"

"No. He was a gamester, his zeal far exceeding his skill. He believed that no duke would allow his father-in-law to either flee the country or languish in debtor's prison, so he foresaw a rosy future."

"I cannot believe you would allow such predation," she commented, breaking into a chuckle. "Your backbone is far stiffer than that."

"You are right." He sighed. "Even before the marriage, I was having second thoughts about allowing him to rush me into signing the settlements. When my solicitor saw them, he nearly exploded. Fortunately, Annabelle's father made one mistake—he forgot that I was not legally of age. We overturned the initial document, replacing it with one that would protect Annabelle but not allow her father to coerce anything from her. Yet even that was not enough. I had assumed that she cared for me, of course. In reality, she quickly became a pawn in a power struggle between me and my father-in-law. He applied enormous pressure on her to turn me up sweet. I eventually barred the house to him. But I was hardly better, refusing to allow her to give so much as a groat to the man. The situation made an already bad relationship worse. Her hatred grew until, at the end, she would not even allow me to enter her room as she lay dying."

"It is over," she reminded him, noting the sheen of tears in his eyes. "I do not believe that you were ever cruel to her. Nor do I believe that she truly hated you. She was very young and probably deflected her fury at the situation and her frustrations over her own imperfect scheme in your direction. You were as much a victim as she, all of you prey to her father's obsession."

"I should have known better," he insisted. "If only I had not let my enthusiasm run away with me."

"If, if, if," she chided him. "If wishes were horses, and so on. Who can blame anyone for acting his age? Don't hate yourself for falling prey to youthful misjudgment. You could not be expected to recognize her desperation."

"But I should have. Poor Annabelle. She was so miserable. How can fate be so cruel?" His control snapped, allowing a sob to escape.

"Cry it out, your grace," she urged him, sliding close enough that she could gently pull his head against her to muffle the heart-wrenching sobs. For ten years he had been carrying the pain and guilt. But he was not the Iron Duke, charged with securing Europe's future. Norwood had no reason to hide his own emotions. She absently smoothed his hair and massaged the back of his neck, hoping all the while that Annabelle's father would roast for an eternity. His selfish scheming had destroyed three people. It was clear that Norwood was not at fault in the debacle. Nor were Annabelle or her young man.

As the duke's tears slowed, she slipped out of the arms
that had wound around her and moved to add coal to the
fire.

Norwood was in shock over his breakdown, yet he had to
admit that he felt better. Mrs. Morrison had made him look
at his marriage from a different point of view. He had been
too busy blaming himself to remember that Crompton was
the real villain. Yes, he had been naive—and impetuous,
foolish, and way too arrogant. But it was Crompton's ve-
nality that had engineered the fiasco. Poor Annabelle had
found herself in a hopeless coil, her father's pressure threat-
ening her own happiness. Lacking the courage that had allowed Lady Amanda to escape in similar circumstances,
Annabelle had taken the only other path open to her—the
faulty plot to sidestep matrimony. She had made only one
mistake—failing to consider that one of the unlikely suitors
might fall in love with her. He must have seemed the perfect tool in her attempt to stymie her father.

If only he had talked to her! Despite their frequent discussions, he had never bared his heart, for proper gentlemen did not expose their feelings. He wiped the tears from
his face. Not once had he considered asking her if she
cared. Why should he? Everyone had fawned over him
since the day he was born, rushing to fulfill his every
whim. He snorted. It was ridiculous to interpret that as caring. If only he had talked to her first! He had not even taken
the time to think through his decision, impetuously offering
for her only a fortnight after meeting her. Had he even
loved her? The unthinkable question slipped into his mind
so quickly that he gasped in shock.

She had been beautiful, vivacious, witty, and carefree.
But it had been a facade. She was good-looking, of course,
but the real Annabelle was a perplexing mixture of timidity
and iron determination, of boldness and terror. Crompton
wore the face of a bluff, hearty man, but Norwood now
knew that the facade hid a selfishness that often stooped to
dishonor and outright brutality to achieve its ends. Nicholas
had been horrified to discover his wife with a black eye and
bruised jaw one day. That was when he barred the viscount
from the house, though he could not prevent the man from
lurking to accost Annabelle when she went out. He had fi-

nally hired a bodyguard to escort her everywhere, but the continued friction exacerbated an already deteriorating relationship.

If he had been more experienced, perhaps he could have averted the disaster he had visited on her. In retrospect, his great love had been nothing but infatuation with the face Annabelle showed to society. He neither knew nor understood the woman behind the mask. And yet his naiveté was not the only contributor to their disaster. If she had been more worldly, she would have found a way to announce that she was not looking for marriage, or to inform her court that any suitor must speak to her first. He had met two young ladies this past Season who had done just that. He could only conclude that he and Annabelle were both victims of innocence. If he had been older, he would never have offered for her. He would have been suspicious of her flirtation, assuming that she was angling for a position as duchess. Investigation would have revealed Crompton's debts and might even have turned up her attachment. No wonder parents refused to grant their children control of their lives at so tender an age. Judgment did not mature until later.

Something had been tickling his mind and finally stepped into full view. There was a second flaw in Annabelle's scheme. What if her scheme had worked? After a full Season of flirting with him, she could never have gone quietly home with no betrothal. Crompton would have vented his fury on her. She would not have survived long enough to marry Hensley. Elopement had been her only chance for happiness, but she had lacked the courage. He mopped up the last of his tears and shook his head, his eyes focusing gratefully on Mrs. Morrison.

Amanda poked idly at the fire until Norwood had regained his composure. Only then did she return to her chair.

"It is over, your grace," she said again. "Annabelle has been at rest for ten years. It is time for you to move on."

"You understand so much," he agreed, his voice still raspy. "Did you learn it all by experience, or were you born wise?"

"If I had been born wise, my life would doubtless have proceeded along much different lines," she admitted.

"Was your marriage also a mistake, then?"

"Not in that sense. My biggest mistakes occurred much earlier, like refusing to give in to my father's demands. I proved so intransigent that he finally decided I would only embarrass him if he introduced me to society, so he arranged a betrothal to a gentleman I had met once. Once was enough to know that he would have abused me roundly, so I left."

"Were you in love with Colonel Morrison?" Why was he prying like this? he suddenly wondered. It was none of his business. But he couldn't help himself. His recent storm of tears had broken down the barriers he usually hid behind. But beyond that lurked the certainty that she also needed to talk.

"Not then. That grew later. We started as friends. Jack was always kind and gentle, and he spent an enormous amount of time correcting the deficiencies in my education. By the time we reached Portugal a year later, we were very close. There were no real problems until Vienna." She closed her mouth, having already said too much. That was a period she was determined to expunge from memory. It was hard enough to accept her misjudgment of Jack's character and cope with her grief over his death. She wasn't ready to face the anger, guilt, and pain of Vienna.

"What happened?" he asked, sensing her withdrawal.

"I can scarcely burden you with my own problems," she protested, going to check on Oliver.

"It would be an honor, not a burden," he assured her. "Major Humphries mentioned that you played confidante for your husband's regiment. If you've so much sense, you must realize that discussing your own trials might help resolve them."

Finding nothing wrong with Mr. Stevens, she was forced to turn back to the duke. "It was nothing, really. Vienna was such a hectic period that there were bound to be disagreements at times."

"Such as—" he persisted. Her very reluctance to discuss it increased his determination.

Amanda tried to change the subject, but again he seemed to pull words from her mouth without her permission. "Jack often berated me for flirting with other gentlemen. We were socializing more than we had ever done in the past, and with a much higher class of people. He didn't like it."

"Was he unhappy because he knew you belonged in those circles?"

She frowned. "That might have been part of it, though he should have known that I had no aspirations to the polite world. Even as a child, I did not belong there. Father made it clear from the beginning that I was a disgrace to my breeding. Yet I could never change. If following his edicts was what it took to join society, I wanted none of it. But that was not the real problem. In fact, none of the things we fought about during those months were important."

"Besides flirting, what did he object to?" asked Norwood as Amanda wandered over to stare sightlessly out of the window.

"Stupid things." She sighed. "Which parties to go to; who our friends should be; money—we never had any; clothes; schedules . . . It doesn't matter. After a while, it got so we fought about anything and everything." Her voice cracked.

"What was the real problem?" he asked softly.

"Jack's job. Wellington is the one who opened my eyes to that, just last week. Jack was very unhappy. He was not a man who enjoyed spending his days in diplomacy and report writing."

"I suppose he found it boring."

"Of course, though that was not the crux of the matter, either. He needed action and competition, but he was so tied down in Vienna he couldn't even get free to go hunting. All he could do was create conflict to replace the danger that Napoleon's abdication had removed from his life."

"Arguing with you was a substitute for war?" he asked incredulously.

"In part, though it was more complicated than that. The situation was very odd, and I doubt anyone who did not know Jack could understand it. Even Wellington contributed to the problems. When he recruited me to help him, he forbade me to tell Jack."

"You mean your husband did not know about your spying?"

"No. Much of the socializing I was doing was in pursuit

of information. Wellington used Jack's jealousy as a cover."

Norwood shivered. Of all the cold-blooded . . .

"And it worked, of course. A typical scene occurred at the Countess of Worth's ball. Jack accosted me in a deserted hallway and immediately assumed that I was heading for an assignation. I was torn between relief that it was Jack and anger that he had appeared at all. A second gentleman arrived moments later who thought nothing of discovering us in furious argument but who might have arrested me had I been alone. Yet I wish they had both arrived later. I had been trying to overhear a conversation between two men who I suspected had engineered the disappearance of a British officer some days before. I still believe that if Jack had not created such a scene, we might have found the major before they killed him."

"I suppose you are talking of Major Collingsworth. You are not responsible for his death. As you reminded me earlier, that falls under the province of God, and you should not second-guess Him."

"I know, but it is difficult." Amanda's voice dropped to a whisper as she relived those months in Vienna. She rested her forehead against the window. "Poor Jack. He was caught in a web of discontent. Nothing he did was interesting. I was carrying on in a way he could only interpret as repudiating him. It is no wonder he began to spend his time with others, but it hurt to see him drifting away from me."

That was the real problem. "So he retaliated against your socializing by doing some of his own?" he asked obliquely.

Her shoulders twitched as she choked back a sob. She nodded.

"Painful, but you must have known the reason," he said calmly.

"I suppose it was the last straw," she murmured. "I had hoped that the end of the war would allow us to grow closer."

"I thought you were already close."

"It is difficult to explain," she said brokenly. "Those first months, I was everything to Jack, but it wasn't real. He was still recovering from his injuries and devilishly frustrated. I was the new toy that allowed him to retain his sanity."

Norwood shivered.

"But once we got to Portugal, I was always second. Don't get the wrong idea," she added as he drew breath to protest. "The army came first. It had to, with both of us. He never ignored me, but I was always an afterthought to the job at hand."

"So you looked forward to peace and a more normal life."

"Foolishly, it turns out. Jack never needed me. He was only truly alive when faced with danger."

Norwood had come up behind her and now laid his hands gently on her shoulders. "Aren't you exaggerating just a bit?"

"No," she choked. "He only put up with me because I had slightly more uses than his batman. It was nought but a quixotic gesture to marry me at all."

Another sob shook her, prompting Norwood to turn her and press her face into his coat. He felt out of his depth. "Go ahead and cry," he murmured.

"Why does no one care about me?" she sobbed bitterly. As Norwood's arms tightened in protest, she continued. "They all appreciated me, but none truly cared. I am as much a dreamer as Jack. He never loved me. For years I deluded myself into believing he did, but it wasn't true. Perhaps Father was right. No one could possibly love someone as abnormal as I."

Norwood felt like he was teetering along a narrow path in a dense fog with no idea what lurked below. Never had he thought about other people as individuals, let alone about their problems or needs. But as Mrs. Morrison sobbed brokenly into his coat, he wanted nothing more than to remove all her pain and somehow set her on a road to happiness. How could a woman who possessed so much worth and so much love believe herself to be a failure?

As her tears eased, Amanda reviewed her words in amazement. She really had been Jack's new toy, she admitted, still shocked that such a description had tumbled out when she had never considered herself in that light. But it was true. Once he recovered, he had no real need of the distraction she had offered, but he kept her around because she had proven to be useful. He could just as easily have left

her behind when the regiment sailed—and would have if
she had caused him any distress. But she had been caught
up in the excitement of traveling to exotic new places and
the warmth of romantic love. So she buried her own needs,
content to live by Jack's rules. Not until the crisis atmosphere of war had eased into peace did she demand more
than he was willing to give.

The thought whirled in from nowhere, opening her eyes
in shock. It was not just his job that drove Jack to argument. For the first time since their marriage, she had made
demands on him.

She hiccuped, accepting Norwood's handkerchief and
drying her face.

"Were you never able to discuss this with Jack?" he
asked.

"There was never an opportunity," she admitted. "We
packed up in a dreadful hurry one day and went to Brussels.
I hardly saw him during the six weeks before Waterloo. He
was racing around delivering messages to troops scattered
across a wide area. It was better for him, of course, but the
constant recriminations of the previous months prevented
us from ever really talking. More than often not, we wound
up fighting."

"Don't blame yourself," he admonished her. "It would
have come right eventually. You are too sensible to have
allowed it to continue once life settled down again. And
you would have reached a comfortable arrangement."

"I'm not so sure," she countered. "Jack was not a man
suited to a peacetime existence. Many men are addicted to
destructive behavior—drunkards and inveterate gamesters,
for example. Jack was another. But with him it was competition. He needed action, danger, and constant challenge.
Combat intoxicated him, as did pitting himself against others. Not even love and the lighthearted whimsy that he
brought to the rest of his life could compensate for peace."
She trembled, grateful for the warm arms that still pressed
her head to his shoulder. The comfort and safety Norwood
offered allowed her to finally examine those last months.
And he seemed to understand her need to do so, for he remained silent, content to stroke her hair.

Poor Jack. Restlessness had driven him to increasingly

reckless behavior. He had run wild in Vienna, flaunting an endless parade of women. Not that he repudiated her. If anything, his attentions increased, their verbal sparring often lending an extra spark of passion to their lovemaking. But she alone could not compensate for the lack of warfare. So he had courted as much danger as possible, relieving his frustrations through discord at home and creating strife at every turn by publicly cheating on his wife and by cuckolding other men. At least half of his women were married, and he had reportedly been involved in several duels as a result. Wellington deplored such behavior and must have castigated him for it, placing his commission in jeopardy.

She might as well face the truth and be done with it. A deep, abiding love might have helped him cope, but neither of them felt that strongly. She could accept that now. Jack's affection had never wavered and he had always been proud of her accomplishments. Had he known of her spying, he would have supported her without reservation. But with him, friendship had never ripened into love. Nor were her own feelings strong enough. She had accepted the fact that she loved him without ever considering just what that meant. In the beginning, it had been a form of gratitude for rescuing her from a miserable future. Despite his injuries, he had been a dashing, worldly man, the scars on his face adding a piratical look that made him even more attractive. His teasing ways made her feel desirable, and he offered travel and new experiences, both of which she had long coveted. But her father had been at least partially right. Jack was a hero many times over. As a soldier, he had always been larger than life, leading his men against seemingly impossible odds, achieving his goals, and coming out alive. She had worshiped him, awed at his prowess even when she feared for his safety. But she had never learned to know the inner Jack. What had driven him? It was too late to find out. Perhaps that explained why she felt so empty now. Her love was shallow and limited, never really encompassing the whole man.

She shivered and Norwood's arms tightened. Blinking away one last tear, she sighed. "Wellington described Jack as the perfect knight-errant, and he was right. Peace would have made him miserable, and that would have permanently impaired our marriage. Much as I miss him, I have accepted that he was better off dying at Waterloo. There are not enough dragons left to keep him busy."

"Perhaps you would be happier if you had had children," he murmured, though how they could have managed a family during a war, he didn't know.

"Perhaps, but I knew before we married that it was impossible. Buenos Aires stole that from him." She pulled away to check on Oliver.

Norwood ignored the tears again shining in her eyes. His own chest seemed suspiciously constricted. Mrs. Morrison was like no other woman he had ever met, and she touched him in ways he had never before experienced. She deserved far more than life in a country market town, tending the sick and teaching music to the gentry. In that moment he decided that he would find her something better. Once he was married to Emily, he would bring her to London to look for the husband she deserved. He did not believe that Jack Morrison had been that man. He might have been a great hero, but he was not a good spouse. And if Thorne objected, he would accept a family rift. Lady Amanda was too precious to bury in the country.

He changed the subject to Mr. Stevens's injuries and excused himself some minutes later when she had regained her composure.

Chapter Fourteen

Norwood gave up trying to find a comfortable position. Pushing the coverlet to one side, he climbed down and drew on his dressing gown. It was going to be another night when sleep did not come easily. There had been too many of them lately.

He paced the floor for several minutes, his mind churning uselessly. Annabelle had occupied his thoughts more in the past fortnight than she had in years. It was probably inevitable since he was embarking on matrimony again, but there was no excuse for discussing her with someone else. He felt powerless, unable to control even his own tongue.

Or perhaps Lady Amanda really was a witch. She had induced him to relate things he had never shared with another living soul and had forced him to honestly evaluate his life. He was beginning to realize that he had been all but dead since his first marriage. The lessons he had drawn from his mishandling of Annabelle were important, but he had carried them too far. By preventing any possibility of further pain, he had also eliminated all potential for enjoyment.

He stopped to gaze out the window. The storm had moved on. A full moon bathed the gardens in silvery light, glinting invitingly off a distant lake. Impulsively, he threw on his clothes and left the house.

Laying Annabelle's ghost to rest had removed an enormous weight from his heart. That explained his restlessness. Excitement and energy were bubbling up, making him feel twenty again. He had Amanda to thank for it. Her caring compassion was new to his experience. She promised to make an admirable sister-in-law.

And what kind of wife would Emily make? His euphoria faded. Unfortunately, his ideas about marriage had undergone considerable change. The cold, emotionless facade he had hidden behind for the last ten years was not his true self. Drifting was unrewarding. He needed to inject some commitment into his life, to build a loving relationship with Emily.

But the prospects were daunting. He frowned into a reflecting pool as he recited the attributes that had led him to choose her in the first place—proper, unemotional, undemanding. What a negative list, and the discussion they had held after dinner that evening did not relieve his anxiety. He had been trying to discover some mutual interests that would provide a foundation for friendship. But he was not having much luck.

"Papa has very definite ideas on education," she stated coldly. "He despises bluestockings and would never countenance rearing one."

"But knowing a little Shakespeare is hardly blue," he countered. "Every lady in London attends his plays regularly. One must be able to discuss the theater."

"I don't see why. It is such a bore," she said on a long sigh.

"What did you enjoy during the Season, then?" he asked.

"All that is proper, of course. Almack's, walking in the park, paying calls." She lifted a delicate brow. "One has a duty to participate in society."

"Is that what is important to you then? Duty?"

"Of course. I have been well trained."

"And what do you see as your duty?"

"Obedience to my father and my husband. Wifely duties are very explicit—running the house, dispensing aid to the tenants, providing an heir, upholding my position in the world."

He had dropped the subject, for it all sounded so dull. She had shown no interest in any of it. Life with Emily offered few rewards. Even worse was an overheard snatch of conversation an hour later. He had been heading for his room when he chanced to pass Emily's sitting room. Miss Havershoal was laughing at something Emily had just said.

"But surely you look forward to the intimacy of marriage."

"Victoria!" Emily's shock halted her friend's mirth. "A

lady neither enjoys nor discusses such things. And once I produce an heir, I will not have to concern myself with it. All gentlemen keep mistresses, thank heaven."

"I have heard differently," countered her friend.

"You must have some very low acquaintances," charged Emily, all trace of approval gone. "Mother warned me about keeping low company. Their depraved ideas can rub off, as you have just demonstrated. No one will respect you if you harbor such thoughts. Once she knew she was dying, she made sure I learned all I would need for the future. In truth, that part of marriage is painful and disgusting, but one must tolerate it if one wishes to maintain a proper place in society. There is no other way to fulfill one's duty to provide an heir."

It was that that bedeviled him now. While he had kept mistresses for years, it was not something he had done during even the worst times of his marriage and he had no interest in doing so in the future. He wanted both companionship and commitment from his union, and it did not sound as if he would find either. Was there enough warmth buried beneath Emily's coldness that he could eventually coax a little enjoyment from her? It was doubtful. Emily had dismissed Miss Havershoal in terms that indicated their friendship was over. It brought to mind a tale he had discredited about her terminating another friendship the previous summer because Miss Simpson refused to condemn a prank. The future was beginning to look even worse than the past.

Dr. Robinson arrived near dawn. Amanda smiled in relief. Oliver had awakened several times during the night, continued discomfort making him restless. She had fed him broth, barley water, and a tisane that reduced his pain, but it had not been enough. Until the doctor saw him, she refused to use laudanum, fearing that it might mask something important.

The doctor's diagnosis was concussion. He commended her care and prescribed bed rest until the headache eased, but declared that there was no further need for continuous observation. Oliver's thinking was rational, his memory unimpaired.

Amanda returned home immediately, but sleep eluded her. It was not the strain of nursing, for that had never been troublesome. This was worse. All the emptiness of her life was tormenting her. What was it that made her unlovable? Her family had never cared. Her husband could not. Even Granny Gossich had harbored no deep attachment. Theirs had been a complicated relationship. She suspected that Granny's interest grew out of an ongoing feud with Thorne. By supporting Amanda's rebellions, she could avenge herself of an unknown injustice.

Amanda had rebelled often as a child, and not always from conviction. Thorne had controlled her behavior as much as if she were obedient. He had only to forbid something to make her do it. Would she have visited Granny if her father had condoned it? Not in the beginning, certainly, though once her interest in herbs and cures was piqued, she went on her own account.

It was time to take herself in hand and plot a course for the future. The truth was that she was lonely. It wasn't only Jack that she missed, but the camaraderie of the regiment. They had been her family for many years. They were her brothers, sharing and caring without restraint, openly grateful for her assistance and concern. In spite of the pain of losing so many of them, the years had been rewarding. Now there was nothing.

Her conversation with Norwood teased her mind. She was amazed that he had induced her to discuss her marriage, especially the confusion at the end. There was something about the man that begged confidences. This was not the first time she had bared her soul in his presence. It was still surprising how much she had told him about Waterloo and her experiences on the Peninsula.

Again she felt the strong arms that cradled her and the soft hands that had stroked her hair—as if he were comforting an injured child, she told herself firmly, though where that image came from, she could not explain. Her own childhood certainly did not produce it. Tingling heat washed through her and she gasped. It had been too long since she had felt a male body pressed so close to her own. Way too long.

Enough! She could not lie quietly in bed with the turmoil

that raged through her breast. Donning an old cloak, she strode toward the woods, her heedless feet crushing damp plants, creating a pungent cloud of herbal scents that swirled around her.

Was this what happened when grief waned? Having come to terms with the past, she was no longer fettered by the blue devils that had dogged her since Waterloo. Surely that was the only explanation for this sudden desire to crawl into bed with Norwood. She blushed, recalling the feel of a muscular shoulder under her cheek. It was insignificant, a natural outgrowth of the situation. And that had been scandalous itself. What had possessed her to remain in a bedchamber for two hours with a gentleman— alone! The sleeping Mr. Stevens could not be considered a chaperone. Not even years of following the drum could excuse such unconventional behavior.

The forest thinned and Amanda leaned against the last tree to watch the brightening eastern sky where a few wisps of pink-tinged clouds still lingered from the storm. There was no point trying to blame the situation or to pass off her desire as a reaction to a year alone. The attraction was to Norwood himself. Not to the haughty duke, of course, but to the unhappy man beneath the shell. They had so much in common. And that would never do. It would be bad enough if he were someone who would soon pass out of her life, but he was to be her brother-in-law. She could not form a *tendre* there.

Yet the feeling would not depart. She wished with all her heart that she could help him regain the happiness she suspected he had known as a boy. His coldness was not natural. His disdain was contrived. He had the potential to become an intensely emotional man if he allowed himself to care. And he had no urge to waste himself by courting constant danger.

She gasped as the full weight of her folly slammed into her heart. She loved him. "Dear God, no!" she whispered even as she acknowledged the truth. Already, her feelings were stronger than she had ever experienced before. How could she have been so stupid? Norwood's future was settled—marriage to her sister. She shivered. Emily was not the wife he needed. Amanda did not want to consider how barren the rest of his life would be.

Sighing, she turned her feet toward home. It was obvious that she could not stay in Middleford. She wanted no continuing relationship with her relatives, for they had little in common. But having acknowledged her as his daughter, Thorne would now feel obligated to include her in family gatherings. With her feelings for Norwood, that would be impossible. She must find a new refuge. Perhaps she could convince Thorne that they would both be happier if she moved elsewhere. He would probably be relieved.

Oliver gingerly prodded the knot on his head. The pain had diminished until it no longer triggered waves of nausea. With luck, he could manage with only one day in bed. Someone rapped on his door.

"Come in," he called, assuming it was the housekeeper with yet another posset or dish of gruel to poke into him.

Emily opened the door and crossed to the bed.

"What are you doing here?" he demanded. "You are the last person to breach propriety to this extent."

"I had to see how you were. Everyone says you will recover, but you were unconscious for so long that I could hardly believe it."

He caught his breath at the fear blazing in her eyes. It was the most emotion she had ever displayed.

"I truly am fine, Lady Emily," he murmured soothingly. "Both your sister and the doctor agree that there will be no problems, so you may set your mind at rest. I owe a great debt to Norwood, of course. If he had not happened along, things would have gone quite differently."

She ignored the reference to her betrothed. "You are truly all right? You are not just saying that to ease my mind?" Her hand fluttered in agitation with the words.

"Truly, my dear," he assured her, drawing the hand to his lips.

She let out her breath in a long sigh of relief.

"Do you care that much?" he asked, almost without volition.

"You are one of my dearest friends," she replied primly.

"No, Emily, that won't do," he exploded, his voice suddenly harsh. "I cannot allow this farce to continue. You must know how much I love you. And you love me as well, don't you?"

Tears started in her eyes. She remained silent but her head moved in the barest of nods.

"Emily, my dearest girl," he choked, pulling her down where he could kiss her. And she responded, one hand threading his hair as her mouth opened to his own. For nearly a minute she clung to him until reality returned.

"No, we mustn't," she cried, appalled at her actions.

"Don't leave," he commanded as she broke away and ran for the door. She paused to look back. "Think well, my love. If you marry Norwood, you will spend the rest of your life in misery. You cannot possibly care for him. I've seen the way you avoid his company. Do you think anything will change later on?"

"Of course not. He has no interest in anything beyond an heir."

"Emily, my love," he pleaded. "You deserve so much better. And I can give it to you."

"There is nothing to be done," she stated, her voice cracking into a sob. "It is my duty to marry well. The betrothal is already arranged. You cannot deny that the connection is all that is proper."

He sighed in resignation. "No, not if all that matters is a list of assets and liabilities on a piece of paper. But I thought you wanted more than that, like love and tenderness and warmth. You are a person, Emily. A living, breathing being with needs and interests and desires of your own. So is Norwood. So am I. The duke can give you a title, but never his heart. A title can be a cold, empty commodity when you are facing yet another night alone. You and I belong together, as you must admit if you examine your heart. It is not too late."

"You do not know my father," she cried, stumbling out of the room. "It was too late the day I was born."

He sighed. Why had he even tried? Poor Emily. She had been taught to revere duty above all else, even if that meant burying her real self under an icy facade that all too soon would freeze both heart and soul. As soon as he rose from his bed, he must leave. He could not remain to listen as her betrothal was announced to the public. Even his usual good humor could not survive that.

"Yes, Ellen?" asked Amanda when the maid appeared in her doorway. She had just returned from teaching and hoped this was not a call for medical attention. After being up all night, she was tired.

"A Mr. Grayson to see you, ma'am," reported Ellen, bobbing a curtsy. She held out a calling card.

"Show him in." She stared at the engraved card. W. M. Grayson of Grayson, Grayson, & Smith, solicitors. Had her father discovered some new way to command obedience?

Mr. Grayson was nonthreatening, a lean, modest man in his fifties whose thinning gray hair and thick spectacles complemented his thin-lipped mouth and permanently stooped shoulders. They exchanged pleasantries for some minutes until Ellen had delivered a tea tray and withdrawn from the room.

"Your husband was John Peter Morrison, son of Edward Rawlings Morrison of Herefordshire?" he asked.

"I believe that was his father's name, though Jack never spoke of his family. There was a well-established rift between them."

"What do you know of his family?"

"His mother was the youngest daughter of Viscount Brodley. Her maternal uncle was Mr. George Comfray, who owned an estate some fifteen miles from here. And Jack had a brother, William, who refused to acknowledge any relationship between them. I fear that is all."

"Have you met none of them then?"

"Only Uncle George. We stayed with him for some months after our marriage."

"And when were you wed?"

"March 22, 1807. What is this to the purpose?"

"I must establish your identity. Have you your marriage lines?"

Amanda retrieved them from her desk. Mr. Grayson compared Jack's signature to a paper he pulled from his pocket and nodded.

"What is this about?" asked Amanda again.

"You are aware that Mr. Comfray died?"

"Of course. Nearly two years ago."

"His will mentioned your husband, Mrs. Morrison."

"Then how comes it that we heard nothing earlier?" she asked sharply, thinking how nice it would have been to have had a bit more in Vienna than Jack's pay. It was one reason she had agreed to spy. They had needed the money it brought.

Mr. Grayson sighed. "It is rather involved. The wheels of the law turn slowly in the best of times, and even worse in this case. I was ill when Mr. Comfray died. My son took care of the routine of reading the will and settling with the servants, but the task of contacting heirs was left until I returned many weeks later. I sent a letter to Mr. Morrison in care of his regiment, not realizing that he was no longer with them. By the time I learned that he had transferred to Wellington's staff, he had died at Waterloo."

Amanda said nothing, wishing that the man would reach his point. The dry, ponderous voice resumed.

"Once I ascertained that he had drafted a will leaving all he possessed to his wife, I set in motion an effort to discover your whereabouts."

"It has taken you more than a year to find me?" she asked skeptically.

"No. The search was suspended for some months when Mr. William Morrison filed suit contesting the validity of both wills."

"He would," grumbled Amanda. "My impression was that William would begrudge Jack even a penny-piece."

"An admirable description," agreed the solicitor with a slight smile.

"But why was I never informed?"

"You have done a marvelous job of hiding yourself from the world, Mrs. Morrison. Even my client, Mr. Comfray, knew nothing of your background. Mr. Morrison's military associates lost sight of you after Brussels. I only discovered your direction some days ago when his grace of Wellington informed me of meeting you here. Mr. William Morrison's suit was denied last month so the will is now proved."

"What exactly is this inheritance?" she asked, suspicious at the time and money that must have gone into the search.

"Mr. Comfray's estate."

Her eyes widened. "You mean Beau Cime?" It was a lovely property, sited on a hilltop, with an Elizabethan manor that had been updated in Uncle George's youth to improve its comfort without sacrificing its charm.

"In part. Aside from legacies to several servants, he left everything to Mr. John Morrison. The estate is profitable and the investments bring in around five thousand a year."

Amanda was having trouble breathing. Five thousand? The principal must be well over a hundred thousand to produce that much. Had Jack known that he was George's heir? She doubted it. Thinking of the future was not one of his habits. She was amazed that he had made out a formal will of his own.

"I am stunned," she admitted at last.

"You need to come to Beau Cime to look over the property. I have kept an eye on it for nearly two years, but it is not the same as having an owner there."

"I will arrange to visit next week. We can discuss the future then."

Amanda sat in thought long after the solicitor had left. It was the answer to a prayer, the solution to all her problems. She must leave Middleford. Now she not only had a place to go, but the means to support herself without help from Thorne. The only question was whether to leave immediately or to discuss the situation with her father first.

Chapter Fifteen

Norwood stared sightlessly at the portrait above the fireplace. The morning room was gloomier than ever this evening, the overcast that had threatened rain all day bringing on dusk an hour early. He ought to be in the drawing room awaiting the summons to dinner, but he had no heart for company.

The house was crawling with people as more and more guests arrived for the ball. Coquettish giggles and young men's laughter echoed down hallways unaccustomed to merriment. Public rooms overflowed with gossiping ladies and pompous gentlemen.

How had he gotten himself into this coil? A fortnight earlier he had stood in this very spot, offering marriage to a chit he neither knew nor loved. He must have been suffering from brain fever for the last six months. Cutting all emotion from one's heart might work for someone intrinsically cold like his father or Thorne, but not for him. His life was empty. Acquiring a wife with whom he planned to spend no time would never change that. His stupidity was appalling. And this time he could not claim naiveté or inexperience. Only bad judgment.

The future was daunting. Emily avoided him whenever possible. As Thorne's very dutiful daughter, he could hardly expect her to become the loving woman her half-sister was. Each lady too closely resembled her own mother. If only he had talked at length with his grandmother before embarking on this expedition. The very fact that she had agreed with the duchess should have warned him that something was wrong. But it would have made no difference if he had, he reminded himself. There was no deceit. His own ridiculous notions had welcomed Emily's demeanor.

Running footsteps sounded in the hall, startling him out of his reverie. "Jameson!" shouted a voice.

Norwood could picture the haughty stare that must respond to such disrespect. Jameson was at least as high in the instep as Thorne.

"Falston sent me," panted the newcomer. "Wilson's house is on fire. Can you spare two or three footmen to help?"

"I will send Willy and Frank," agreed Jameson coolly.

Norwood stepped from the morning room as the groom turned to retrace his steps. "Where is the fire?" he demanded sharply.

"A tenant farm about two miles away, your grace."

"I am coming with you. Did the family get out?"

The groom wore an expression of shock, but he dared not counter a duke. "I do not know, your grace."

The stable yard was bustling with activity as horses were harnessed to a wagon into which buckets and tools had been tossed. Two footmen rushed to join half a dozen men in the wagon bed. Norwood climbed onto the box and they were off.

By the time they arrived at the fire, Norwood had gleaned quite a bit of information from Falston. The Wilsons were the most prosperous of the tenant farmers, occupying a stone-walled cottage large enough to qualify as a manor house. The family was extensive, including eight children and two of Mr. Wilson's brothers.

The house was too involved to save, decided Norwood in a single glance. It was already three-quarters ablaze, with little hope of stopping the flames. The farm buildings were another story. Close enough to be endangered by sparks from the fire, and with thatched roofs that made them particularly vulnerable, they needed immediate attention.

Falston had reached the same conclusion. "Let's go to work on the barn," he ordered his minions. "The stream is just over there." He pointed beyond a mosaic of pig pens.

Norwood was moving off with the others when a scream rent the air. He froze a moment, then raced toward the house.

"Let go!" demanded Amanda sharply, beating her hands against a man's shoulder. "Ben is still in there, in the end not yet ablaze. There is no way he can get out by himself. He has a broken leg. You cannot condemn him to die."

"Be reasonable, Mrs. Morrison," countered her opponent. "The stairs will go any second. You'll be trapped, too."

"Where is he?" asked Norwood.

"Oh, thank God you are here, your grace," sobbed Amanda. "There is a boy upstairs in that corner room." She pointed.

"I'll get him," he promised.

"The stairs will be in flames soon," protested the other.

"Get the men to throw water on them," ordered Norwood. "All I need is two or three minutes." And he was off.

Amanda was frozen in place by shock. Everything had happened too quickly. Though she had been on the scene only ten minutes, it seemed more like ten hours.

She had been driving home when she saw the smoke and knew immediately that it came from the Wilson farm. It hadn't taken her long to reach the site.

Her first action was to gather the women and children together and assure herself that everyone had escaped. It was a difficult task, for the Wilson family was large, with several workers and servants also living in the rambling old building. The men were scrambling to fight the flames, so she could not tell if any were missing. Within minutes, the dry wood had spread the fire far enough to drive them all out.

"The house is a loss!" shouted Mr. Wilson. "Get the animals out of the barn."

Amanda patiently counted heads. The two oldest boys were with the men. The next two had ridden to get help from other tenants and the Court. Mrs. Wilson had been carried in hysterics to a neighbor's house, along with the baby and an expectant sister-in-law. Not until Amanda came to the nurse did she discover that Ben had been left behind.

"I got the little ones out," the woman sobbed, "but I cain't carry Ben with his leg all done up in splints. I thought one of the men could run up and get him, but they all refused."

The nurse had not asked the right people, but Amanda refrained from voicing the thought. Mr. Wilson or either of his brothers would have been in the house in a flash if they had known, but they were busy trying to keep the blaze from spreading. Neighbors and farm workers were loathe to risk their own necks. And so she had headed in herself.

Entering through the kitchen proved impossible, though the fire was not yet burning there. She got as far as the pantry door when a beam collapsed, raining fiery debris upon her and blocking access to the back stairs. Brushing off the cinders that threatened to ignite her gown, and choking from the heavy smoke, she retreated.

But her determination was firmer than ever. Horror was back, memories swirling through her head in a maelstrom of sights and sounds. The crash of the beam sounded like distant cannon fire. Men scurried around, shouting orders. Jack's voice echoed through her mind. *Never retreat until all options are exhausted . . . There is always a way to achieve victory . . .* Crackling flames raised the specter of the Blue Boar in the overheated air. And Ben. Poor Ben. He was such an intrepid boy. How could she let him die?

"No!" she screamed, racing around to the front entrance. She was pushing her way into the building when Jem grabbed her and dragged her back.

"No!" she shouted again. "Ben is still in there. I must get him."

"It is useless, Mrs. Morrison," Jem countered harshly. "The stairs will be burning any second."

"You can't abandon him!" she sobbed, beating against the arms that restrained her.

They argued for nearly a minute, her desperation growing when she could not break free. Then, miraculously, Norwood appeared and headed into the house.

Now her fear was trebled. With startling clarity, every detail imprinted on her mind. Jem had been right, of course. There was little chance the stairs would remain open long enough for anyone to get upstairs and return. Flames already raged in the sitting room and flickered across the ceiling, burning fiercely through beams that must soon crash down. A glance at the windows showed that most of the upper floor was engulfed.

Why had he gone in? If he was trapped in there, she would never forgive herself. Nor could she live with the knowledge that her demands had killed him.

Norwood was reliving his own hell. The blast of hot, choking air that surrounded him the moment he passed through the front door brought back all the terror of the fire at the Blue Boar and every flaming nightmare he had suffered since. What was he doing here? It was not a question he could answer without thought, and there was no time for reflection.

He cast a fearful look at the burning beams overhead and dashed up the stairs. The smoke was even heavier up there. Holding his handkerchief to his mouth, he coughed and turned left. The hallway to the right was fully involved, part of the ceiling already collapsed.

The boy was in the end bedroom, but he lay as though dead, sprawled on the floor, having apparently tried to crawl to the door. Norwood recognized him instantly—the lad who had fallen in front of his horse. Tearing at the bedgown, he pressed an ear to that small chest, gasping in relief when he heard a heartbeat. Tossing the boy awkwardly over his shoulder, he headed for the stairs.

More of the roof collapsed, dropping fire into the hall. He briefly considered going back and trying to jump, but a glance over his shoulder revealed flames racing up from below.

"Please, God," he prayed. "Let the stairs be open."

Leaping across a blazing beam, he dodged a burning stretch of wall, weaving his way through the worsening fire. His head swirled dizzily as more and more smoke clogged his lungs. But the stairs were still clear.

"Watch out!" shouted one of the men who clustered near the door.

Norwood looked up. The ceiling seemed ready to come down. Increasing his speed, he took the stairs three at a time, slipping when he hit the water that had been thrown on the floor to impede the fire. As he sprawled full-length in the hall, Ben flew forward to smash head first into the wall. The ceiling collapsed, scattering debris across the duke.

Amanda watched in horror as Norwood tripped. Time screeched to a halt as the ceiling slowly tumbled down to cover him.

"No!" she screamed. "Dear God, no!"

It seemed an eternity before Jem reached down and pulled the duke free of the wreckage, slapping out fire on his sleeve.

"I-is he alive?" she asked haltingly.

"I s'pect he's just stunned," reported the farmer.

"Thank God. Get someone to help you carry him to the orchard. I'll bring Ben. If anyone else is hurt, send them there as well."

By the time she had carried Ben to the relative coolness under the apple trees, the boy was stirring.

"How is he?" asked Norwood, again coughing.

She looked up in surprise. "Are you all right?"

"I'll live. How is Ben?"

"A little singed around the edges. Can you get my bag?"

Her gig was parked close at hand. By the time he had retrieved the bag, she had pulled the torn bedgown from Ben's shoulders and was examining a scrape.

"How did you recover so fast?" she asked, smoothing salve into the wound.

"I wasn't unconscious," he replied. "Just stunned and in need of some air. The smoke was rather thick upstairs."

"I don't know how to thank you."

"Don't try. Where are the other children?"

"At a neighbor's house. There wasn't anything they could do here except get in the way."

He nodded. "I had best go throw water on the barn."

"First let me take a look at your arm." She finished applying a soothing cream to Ben's burns, none of which looked to be very serious. He was breathing easier but had slipped back into unconsciousness, the growing knot on his head evidence of his skid into the wall.

"I am fine," he protested.

"Hardly, your grace. You've a scrape on your forehead and that sleeve is burned through to the skin."

Norwood looked down in surprise, suddenly aware that there were pains in several parts of his body. "Dear Lord, I never felt a thing."

"That is quite normal under the circumstances," she assured him, pulling off his coat and cutting away the remains of his shirtsleeve. "It happened often on the Peninsula. The mind becomes so engrossed in the job at hand that ordinary pain does not register."

"It comes back with a vengeance," he admitted, gritting his teeth as she applied ointment to his arm and wrapped it in a strip of linen.

"You've changed," she commented as she treated several other cuts and scrapes. "What happened to the icy arrogance?"

"You taught me to care about people." He caught her eyes with his own and held them. Something swelled in his heart at the look in those brown depths. "It's something I did as a boy but had grown away from."

"It has only just occurred to me to wonder what you are doing here. Oughtn't you to be at dinner?"

He shrugged. "I picked up a copy of Donne's *Devotions* in Middleford yesterday. You were right, of course. *No man is an island*. Like him, I must now proclaim that *I am involved in Mankinde*. It seemed natural to lend a hand when I heard about the fire."

She opened her mouth to reply, but was interrupted. Jem and Frank arrived with a third man suspended between them. Behind them the last of the roof collapsed, sending sparks and flames high into the air. The kitchen wall was down and louder shouting arose from the direction of the barn. Frank raced back to the fire.

"Rob was kicked by one of the draught horses," reported Jem. "Part of the barn is burning, but I think we can stop it there."

"Is anyone else injured?" asked Amanda, ripping away Rob's shirt. The blow had hit the shoulder after glancing off the side of his head.

"Nothing serious." He left at a run.

"That shoulder looks dislocated," commented Norwood, kneeling on the other side of Rob's inert body.

"We'll have to send for Dr. Robinson." Amanda shook her head. "But not until one of the men can be spared."

"In the meantime, let me see if I can do anything for it. A friend had this happen while hunting a couple of years ago." He was feeling along the bones as he spoke. With a sudden twist, he snapped the shoulder back into position.

"You've a talent for this," observed Amanda, wrapping Rob tightly to keep it from shifting out of place again. "I hope his head is all right. He is incredibly lucky. A kick there is usually fatal."

"It doesn't look like much," commented Norwood. "He seems to be breathing normally."

Amanda gently prodded the swelling on the side of Rob's head and nodded. "It is not as bad as the knot you had that day. Or Oliver's."

Another crash was accompanied by a scream. Both of them looked toward the house, but nothing had changed on the near side.

"Dear Lord," murmured Amanda. "That sounded like the Blue Boar."

"I keep seeing that fire," agreed Norwood. "It froze me for a moment upstairs."

"How did you get out that night?" she asked.

"Fitch pounded on my door to wake me," he replied slowly, determined not to allow emotion into his voice. "But by the time I realized what was going on and had dragged on some clothes, the hall was filled with flames. So was the window. I had to break through a locked door into the corner room before I found a window that was clear so I could jump. It overlooked the ravine holding the stream."

"So that was the picture that returned—the flame-filled window."

He nodded. "And the hall was burning by the time I got Ben. It was much too similar. How did you awaken so much earlier?"

"Too much war. The smoke triggered my Waterloo nightmare."

"To the benefit of us all. Ultimately, you saved my life. If I had been roused even two minutes later, I would not have escaped."

She stared at him for a moment, knowing it was true. She wanted to tell him how terrified she had been when he had been buried beneath that ceiling, but she could not. He was betrothed to her sister. In fact, the announcement would occur on the morrow. His eyes again met hers and she gasped to see the anguish blazing there. His hand reached out to lightly stroke her own and she knew her tears showed.

"Help," begged a strained voice, breaking the spell and returning their attention to the immediate crisis.

Norwood sprang up and caught the man Jem was carrying alone.

"What happened?" the duke demanded sharply.

"A corner of the barn come down, trapping Jacob here. There are several others who were hurt, but he's the worst. The good news is that I think we've got it stopped."

"Thank heaven," responded Amanda.

"Dear God!" choked Norwood as he lay Jacob down under the trees. One side of his body was burned and a broken arm twisted grotesquely.

"Cut his clothes off," ordered Amanda. "Jem, can someone be spared to fetch blankets from the Court? And Dr. Robinson must be found, if he has not already been summoned."

"Immediately," promised Jem.

"Will he survive?" asked Norwood as he helped her spread greasy salve over the burns.

"It is possible, though his chances are not good," she said softly. "Burns are the worst kind of injury. Deep ones like these frequently turn putrid. If that happens, there is nothing that will save him."

"Why do you use grease?"

"It seems to help. I suspect that it forms a barrier between the wound and the air. It does not dissipate like liquids do."

They worked in silence for some time. Amanda finally stood up with a sigh.

"That is all I can do," she said. "The arm will require Dr. Robinson's attention. It is too mangled to try and set it myself."

More patients were heading their way, for as the fire

waned, they could be spared from the fight. Norwood
found himself treating burns and wrapping up cuts. Most of
the men returned to the farmyard as soon as he was done
with them. Ben stirred and he went to sit with the boy for a
few minutes when Amanda did not need him.

His mind churned as he glanced around. The shell of the
house was growing dark as the flames dwindled inside.
Four men and a boy remained in the improvised hospital
under the orchard trees. The shouts of those fighting to save
the barn had grown less urgent and more tired as the reflected flickering from the farmyard waned.

He thought again about Donne's powerful words and had
to admit that he truly believed them, though he knew that
much of the *ton* did not. But titles were compatible with
compassion, and not just for a few pet causes. Wellington
had argued fiercely in favor of a pension bill for Peninsula
veterans, yet decried Whig efforts to improve the lives of
ordinary people. With that thought, the blinders finally fell
from his eyes and he realized that the Whigs were right. It
would cause a nine-days-wonder, but he would have to
come out as a reformer. He was not the man he had been at
the end of the Season, and it was mostly Amanda's doing.
She had challenged him to look outside of himself, to see
the world as a collection of people, each with a different
position, but all worthwhile. His own high place did not ex-
empt him from being human.

Chapter Sixteen

Norwood was binding up Jem's arm when he felt the farmer stiffen. An elegant coach drew up at the edge of the orchard, disgorging Lord Thorne. The marquess's face reflected resignation to an unpleasant duty, with no hint of warmth or sympathy. It stiffened even further when he caught sight of Amanda, who was soothing a wailing Ben.

"You are here?" gasped Thorne disapprovingly, his expression changing to shock as he identified Norwood.

"As you see," said Norwood, drawing Thorne's attention from Amanda.

"Who had the effrontery to force you into this?" demanded Thorne.

"No one. I volunteered," said Norwood calmly. "Who could watch a tragedy unfold and not try to avert it? Certainly not I, nor any other who claims to be human. I presume you are also here to offer support and assistance to the family."

Thorne's face appeared thunderous, but he could find no rejoinder. Turning abruptly, he went to examine the damage.

"You are lucky to be a duke," murmured Amanda as Jem departed. "He would have combed your hair with a joint stool if you did not outrank him."

"He has already done so—when I insisted on summoning you to attend Mr. Stevens. But he would have had no cause three months ago," admitted Norwood. "I must thank you for your salubrious lessons in compassion. It is a concept I had forgotten, much to my mother's delight. She is very like your father."

"I cannot imagine enjoying life insulated from other people. Nor can I remain aloof from those whose birth is below my own. Not that I think we should erase the class boundaries, but it is possible to treat those lower than oneself with dignity and respect. And one can learn lessons from them. It was Granny Gossich who taught me to care."

"Would there were more like you."

"Has your mother always been so cold?" she asked, pursuing that flash of camaraderie she had felt before.

"Always. She was the perfect match for my father. If anything, he was worse."

"Yet you spent years patterning your behavior after them."

"I must have been mad. But I needed the facade at the time."

"To cover your pain?"

He nodded.

"That is understandable. Your only mistake was in forgetting that it was, in fact, a facade."

"So wise. I wish—"

"No you don't," she interrupted firmly. "Just live the remainder your life with compassion, your grace. And teach Emily to care. The capacity is there, but she has lived for seventeen years under Thorne's thumb. You will need patience." She went to check on Jacob and Rob, leaving him with Ben.

Thorne was talking with Mr. Wilson. He glanced back at Norwood in surprise, then continued the discussion. Even from the orchard, they could see that his posture had relaxed, lending him a less dutiful look.

Dr. Robinson arrived at last, shaking his head over Jacob but offering the hope that perhaps he would pull through. Ben had not reinjured the leg, but he had several burns that would torment him in the days ahead.

Thorne had moved on to talk to the other men who had fought the fire. Mr. Wilson headed hesitantly for the orchard.

"My condolences, sir, on the loss of your home," offered Norwood after Amanda had introduced him.

The farmer shrugged. "How can I ever repay you for saving my son, your grace?" he asked, tears evident in his eyes.

"It was nothing," said Norwood.

"It's a saint, you are," declared Wilson fervently. "Why would a duke risk his life for the child of a tenant?"

Norwood was feeling very uncomfortable under such obvious emotion, but a glance at Amanda stayed any argument. "A title is an empty thing unless one cares about the world," he said slowly. "And that includes caring about one's fellow man. Besides," he added, trying for a lighter tone, "I met the scamp several days ago."

Mr. Wilson seemed surprised, but he did not ask questions. After a few more words, he collected Ben so he could return him to the rest of his family. Amanda was packing her bag into the gig when the marquess returned.

"May I escort you home?" Thorne asked Amanda.

She raised her brows in surprise, but nodded.

The marquess turned to Norwood. "My carriage can return you to the Court. I only ask that you send it to collect me when you have no further use for it."

Norwood nodded, speculation lighting his eyes.

Thorne remained silent for the first mile. "How did you come to be there?" he asked at last.

"I saw the smoke and knew they would need help." She kept her eyes on the road and her concentration on controlling her horse.

"Your mother would have done the same," he observed softly, no censure evident in his voice.

"Another reason you have always disliked her."

"So I have always believed," he replied slowly. "And yet, I can no longer do so. It was a terrible shock to see you that day in the library, Amanda. You look exactly like her. She was always the most beautiful woman in the world."

"What fustian is this, Father?" she scoffed. "My looks are passable, but no one in his right mind would call me beautiful."

"Then I belong in Bedlam. There is more to beauty than looks, Amanda. Your mother's spirit shone with a radiance that I cannot describe. You are the same. If only I had been more understanding, perhaps we could have been happier, but I was not. It never occurred to me that what I admired most about her arose from those very traits that I had been taught were inconsistent with my position."

Amanda felt tears sting the backs of her eyes and fought them down. ".You loved her." It was not a question.

"Yes, though I did not realize it myself and would never have admitted it if I had. She was the joy of my life, yet I made her own life a living hell and ultimately killed her." His voice broke.

She glanced surreptitiously at his face, shocked to discover that he too was on the verge of tears.

"You cannot blame yourself for that, surely," she protested. "Women die in childbirth every day."

"But if she had been happier, she might have lived. If I had been there, she might have lived."

"Tell me about it," she urged him softly. If there was any truth in his self-accusation, she had to know. But more importantly, if he was deluding himself, she must remove his guilt. She sensed that they were on the verge of a new relationship. It gave her hope, at the same time filling her with terror. She had resigned herself to lifelong antagonism. There was no guarantee that she was capable of changing.

In the dark of the gently rocking gig, Thorne found it easier to talk than if they were facing each other in a brightly lit drawing room. "My upbringing was very strict," he began softly. "You may remember my father. From the day I was born, he drilled me on the behavior expected of one who would become the Marquess of Thorne. His word was law; even my mother was unable to bend his will. One of his strictures was that displaying emotion was indicative of low breeding."

Amanda nodded silently. She had often been on the receiving end of that edict.

He continued, almost to himself. "I did not meet your mother until after the betrothal was arranged. The future of my father's line was far too important to trust to fate, so he researched her breeding and upbringing until he was satisfied that she would make an impeccable marchioness. He was as appalled as I to discover too late that she harbored traits that ran counter to all of his dictates. I had been too well taught to question his fury at being thus deceived."

They drove in silence for several minutes, Amanda's heart breaking for her father. In a way, he had been worse served by his father than she had been. She now saw that much of his mother's buried compassion was present in her son, but it had been completely suppressed in the course of his childhood.

"She lived for fifteen months after our marriage," Thorne continued, his voice harshening in self-reproach. "Not a day went by that I didn't castigate her for something, and I know that my father did likewise. She grew to fear my presence. My God! How much pain did I cause her? I think it was the fear that finally convinced me that I hated her, and so I redoubled my efforts to mold her into the proper lady I thought I wanted. But like you, she refused to break. Her intransigence led to almost daily battles—between us, between her and my father, between me and my father. In retrospect, I should have insisted on living elsewhere, on allowing her to be the mistress of her own home instead of a resident in my father's. Perhaps her influence would have softened me and things might have been different."

"It is too late to change the past, Father," Amanda murmured soothingly. "Whatever decisions were made are beyond rectifying." It was difficult to picture her larger-than-life father under the thumb of another man, but the memories of her grandfather—who had died when she was ten—fit his narrative.

He ignored her remark. "The last battle was a shouting match that must have been overheard by nearly every servant in the house." He sighed. "I don't even remember what it was about. Something trivial, I've no doubt. I stormed away in the blackest temper I ever remember, and rode the moor for hours cursing fate, cursing her, cursing God, and whoever else came to mind. I nearly foundered my horse, finally stopping to allow him to rest when I stumbled across an abandoned hut about fifteen miles from here. But the exertions of the day left me so exhausted that once my temper cooled, I fell asleep."

Amanda shivered, knowing what was to come.

"I did not return home until nearly noon the next day," he said, voice again cracking. "The butler informed me that my wife had been brought to bed of a daughter, and had died an hour earlier. Her last words were a plea to see me."

She ignored the sob that escaped, unable to speak without revealing that her own face was covered with tears. The silence stretched until they were nearly at Middleford. "How does that make you responsible?" she asked at last.

"I wondered if her death was my punishment for mistreating her so badly," he said. "The thought even crossed my mind that she was taken to rescue her from further pain."

"I doubt it."

"Whatever the reason, I learned nothing from the experience," he stated coldly. "In the weeks that followed, I honed her faults until I rejoiced at being delivered from so unsuitable a wife."

"It is a common way of dealing with grief, unfortunately," said Amanda. "One transforms the pain into something easier to bear."

"You make me sound human," he said ironically.

"We are all human."

"The process intensified once I married again. This time, I attended the London Season so that there would be no more unpleasant surprises, deliberately choosing a woman who met all my father's ideals for a marchioness. There was no reason to expect that anything would mar the future. But thoughts of Amanda kept returning, often wistfully. I repeated the litany of her faults with more diligence, furious that my wayward mind could compare the perfect wife unfavorably with the imperfect one. It took several years before I banished her from my life. By then, it was obvious that you had inherited most of her character. And so I began the process again, trying to force you into the pattern that I believed to be essential to a highborn lady."

She arrived home, pulling the gig up before her stable so the boy could unharness the horse. They spoke no further until they were ensconced in her sitting room with a tea tray and some sandwiches.

"It is too late to change the past, Father," she reminded him again, "though I thank you for sharing it with me. It explains much."

"Some of the mistakes of the past can be rectified, Amanda," he countered. "I was wrong in many of my judgments of you, and I was wrong in expelling you from the family. There is shame in admitting that all the world recognizes your excellence and condemns me for cruel stubbornness. There is even more shame that it took two dukes singing your praises before I would come to my senses, but I believe I have now done so. If you choose it, I would welcome your return."

Amanda smiled, tears again stinging her eyes. "I would like to get to know you better," she said softly. "But I cannot allow you to assume all the blame for this rift. My own behavior was far worse than was necessary. I often flouted your edicts, not because I preferred another course but merely to aggravate you."

"The stubbornness you inherited from me, I fear." He sighed.

"Very likely. But I would beg forgiveness for my behavior. You would not have recognized me in Spain, willingly adhering to the strictest regulations even through discomfort and fear."

Pain flashed across Thorne's face.

"Not to worry, Father. I survived intact. And I will gladly rejoin the family. But you must not expect me to move permanently into your world. I am happy with the life I have chosen."

"There are two things I would ask you to consider. This is unpardonably late, but I would like you to attend the ball tomorrow night where Emily's betrothal will be announced."

"I would be delighted," she agreed.

"The other concerns your allowance. I would prefer to settle upon you the amount that I had set aside for your dowry. It would bring in more than the paltry sum I grudgingly allowed you that day and would free you of all of my strictures."

"It is something we can discuss later," said Amanda. "In fact, I would welcome your advice on several financial matters. Jack's great-uncle died two years ago. The man's solicitor called this morning. It seems George left his entire estate to Jack, so it is now mine. Some legal difficulties and challenges to the various wills were resolved recently, and the authorities finally discovered my direction."

"How much is involved?" asked Thorne in surprise.

"Beau Cime and investments that return about five thousand a year."

"Mr. Comfray was Morrison's uncle?"

"Great-uncle. You knew him?"

"Not well. Our philosophies were too different, but he was related in some roundabout fashion to your grandmother—second cousin, or some such. Beau Cime is a beautiful property."

"I know. We lived there for several months after our marriage. Uncle George is largely responsible for my education."

Chagrin flickered on Thorne's face at the reminder of his refusal to send her to school. "You will be living there, then?"

"I expect so, but nothing is yet decided. I will be meeting with the solicitor and the steward next week. It will be time enough to plan the future after I discover what the situation is."

"Do you wish company?"

"Not this time, but there may be need later," she admitted, surprised at how willingly she considered his offer. The revelations of the evening had changed her views so thoroughly that she could no longer see him as her enemy.

Talk moved into less personal channels, including a discussion of the fire and what needed to be done to help the Wilsons. It wasn't long before Thorne's carriage arrived and he took his leave.

Norwood was suffering another sleepless night. Every time he closed his eyes, flames danced around him and his throat constricted. After two abortive attempts to rest ended in screaming nightmare, he gave up the effort and now paced his room.

The future loomed as a continuous hell of his own devising. He shuddered every time he thought of Emily. Despite Mrs. Morrison's words, he did not believe she harbored any trace of compassion. What kind of miasma had he been suffering from for the past ten years that he could have expected such a wife to meet even the least of his needs?

The brutal truth could not be ignored. He loved Amanda as he had never expected to love anyone. And yet he lived in a world where even a duke could not ignore convention with impunity. If he cried off his betrothal to Emily, she would be ruined. He could not cause an innocent to be ostracized from the only society she knew. Compounding the problem, both he and Amanda would likewise be ruined. For himself, it did not matter. After all, he had eschewed that very society for ten years. But he did not want to cause embarrassment to the one he loved, and he had no idea what stigma would attach to his children.

It was an impossible coil, and not one for which he could envision a solution. Even taking the dishonorable step of trying to talk Lady Emily into accepting the blame—which would damage them both, but not irreparably—would not work. He had been very open when he proposed, offering nothing but position and wealth. She had been satisfied by those terms. Nothing had changed.

So what was he to do? There was no use hoping that Emily would prove as weak as Annabelle. Even if she died, he would be prohibited by law from marrying Amanda. Nor did he know if Amanda returned his regard, though he suspected she did. Her eyes were too expressive. They had held not just affection, but agony. Only the fact that he was betrothed to her sister could account for such a strong emotion. And she had stopped him from putting their predicament into words, knowing exactly what he had been trying to say.

His pacing accelerated. There had to be a solution! He could not walk into a trap that must make at least three people miserable. He would speak with Emily in the morning, he decided at last. Perhaps her lust for becoming a duchess was not quite strong enough for her to force marriage onto someone who admitted loving another.

Chapter Seventeen

Shrieks echoed throughout the family wing, spilling into the corridor housing the higher-ranking guests. Norwood had not yet managed to fall asleep. Noting that it was half-past six, he gave up and summoned his valet. He would await Emily in the breakfast room. It was time for a frank discussion.

Norwood was not the only early riser this day. The wailing maid woke Thorne from the deepest sleep he had experienced in years. He was not pleased, and even less so when he discovered the cause.

"Sir Harold Stevens," announced Jameson woodenly, pulling the library doors closed behind the baronet.

Thorne ceased his pacing to glare at his visitor.

"What is so important that I must be dragged out at dawn?" groused Sir Harold.

"You are lucky I don't call you out," snapped Thorne, shoving a paper into the man's hands. "Read this."

All color had left the baronet's face by the time he finished the brief note. "My God!"

"Exactly. That scapegrace son of yours is not fit to call himself a gentleman. How dare he insult me under my own roof!"

"How dare you blame him!" Sir Harold waved the paper under Thorne's nose. "Look at this—'*ruining my life . . . forcing me into everlasting unhappiness.*' Clearly the blame rests on your shoulders."

"Ingrate! I should never have invited one so low as you to my home. No wonder the boy has no concept of honor."

Sir Harold appeared ready to explode into fisticuffs, but

further argument was forestalled when Jameson again opened the door.

"His grace of Norwood," the butler announced.

"Dear Lord, no," murmured Thorne under his breath.

Norwood took a moment to survey the purple-faced combatants. Both appeared on the verge of apoplexy. With their last exchange ringing in his ears, he had no trouble picturing what the meeting had been like thus far. Repressing his own emotions, he assumed the ducal hauteur that had been his cloak for the past ten years.

"It would seem we have a problem," he observed coldly.

"You know?" asked Thorne, blanching.

Norwood tossed his own note onto the marquess's desk, waiting silently until the man had read it. He need not see it to recall every word.

> *My Lord Duke,*
>
> *After much consideration, I must withdraw my acceptance of your offer. It would be unfair to marry you when I love another. I apologize for placing you in the uncomfortable position of being jilted, but I trust your title will enable you to recover quickly. As I know your heart is not engaged, you should suffer no more than embarrassment.*
>
> *By the time you receive this, I will be gone. It would have been better for us both if my father had not forced me into sacrificing happiness to duty.*
>
> *Lady Emily Sterne*

"You cannot believe she means it," declared Thorne. "It is merely a childish whim. I trust you will not hold it against her."

"On the contrary. I do not believe it to be a whim, nor am I pleased to discover that she only accepted my suit because of some misplaced notion of duty drummed into her by an arrogant, tyrannical parent. I will never consider marriage to a girl who is not wholly committed to the union. Nor can I condone forcing her to abandon the man she loves because you decided the gentleman was unworthy."

"You mistake the matter, your grace," said Thorne, visibly fighting to control his temper. "I had not the slightest inkling that her affections were engaged until I received my own note half an hour ago."

Norwood stared at the marquess for nearly a minute, finally nodding. "I presume the gentleman in question is young Stevens." He turned to the baronet. "Have they eloped?"

"Yes."

"Let us sit down and discuss this calmly," urged Norwood. "I expect we all agree that an elopement is out of the question. Their credit cannot stand the approbation."

"It is out of the question because she cannot be allowed to make such a mésalliance," growled Thorne.

"When did they leave?" asked Norwood, ignoring the outburst.

"Sometime after three," admitted the marquess. "Your traveling carriage is missing, Sir Harold, but it was still there when the grooms returned from fighting a fire at one of the tenant farms."

"What else could he have taken?" murmured Sir Harold. "His own was destroyed in the accident. I can only assume the blow to his head addled his wits."

"Are you implying that Emily is not good enough for him?" stormed Thorne.

"Has anyone been sent after them?" demanded Norwood, cutting into the argument before the principals came to blows.

Thorne inhaled deeply to calm himself. "Not yet. Englewood should be down shortly. It seems best to send him in pursuit. If they do not return by tonight, I must be here to make excuses to the guests."

Norwood nodded. "You will have to permit them to wed," he stated, staring daggers at Thorne until the marquess closed his mouth against his protests. "Think. There are upwards of sixty people staying at the Court, with more due to arrive today. Stevens and Emily probably have a four-hour start on Englewood. Even if he rides, he is unlikely to catch up to them until this afternoon. The most we can hope for is that they will return in time to open the ball. There is no possibility that Emily's absence will not raise comments from the houseguests."

"His grace is right," said Sir Harold. "I too oppose this marriage, but I cannot see how to avoid it. Oliver has compromised her too thoroughly by now. Since Norwood refuses to reinstate his betrothal, you will never find another match."

"You oppose it?" repeated Thorne incredulously.

"Yes, though on different grounds than yourself. I find Lady Emily too cold for my tastes. I cannot believe she will make Oliver happy. He is so open and caring that I wonder what he sees in her."

A knock sounded on the library door.

"Are we agreed that the marriage must take place?" asked Norwood.

The others reluctantly nodded.

"Enter," called Thorne.

Englewood stood in the doorway, sleep fighting for control of his eyes. The marquess quickly put him in possession of the facts.

"Try to get them back in time for the ball," urged Thorne when he had finished. He looked at Norwood.

"It would be best if it remains a betrothal ball," the duke said in response to the unspoken question. "Its nature is no secret, but rumor often lies, so we should brush through fairly well when the groom's name is announced."

Sir Harold inhaled deeply and tried to smile. "Inform them that they can expect a cordial welcome upon return."

Norwood nodded. "My only sorrow is that your sister felt unable to explain her problem to me in person."

"Take Black Thunder," ordered Thorne, naming his own stallion. "He should carry you at least four stages."

"I will leave at once," promised Englewood.

"How are we going to minimize the scandal?" asked Thorne, pouring brandy for the other men before claiming his favorite wingback chair.

"It depends on whether they return before the ball," said Sir Harold with a sigh. "If not, I suppose nothing but the truth will do."

"Society knows that Stevens was dangling after Lady Emily last Season," observed Norwood. "At least we have a history to work with."

"Are you suggesting that this house party was arranged to bring Oliver up to scratch?" exclaimed Sir Harold. "Not to denigrate my son, but no one would believe it. And how can we explain your presence?"

Thorne shook his head. "No one will believe that I approved the suit of a younger son of a baronet. The lad is barely two-and-twenty."

"Not necessarily," protested Norwood. "Naturally, you had higher aspirations, but you love your daughter. You also deplore the London Season, my lord. You have hardly been in town more than I, so an antipathy to the giddy social rounds is understandable."

"Where is this peroration heading?" asked Thorne sourly.

"Having endured an exhausting Season in town, you discovered that Emily favored the least likely member of her court. Being a loving father, you disliked barring the boy from your door, but being a prudent parent, you demanded that she take the time to study all of her suitors. So you arranged these house parties. Who did you invite last summer?"

"Lord Peter Barnhard and Mr. Raintree," he grudgingly replied.

"So I thought. They were the most eligible half of her court. And this time you invited Lord Geoffrey and Stevens. You have given her an opportunity to become well acquainted with all her beaux. And in the end, she insisted upon Stevens. You cannot wholly approve, of course, but since Stevens has a reasonable fortune of his own and at least one marquess in his background, he is not ineligible. Your first consideration must be your daughter's happiness."

Sir Harold chuckled.

Thorne sighed. "Very well. But how am I to explain your presence? Who can expect any girl to spurn the hand of a duke?"

"But I am not here to court Lady Emily," announced Norwood placidly. "We can discuss my visit later." He nodded toward Sir Harold. "After all, my attentions were not pointed last Season. There are at least four other ladies who might claim equal expectations. Any guest will testify that Emily paid little attention to me or I to her these past weeks. In fact, she has split her time almost evenly between Lord Geoffrey and Stevens."

"That seems to settle everything," observed Sir Harold. "If you will excuse me, I will retire to my room. If they are not back by dinner, I suppose we will have to devise a new story. Where are they today, by the way?"

"Emily is helping her sister deal with the aftermath of a fire that destroyed the house of one of my tenants last night," replied Thorne in resignation.

"Stevens mentioned having friends in the area," recalled Norwood. "Perhaps he decided to spend the day with them and thus avoid a house at sixes and sevens as it prepares for a grand ball, especially as he has no wish to anticipate the announcement that will be made at that ball."

Sir Harold laughed. "You are a complete hand, your grace. I can only thank you for accepting what must be an insult with such aplomb."

"Believe me, sir, I do not view it as an insult but rather as a deliverance at almost the last moment from a situation that must have made us both unhappy."

Sir Harold departed, leaving Norwood and Thorne together. Thorne immediately reverted to embarrassment.

"He is right," he observed. "You are taking this much differently than I would have expected."

Norwood wandered over to the window and stared down at the formal gardens. His earlier geniality was gone. "Men like us, who possess high titles, are often beset by those who covet either the title or association with it. Both you and your daughter are such persons. Neither of you looked beyond the dukedom to see whether marriage might be agreeable. Nor did I see beyond the marquess's daughter."

The last sentence prevented Thorne from slipping into rage. His sputtered protest died.

"One would think that I might have learned the lesson from my first marriage," Norwood continued. "She was another who was forced into accepting my offer despite the fact that her father knew full well that she had long loved someone else—another baronet's younger son, by the way; what is it about them that appeals to girls? She suffered miserably for over a year before dying in childbirth. Unfortunately, the lesson I took away from that union was a cynicism that ultimately made me no better than my father-in-law. But I cannot allow that to happen again. I had already decided to speak with Emily this morning and terminate our betrothal." Much as he hated to bare his soul, he had already realized that it was the only way to rescue Emily from the consequences of her elopement. He owed her that, in gratitude."

"What?" croaked Thorne. "You knew of her attraction before?"

"No, I did not. But I have discovered that my own affections are engaged elsewhere. It would have been unfair to Emily to condemn her to marriage under those circumstances."

Thorne poured himself another brandy and drank half of it in a single gulp. "You would have put her through the humiliation of being jilted by a duke?"

"I hoped that we could contrive to prevent that." Norwood sighed. "You can see why I am not displeased over this elopement."

"Certainly. It must seem the answer to a prayer. Forgive me if I am a little brittle. There have been too many shocks recently. But out of curiosity, how did you envision explaining away a betrothal ball where no betrothal is announced and the daughter of the house claims no attachment?"

"It was always a long shot. And it is difficult to think clearly at four in the morning after an evening such as I suffered yesterday."

"I should have thanked you sooner for everything you did last night," interrupted Thorne. "I understand you actually went in and rescued a boy."

"I am sure Mr. Wilson made it seem more heroic than it was. In actual fact, that portion of the house was not yet burning."

Thorne shook his head. "Returning to the question of the hour, how did you expect to extricate yourself without harming Emily?"

"I knew that Emily did not care for me. The lady I love is Amanda. I had hoped that if Emily was agreeable and if Amanda would have me, that we might announce the other betrothal at the ball—perfectly logical as she is also your daughter. That explains my presence here, by the way. I came to court Mrs. Morrison."

"Did you?"

"Of course not. I had no idea she lived here until she

found me lying unconscious in a muddy field. And I had no idea who she was until the major's dinner party. This is as much a surprise to me as it is to you. She will turn my staid existence upside down if she'll have me."

"Then you don't know what her feelings are."

"Now *that* is an insult." He glared at Thorne until the man reddened. "I am not so dishonorable. One thing I do know is that she will send me away with a flea in my ear if she does not return my regard. Amanda is one person who will toadeat no one. She loved Jack, and will never settle for less. That is why the plan was such a gamble. She is still mourning him. It may be months before she is ready to consider marrying again. I hope this confession does not lengthen your list of complaints against her, by the way. She has never done a thing to attract my attention."

"You fell in love with her in the short time you have been here?" asked Thorne incredulously.

Norwood ran frustrated fingers through his hair. "No. Actually, she has been plaguing me for months, though I never considered her as aught but a witch and a nuisance. I met her last summer."

"The night you were injured," recalled Thorne.

"Amanda was treating the casualties. I broke my arm, among other things, and came the duke quite horridly at her. She not only refused me instant attention, but coerced me into assisting with an amputation."

Thorne's choking resolved into laughter. "Her mother would have done just the same," he admitted. "I made her life miserable trying to change her into the haughty aristocrat my father demanded. I trust you won't make that mistake."

"You approve the connection, then?" asked Norwood.

"I have admitted my own errors. Amanda and I reconciled when I took her home last night."

"Thank you," said Norwood softly. "That will do more to further my suit than anything I could say. She has been badly hurt by the rancor that existed between you for so long."

"I invited her to the ball," said Thorne. "Do you wish to talk with her beforehand?"

"No. That would be rushing my fences unpardonably. Now that the urgency is gone, I would rather get Emily's betrothal out of the way and then court Amanda properly. I have little doubt that Englewood will return in time. I suspect they did not leave until five. A carriage departed about then. He should have them back this afternoon. In the meantime, I will speak to some friends and start enough rumors that we can cover this debacle in the eyes of society."

"Do you feel as out of control as I at the moment?" asked Thorne unexpectedly.

"Possibly," agreed Norwood. "Amanda seems to have that affect on the pretentious. Since I met her, I have found myself nursing injured peasants, fighting fires, hauling coxcombs out of rivers—which has to be the most useful thing I've done in my life—and questioning everything I thought I believed. Three months ago I was a typical, arrogant duke. Now I don't know what I am."

"You understand, then. I have lost my temper more in the past three months than in the previous fifty years. Her return has forced me to reexamine events I thought I had buried. My mother has complained about my behavior, two dukes have spoken to me as to a wayward child, my neighbors and tenants look at me as if I were Judas, and my usually obedient daughter has eloped with another impossible suitor."

"Stevens isn't that bad," objected Norwood. "I've no reason to decry him as a brother-in-law, and not just because he saved me from a sticky situation."

"Maybe it will work," conceded Thorne. "Amanda seems to have done well with hers. I had best try a different approach with Marianne. I doubt I could cover up a third flit."

"Stress affection instead of consequence. That should take care of matters."

Thorne poured another brandy. "I feel better about the way Amanda has overset my life now that I know she's done the same to you."

"Young Taylor called her a witch," murmured Norwood. "I believe she is. There is something about her that restores youthful idealism to even the starchiest prig. No wonder Jack was such a hero. With Amanda around, he couldn't be anything else."

Chapter Eighteen

Norwood returned to his room and finally managed a couple of hours of sleep, awakening refreshed and more in charity with the world than he had been in years. The breakfast room was occupied only by an earl who had arrived late the evening before. The men were long-standing acquaintances, though they had never been close.

"Morning, Norwood." He nodded his head as the duke entered.

"Penleigh."

"Congratulations," the earl said once Norwood had been served and the footman had retired.

"For what?"

"It is no secret that this is a betrothal ball," scoffed Penleigh.

"True, but not mine."

The earl stared in astonishment. "But everyone in town knows you are marrying Thorne's oldest daughter."

"As usual, rumor exaggerates," explained Norwood with a sigh. "It is true that I have been courting the lady, but I have not yet made an offer. She is still grieving the death of her husband at Waterloo."

"But she only came out last Season."

"You must not know the family very well. Lady Emily did indeed make her bows recently, but she is Thorne's second daughter, the first by his second wife. She will be announcing her betrothal tonight."

"I could swear you were courting her last Season."

"Just keeping a paternal eye on the chit," Norwood assured him. "After all, I'm nearly twice her age and hope she will be my sister." He turned the conversation to other topics, refusing to say anything further about the situation at Thornridge.

Norwood was more open with Geoffrey. They wandered through the gardens while he explained events and extracted a promise to support the planned story.

"My condolences," Geoffrey said when the tale was finished.

"Not necessary," replied Norwood. "I had already discovered that it was an ill-fated match and was looking for a way out."

"How are you going to explain your presence?" his friend asked, raising a quizzical eyebrow.

"I am courting someone who lives in the neighborhood."

"It won't wash, Nicholas. Aside from the fact that Lady Emily is the only one around here who merits consideration as a duchess, you have made no effort to see anyone else."

"Ah, but you're not thinking, Geoff," he protested, shaking his head. "Not only have I been seeing someone else, I've actually fallen in love with her."

"Who?"

"Lady Amanda."

"I had forgotten about her," he admitted. "What luck that she is also Thorne's daughter."

"Quite. I only hope she'll have me."

"You sound uncertain. How could anyone turn down a duke's offer?" asked Geoffrey. "And a wealthy one, at that."

"She would if she does not return my love."

"You don't know?"

"What do you take me for?" demanded Norwood angrily, turning a flashing eye on his friend. "I've not been in a position to discuss the matter with her. In fact, the only reason I am mentioning it is to explain my presence and protect Emily's reputation."

"But you are serious?"

"Absolutely. And devilishly nervous. I don't know how to broach the subject, or even when."

"She is not at all what you were looking for when you came to town last Season," observed Geoffrey.

"No, she's not, thank God. I must have been mad."

"I wish you the best. In the meantime, I will correct the

confusion about Lady Emily's position in the family." He grinned.

With that conversation over, Norwood had only one other guest to see. Thorne was apprising his relatives of the change. After asking Jameson, he found his quarry in the music room, idly playing Mozart.

"Your grace!" she exclaimed when he appeared in the doorway.

"Miss Havershoal." He nodded. "Have you and Lady Emily made up yesterday's quarrel?"

"What?"

"I inadvertently overheard your conversation yesterday."

"Oh." She meticulously closed the cover on the keyboard and restored the music to a cabinet while she groped for a response. Even from across the room he could see the blush that extended to the back of her neck. "I have not seen her today, your grace."

"That is not surprising. She isn't here."

Her eyes flew to meet his, and he could see that she had not known of Emily's elopement.

"She has learned much about herself and the world since your unfortunate spat. I presume you wish to continue you friendship?"

Miss Havershoal nodded.

"Excellent. You can do her a considerable service if you would." And he gave her an expurgated account of events, accompanied by the innocuous explanation for Emily's summer entertaining.

"Good heavens!" She shook her head. "Of course I will help. The poor girl has certainly flung herself into a coil."

"Thank you. By keeping our heads, we can extricate her from it."

Norwood had asked to be informed the moment that Englewood returned. A footman found him in the library shortly after two and escorted Emily to him a few minutes later. Oliver was already on his way to the study to meet with Thorne.

"Don't look at me like that," begged Norwood once the door had closed. Emily's eyes were filled with terror. "Did your brother not tell you there was nothing to fear?"

"Yes, your grace, but I cannot help it."

"I wish you had found the courage to come to me and explain instead of running off." He sighed. "I have done you a grave disservice by assuming that a dispassionate marriage would satisfy either of us. As things stand, your preference for Stevens is the best thing that could have happened, for I have discovered that my own affections are elsewhere engaged."

"They are?"

"Yes, so you must see that you have nothing to fear from me. I hope that we can eventually become friends, for if things work out, we will be in-laws."

"You cannot mean that you love Amanda!" she blurted out.

"I do."

"She will lead you a merry chase, and she is not at all what you claimed to seek in a wife."

"She is not. But enough of that. Time alone will resolve that problem. Now pay attention so we can all tell the same story." He quickly put her in possession of the new facts. "Your betrothal to Mr. Stevens will be announced tonight at the ball. You have spent the morning helping Amanda see after the Wilsons. Their house burned down last night, injuring several people, one of whom may not survive."

"How do you know that?" she asked in surprise.

"I was helping Amanda treat the wounded. We can discuss the details later. For now, you must join your father and Mr. Stevens in the study. They should have come to terms. I wish you very happy, my dear, and am delighted that you have discovered someone you truly care about. I should have made you a devil of a husband."

"Thank you, your g-grace," she stammered. "For everything."

Norwood quickly gave up any hope of staying in the house. He was as nervous as a blood horse in a thunderstorm, unable to sit, unable to keep his mind on a conversation long enough to participate, unable to appear at all normal. Thinking a hard ride might help, he ordered a horse.

Would she accept him? Had she even thought of him in

that way? She had undoubtedly known since returning home last summer that he was offering for her sister. Every time he thought of his stupidity, he wanted to wring his own neck.

He set the horse at a high wall and galloped furiously across the newly harvested field on the other side. *Patience!* Amanda's voice echoed through his ears. She would probably label his present desire to charge into her house and claim her as further proof of his arrogance. And he was not even sure where she lived. Damnation!

He topped a rise and saw the blackened ruins of the Wilson farm in the distance. A shudder tickled his spine as the evening's events returned. That had been another piece of utter insanity. He could have died. Yet he would do it again if the situation recurred. He had changed drastically in only three months. Amanda, the witch. Amanda, the charmer. She would provide something that the dukedom had lacked for a long time—compassion. *Please*, he prayed. He felt like a callow youth, his mind bouncing from one thought to another, without rhyme or reason.

The horse was showing signs of weariness, so he slowed, circling back toward the Court as he tried to plan how to confront Amanda. She had been invited to the ball, so he would see her that evening. Had the invitation included dinner? It was necessary to his own story that it did. Amanda also must learn what had transpired between Emily and Mr. Stevens, else she might mention the truth and brush them all with scandal.

Was that really necessary? he wondered as he turned his horse toward the estate gates and Middleford. Or was he looking for an excuse to call on her? If he was honest, he rather suspected the latter, but there was no point wasting such a good one. Accosting her as soon as she arrived at the Court was too chancey.

Ten minutes later, he halted in surprise. Amanda's gig was pulled to the side of the lane, very near the clearing where he had discovered her in the throes of nightmare a fortnight before.

Amanda spent the morning visiting the fire victims. On the way home, she called on her grandmother.

Lady Thorne was delighted to learn that her son and granddaughter had buried their differences, and she was even more delighted to discover Amanda's inheritance and Jack's relationship to Mr. Comfray. They chatted companionably over a light luncheon before Amanda excused herself to prepare for the ball.

But she had not gone home. Her spirits were too low. It was doubtful she could make it through the evening without betraying her foolish attachment to the duke. Yet she could not avoid attending. Such an action would destroy the tenuous relationship she was beginning to form with her father. It was important to both of their futures that they learn to know each other. So she was faced with trying to hide her love. She sat down on a low boulder, staring over the river, unable to think.

"Lady Amanda?" Norwood murmured from barely ten feet away.

She jumped. "Good afternoon, your grace. You startled me." She hoped her color had not risen. For a moment it had seemed as if her thoughts had conjured him out of nothing. "How are your injuries?"

"As expected." His arm suddenly throbbed at the reminder. "Is there any news of the others?"

"Ben is fine. Rob's shoulder will require at least a fortnight of complete rest. And Jacob is holding his own, though the outcome is very much in question."

"I trust the family will be all right."

"Yes, Father is already arranging things, or so he said when he escorted me home last night. We have decided to overlook the past," she added softly.

"He told me."

Surprise flashed across Amanda's face. "You were discussing me?"

"It has been a strange day at the Court," he admitted, trying to find the words he needed. "While we were engrossed by the Wilson fire, Mr. Stevens and Emily departed for Gretna Green."

"Dear Lord," she breathed, looking as if her closest friend had just died. "Poor Papa—two of us running out on him. And Oliver. I thought he was in love with Lady Sarah.

I am so sorry, your grace. I would never have served you so disgraceful a turn if I had known."

"What are you talking about?"

"He approached me last week, wanting advice about joining the army. I suspected he was running away from something, and eventually won the confidence that he was in love with someone too far above his station to be acceptable to wife. I thought he meant Lady Sarah and counseled him to at least learn her feelings before taking so desperate a step. Please believe me. I never once entertained the notion that it was Emily to whom he referred."

"Do not distress yourself," he murmured soothingly. "You have done me no harm. Surely you must realize that I am the last person to countenance forcing anyone into marriage."

She raised her eyes and saw the truth of the statement. There was something else revealed in his gaze that set her heart racing, but she dared not name it. "I know, your grace. But it was a disservice nonetheless. It cannot but hurt you to be jilted."

"No announcement had yet been made, so I believe that we can muddle through quite nicely." He related again the tale they had concocted to explain recent events. "So you see, if everyone plays his part, there should be no scandal."

"I do not see that at all," she protested. "It cannot explain your presence. You were known to be courting her. You are here. At the very least, choosing another must be seen as a slap in the face."

"I've given out that I had a quite different reason for being here that has nothing to do with Thorne's house party," he said uncertainly. His eyes caught hers and held them.

"And what is that?" She couldn't breathe with her heart pounding in her throat.

"This is hardly the time . . . I mean, I can hardly expect . . . Devil take it, but I'm making a mull of this," he swore softly. "I have fallen in love with you, Amanda."

Words refused to form. She could only stare at him in shock and wonder, but her eyes must have revealed something for he stepped closer, resting his hands on her shoulders.

"Amanda?"

Her arms slid around his neck and he crushed her close, his lips fastening onto hers. Home. She was home at last. Joy rocketed through her. He actually loved her. And he was free. Free. Within seconds she made another discovery—the pleasure she had experienced with Jack was nothing compared to the ecstasy engendered by the duke. She pulled back to scan his face.

"You must feel it, too," he murmured.

She nodded and finally found her voice. "I was leaving next week. I could not bear the thought of seeing you with Emily."

"My God! Where were you going?"

"I just found out yesterday—heavens, it really was only yesterday—that I inherited an estate from Jack's great-uncle. It is far enough away to avoid accidental meetings."

His arms tightened. "That won't be necessary now, I hope. Amanda, it is undoubtedly far too soon, but you already know how impatient I can be. Will you marry me, my love?"

"You won't find me comfortable," she warned him.

"I've discovered that I don't want a conformable wife. Nor do I want one who will allow me to pursue my lonely life in peace. I need someone to talk to and debate with, someone who can share all aspects of my life, including my bed, with enthusiasm. I may even learn to laugh again if you will have me, my dear. You have resurrected that idealistic, impetuous youth I used to be. This time he is tempered by a clearer understanding of the world and the people in it. I love you, Amanda—more than I thought possible. I decided last night to jilt your sister because I could not do her such a foul turn as to marry her under these circumstances. There is no one I can envision spending my life with but you."

"I love you," she admitted. "The real you that lurks beneath the armor you show the world. I recognized it at the Blue Boar, though I did not think in terms of love until we talked in Oliver's room two nights ago. You are worthy of so much more than life has brought you."

"Will you have me then?"

"Yes, your grace, I will."

"Nicholas," he murmured, pulling her into another embrace. "Don't ever treat me like an exalted being again."

"Nicholas, my love."

It felt like a dream, Amanda admitted some hours later. She had dined at the Court, escorted to dinner by Nicholas. Now she stood next to Thorne in the receiving line. The courteous greetings barely hid the delight that beamed in the eyes of neighbors and friends to see her there. Nor did politeness hide the surprise in the eyes of those who had traveled from London and had either forgotten her existence or were ignorant of it.

Nicholas led her out to open the ball, ripples of wonder rolling around the room when people saw him smiling. Amanda glowed under that expression. She had seen it for the first time that afternoon when he released her from his second embrace. It changed his appearance entirely, smoothing out the forbidding lines that usually marred his forehead and lightening his hawkish features into a visage even an impartial observer would call handsome. Her joy must have shown at that moment, for he had groaned and pulled her back into his arms, kissing her more passionately than she had believed possible and not letting her go until both were on the verge of losing control.

Now they swirled through a waltz, eyes locked together, smiling at each other and oblivious to the rest of the world. So it came as no surprise to the gathered crowd when Thorne announced just before supper that his daughter, Lady Emily, would marry Mr. Oliver Stevens at Christmas, and his daughter, Lady Amanda, would become the Duchess of Norwood at a small, private ceremony in the Thornridge chapel the following Tuesday.

"You do not regret missing a big wedding?" asked Norwood when he and Amanda slipped away from the ballroom late in the evening.

"You know I have little use for the *ton*, Nicholas," she reminded him.

"Then what do you say to spending a few weeks—or months—at your new estate, where no one in society will think to look for us?" His eyes gleamed as he led her into the library.

"Perfect."

"It will not bother you that you were there with Jack?" The question had only just now occurred to him.

She smiled. "Jack was a romantic, my love. He would heartily approve."

Nicholas closed the door behind him and pulled her into his arms.